STRANGE
CROSSROADS

D0723669

MYYYANCINTIM

PRAISE FOR *STRANGE CROSSROADS**

"The author paints a shadow side of today's America where, as her local detective says: 'these new immigration laws are cruelty personified.' The tension builds deftly, layer upon layer. The twisting troubles facing her wonderfully personified characters pull the reader deep inside the quagmire that is swallowing a once dignified, Southwest town."

- Scott MacFarlane, author of *The Bone Shrine*
(NichéEco Imprints:2021)

"Colette Ward has truly given us rich characters that we want to aspire to be or truly hate … so real in our world today. The story excites as well as makes us think about our values. Wonderful writing."

- Carol R. Seldin-Bolinski, author of *Something to Wag About*
and co-author of *Pearls Beneath the Rind*

* = *CROSSROADS is a legendary image from Robert Johnson (1911–1938), a Mississippi bluesman, who claims to have sold his soul to the devil at the crossroads in exchange for his talent and success.*

STRANGE CROSSROADS

Colette Ward

JUSTOS PUBLISHING

PRESCOTT, ARIZONA

Copyright © 2020 by Colette Ward.

All rights reserved. No part of this book may be used or reproduced in any manner whatsoever without written permission except in the case of brief quotations embodied in critical articles and reviews.

ISBN 978-0-578-77858-7

Library of Congress Control Number: 2020919782

Book design by Longworth Creative, LLC
www.LongworthCreative.com

First Edition
Printed in the United States of America
JUSTOS PUBLISHING

To my dear parents, Alice and Fred,
my beloved husband, Jack, and our extraordinary kids,
Brian, Sarah, John, Jane, Jacquie and Gretchen.

ACKNOWLEDGEMENTS

Thanks for all kinds of help to Gretchen Phelps, Peggy Falconer, Jacquie Ward, Dusty Sanford, Elaine Jordan, Vaughn Delph Smith, Sue Favia, Janet Hopkins, Sharon Hanson, John Rose and Jennifer Longworth.

But man must light for man
The fires no other can.
And find in his own eye
Where the strange crossroads lie.

- David McCord, *Communion* (1950)

CHAPTER 1

"HEAR THAT?" Luis whispered, paused in semi-darkness as the lights in the old-fashioned Federalist lamp posts flicked on in the streets of Juniper Hills.

Miguel stopped walking, pushed his fingers through waves of black hair, cupped his hand to his ear and pretended to listen. "Woo. Ghosts. Not even Halloween."

Luis ignored his friend's joking but walked faster.

On Friday nights the boys had permission to stay out 'til ten, their mouths salivating for pizza. The sky clear, no threatening monsoons in the Arizona high country, but weather often changed in a nanosecond, as could any situation.

Once the sun slipped beyond the horizon the steamy air cooled and a breeze stirred up. Eerie shadows danced in the graying surroundings. The streets of Juniper Hills lay quiet. Most cars were tucked in garages for the night. The clear July sky threatened no monsoons this night in the Arizona high country.

"Hey. Ain't kiddin'. Listen." Luis' voice trembled.

Stomping and shuffling echoed through the empty street. A mob of white faces advanced on the two friends. Miguel gagged as a stench of beer and body odor fouled the air.

"Let's run," Luis said. "Get away."

"No. Might make it worse."

It wasn't as if they were totally alone. Now and then a car passed on the street. "Step it up. Head for the diner. I see MARIO'S over there."

Behind them the horde of boys and young men began to move faster. A loud voice shouted, "Get them spics!"

Knife blades flashed in the twilight like slivers of lightning strikes. In his mind Luis saw images of evil Ninjas with curved Arabian swords from *A Thousand and One Nights*. Fists and elbows pummeled their heads and bodies.

Luis and Miguel tried to protect their faces as they were choked from behind and forced into contorted tangles of pain. Dirt flew around as if a dust storm had come up. "Shit" and "assholes" drilled into their ears.

"Get that fucker!" Luis heard, as he watched Miguel topple face-first into a rock and onto the pavement.

Sirens screeched in the far distance. The leader of the pack yelled, "Cops! We're outta here."

Bleeding from a slash in his forehead, Luis bent over Miguel's body, his blood dripping on Miguel's yellow shirt they'd bought at Walmart that morning. The sleeves had been torn and the buttons ripped off. He gently rolled his friend over, sat down on the sidewalk and cradled Miguel's head in his lap. He screamed, "HELP, help," but the words died in his throat. There was nobody near enough to hear. He smoothed back Miguel's hair, wincing at the sight of his friend's face. Miguel's right eyeball, dislodged from its socket by the impact of the fall, lay like a large bloody tear on his cheek.

Luis turned away, begging God to keep him from crying. He had to save his friend. He felt for a pulse in Miguel's neck. It was there, but faint. Putting his hand on his friend's heart, he felt a slight beating. That was good, he knew. What to do next? Humming a song from his childhood, he tried not to look at the damaged eye, afraid he would vomit. It was still light, but darkness continued to close in.

More sirens came closer from different directions and splintered the darkening night. He hoped someone had called the cops and they were coming to help.

A low-slung black sports car sped over from the opposite side of the street and slammed on its brakes at the curb. In the fading twilight, Luis watched as a tall redhead in jeans and a white tee jump out and knelt beside him, putting a gentle hand on Miguel's chest. "We'll have help shortly," the man said, still on his knees, assuring the two of them. "I was on my way home when I heard calls on the scanner. What's your name?"

"Luis Gonzales."

"Is this your brother?" The man kept his hand on Miguel's chest.

"No. Miguel Castro. Best friend ... he's still breathing."

"I see that. My name's Dan. I'm a detective with the Juniper Hills Police. How old are you?

"Twelve."

"Documents?" Dan asked. The cop wiped his brow with the back of his hand. Sweat trickled down the sides of the man's face.

"I'm born here." Luis reached for a school crest in his jeans pocket, which his mother insisted he carry at all times.

Dan put his hand over Luis'. "Not necessary. How about your best friend here?"

"He ain't got papers."

"Don't worry. We'll take good care of him at the hospital." With his right hand still on Miguel's chest, Dan, with his left hand, pulled a clean, folded bandana from his jean's pocket and handed it to Luis. "Press this on your forehead. It'll slow the bleeding. Do you know the guys who beat you up?"

"There were maybe ten, all white, I think."

"Dressed in black?"

"Yeah. No writing, everything black ... hats, bandanas, even gloves. A couple had long fencing swords and knives. Two were big, a lot bigger than me and Miguel."

"I know that group." Dan's fists knotted. "Not local, live near the border. First time I've heard of swords. Are you sure about that?"

"Like you see in the movies. I read about them in a book. They were definitely waving around thin swords."

"A bad-news white hate group." The cop sounded mad.

Alerted by the sirens, people appeared in the shadows of the stores and apartments on the next block. One or two covered their mouths in horror. Others clutched each other and turned away. Most stayed at a distance out of respect. Dan warned the jostling others to move back. Luis saw that Dan had the situation under control.

A fire truck followed by an ambulance and three squad cars marked with Juniper Hills' official seals rounded the corner, dazzle flashing from the light-bars atop their roofs, sirens quiet for now.

Medics and police surrounded them. Two officers nodded to Dan as they lined the perimeter of the crime scene with red flares. A uniformed Juniper Hills officer, in the middle of the road, directed the scant traffic around the parked vehicles. Three firemen set up klieg lights that created an oasis of daytime on the area. A police photographer snapped pictures. Three officers searched in and outside the perimeter for clues as to what happened. "We're finding nothin'," Luis heard one cop say to another.

Luis watched a white-uniformed nurse gently ease Miguel's eye toward its socket, wrap his entire head in gauze and strap him to a board. Another medic insisted Luis, now fighting tears, allow her to put him on a stretcher. "Okay," he said, and didn't resist, "but you gotta call our Dads."

"Will do," Dan responded and wrote down the two numbers.

CHAPTER 2

MAGGIE SWEENEY opened her front door.

"I need help!" Rosa's gentle accent thickened with anxiety. In the early morning light, wrapped in a belted beige raincoat, she stood on Maggie's front porch and clutched the hand of her only child, Sophie.

"What's happened?" Maggie asked, peering out at her rain-drizzled housekeeper of many years. "Come in. It's dreadful out there."

"I can't. Carlos lost his passport card when he went to La Paz to see his dying *abuela*. He thinks someone stole it from his back pocket. Border guards grabbed him after he crossed back. Wouldn't accept his driver's license. It's a mistake. He's legal! I need to find my husband, show his papers, before they stuff him in a bus and dump him back over the border. You know he has a bad ... bad back."

Rosa looked small and scared standing on the front porch of the seven-bedroom three-story neo-colonial in Juniper Hills. Maggie always thought of her as a tornado swirling through the huge house with the energy of three women.

"I'm asking you to keep Sophie for a few days." Rosa said. "She'd be in danger where I'm going. The Homeland Security guys are looking for me. ICE agents hit the apartments this morning. Fifteen were rounded up. ... I'm legal, here since I'm twelve. Told you how drug guys in Tijuana killed my father and his brother...."

"I wish the border patrol would stick to drug dealers and gun runners," Maggie mumbled. She knew Carlos had been brought to this country as a small boy and lived in Colorado. He and his parents had become American citizens before moving to Juniper Hills.

Carlos came from a family of warriors. As a young man his great-grandfather had fought with Emiliano Zapata in the Mexican Revolution to force the authorities to return the land they'd usurped from the peasants. Carlos' parents encouraged education. He'd earned two degrees from the University of Colorado in Denver.

Now in Arizona with a Master's, he taught History and English as a Second Language at the Community College and ran a volunteer group to help immigrants navigate the educational system. He had recently finished his thesis, "US and Mexico: A History of Friendship and Distrust," on his way to a Ph.D. that would make him eligible for a full professorship at the local four-year college.

"Please, I need your help," Rosa repeated. She stroked her child's dark silky hair, reminding Maggie, "ICE doesn't know about her. We talked about this."

Yes, we did, Maggie thought with regret. Years earlier, Rosa, even though she was a legal refugee, had been so terrified of the authorities that Maggie couldn't convince her to pay taxes and build up a Social Security Account. Maggie mentally pummeled herself for agreeing to pay Rosa under the table. Disappointed in herself for not insisting that Rosa allow her to properly arrange her legal affairs, she wanted Rosa to come in, sit down and discuss a reasonable course of action.

That was not to be. As panic and tears swelled in Rosa's eyes, she unclasped Sophie's hands from around her waist and gently nudged her toward Maggie. "She is eight and needs to go to regular school. It is almost September. Enroll her in school, *por favor*." Rosa sighed.

Maggie, dressed for work in a stylish gray suit with a lavender silk shirt and scarf, looked up through the swaying trees as the wind tossed her shoulder length blue-black hair. The monsoon season had been raging and the steel-gray sky threatened to dump more sheets of rain. "Come in. We can't solve this standing here."

"I have to go." Rosa moved her child closer to Maggie, who instinctively opened her arms. Sophie nuzzled her face into Maggie's stomach. "See. She is good with you."

Maggie hugged Sophie close, caressing the soft fabric of her summer dress. She had always felt a special attraction to the child, bright and knowing beyond her age. "Rosa, you can't walk off and leave Sophie with me indefinitely. I have a law firm to run."

"I'll call."

"Rosa!" Before Maggie could say another word, the short, stocky brown figure was down the steps and into her car. "Where can I reach you?" Panic clutched Maggie's throat. Sophie was eight! Painful childhood memories swarmed in Maggie's brain.

"I'll call," Rosa shouted through the car window above the rumble of the ten-year-old Ford Escape engine and sped away. The sky ruptured. Rain clattered on the metal window awnings. Maggie's first impulse was to run after Rosa, but realizing the futility of trying to catch Rosa's car, she closed the front door.

Walking through the picture-lined hallway into the kitchen, she felt the warmth of Sophie's hand in hers. Should she ask her how she felt? She knew Sophie'd have a thoughtful opinion. Was this the time to pose the question to a little kid who'd just been left behind?

Estelle, Maggie's grandmother, sat at the kitchen table, straight and elegant as the Navy JAG officer she'd been before she retired from the Service. She was finishing her second cup of coffee and scanning *The Arizona Republic*.

"'Two Latino boys were brutally beaten by a hate gang on William Street last night,'" she read aloud. "What was that about? The detective on the scene said 'no comment.' Doesn't sound like our town. Why the secrecy?"

"Not good," Maggie responded. "I've heard of several incidents against Latinos, attacks and a couple of fires. The authorities think it's an alt-right hate group. They make me sick to my stomach. Our Latinos have contributed so much in the way of services in schools, restaurants, shops, construction, landscaping.... They're doctors, lawyers, scientists, accountants.... What do these dodos want from immigrants?"

Maggie drew in her emotions. It was the shadow of the heartbreak she'd experienced as an eight-year-old, a look her grandmother hadn't seen in a long time ... since ... well ... Maggie's mother, Thelma, had shot and killed Leo, Maggie's father. Maggie had been eight and her brother, Josh, four.

"Look who's come to visit us," Maggie continued in a cheerful voice, hoping, but doubting, that Sophie had missed Estelle's comments about the attacks.

"Hi, Sophie. Is this your day to stay overnight? How about a cookie?" Estelle pried off the lid of a flowered tin in the middle of the breakfast table and offered a chocolate-chip. Sophie refused to be tempted, nuzzling her face under Maggie's arm. "Isn't this Rosa's day off?" Estelle asked.

Maggie, uneasy, sat at the table and lifted Sophie onto her lap. "Rosa and Carlos are in trouble with the authorities. ... It looks like Mama didn't have time to braid your hair, honey." Maggie fiddled with Sophie's dangling tresses. "Would you like me to?"

Sophie smiled up at Maggie and nodded.

"Hand me a couple of those rubber bands," Maggie asked Estelle, pointing to a jar on the counter.

"Are you saying it was ICE?" Estelle asked as she watched Maggie turn Sophie's mass of hair into two long perfect braids.

"Not exactly. It's more complicated. CBP, Customs and Border Protection, a division of ICE, picked up Carlos at the border. Rosa said guards refused to accept his driver's license. He's a citizen, but someone pinched his passport card. ICE raided Rosa's apartment complexes this morning. They may had gotten Carlos' address off his license."

"There's little protection these days." Estelle folded the newspaper. "They're after anyone who looks Latino."

"They're searching for Rosa because she lived at the housing complex. They're checking on everybody. She has permanent residence status on grounds of political asylum. Did you ever see the packet of documents she carries with her?"

Estelle slammed her hand on the table and got up to refill her coffee cup. "Still the authorities harass her!"

"I know, because she looks Mexican. ... She wants us to keep Sophie for a while. She's always said they don't know she works for us. Or that Sophie exists. You know that."

Concerned and glancing at Sophie, Maggie tried to dismiss her negative thoughts. Sophie's situation was bringing back memories, replays of her father's murder that she'd held in her eight-year-old-mind for years.

"I've read that ICE maintains 1,000 detention facilities now," Estelle said "They're everywhere: California, New York, Wyoming, North Carolina. Texas has fifteen! It makes me so angry. Why don't we use that money to feed starving children?" Estelle mixed cream into her coffee with a vengeance. "It's hard to know what's going on. The government is not forthcoming with the facts."

Maggie stroked Sophie's hair. "The saddest story I read last year said that ICE detained thousands of undocumented and documented workers. Rosa is always in danger even with her proper papers. Many are being held in Mexico now, not allowed into our country."

"Maybe we shouldn't continue this in front of our little guest," Estelle said.

"It's okay," Sophie chirped. "I know this stuff. Everyone at the apartments talks about it all the time. My friend Gigi and her Mom were sent back to Honduras. They live with her Grandy. She wrote me a note. Said they hear gun shots at night when they try to sleep."

Maggie wrapped her arms tightly around Sophie. "Oh, honey, you shouldn't have to think about these things."

"It's important to be informed, my Papa says. Gigi likes her bedroom and her new school."

"Your optimism inspires me, my little scholar."

"Papa wants me to grow up to be a scholar," Sophie said, full of vigor.

Maggie squeezed her tighter. Rosa often said Sophie's "brain" scared her.

Estelle continued, "It breaks my heart. We've let the Latinos come in for years, do all our dirty work and then herd them out like cattle. Rosa never became a full citizen because she feared she couldn't pass the English test."

"I read that if you're a Mexican and want to enter this country legally, you have to put your name on a list that got started in 1996. Not sure it's true, but that's how I remember it." Maggie nibbled the edge of the cookie Sophie had refused.

"Doesn't sound too promising. No wonder so many sneak in." Estelle sipped her coffee.

"Let's not complicate this, Mom. The authorities

don't know Rosa worked for us. Sophie may not have papers, but she was born here. Rosa told me years ago. A midwife in Phoenix delivered her."

"But she may have said that so you'd keep her on."

"I'm shocked you'd say that about Rosa!"

"It's just a suspicious old lady talking. Pay me no attention."

Maggie never thought of her grandmother as old, even though she was almost eighty. She had called her Mom since the shooting.

Estelle was upstairs putting baby Josh in his crib for an afternoon nap when a loud noise startled her. She heard the crack. A gun shot. "What the f...?" she shouted, running down the staircase.

Her daughter, Thelma, lounged on the sofa with a derringer on her lap, her face sweet and contented. Leo, her husband, lay on the floor with a bullet hole in the middle of his brow, a pool of blood surrounding his head. Dead.

"He was making a move on Maggie. Trying to get her into the bedroom," Thelma explained. "I told him to stop. He said it was a game. I said STOP. I'd bought a gun for our protection from him. I pulled it out of my purse and shot. I'm not sorry."

Estelle picked up eight-year-old Maggie and hugged her to her heart. She knew the child had witnessed every detail of the scene.

For years after, in the face of panic, Maggie would retreat and get that look of invisibility kids get hoping to remove themselves from an ugly scene. Estelle abruptly retired from her impassioned life as a civil rights attorney to care for Maggie and Josh. Therapy helped them return to a peaceful calm. Thelma admitted to her mother that she was ill. She'd been diagnosed before the shooting with acute myeloid leukemia and died in prison four months later, before her case went to trial. When Thelma died, Estelle legally adopted Maggie and Josh.

Still agile, with stylishly coiffured silver-white hair and energy to match Sophie's, Estelle often overwhelmed Maggie who was more deliberate in her actions and decisions. Estelle tapped her spoon against her coffee cup.

Agitation bore into Maggie's nerves. The muscles in her neck tightened. "I'll take Sophie to work with me until I decide what to do."

"Is it wise to take her to your office? I could stay home today. I was just going to a meeting. A group I know wants to make Juniper Hills a Sanctuary Town to protect our threatened Latino families."

"That would be helpful, but I'm not sure about her legal standing." A clap of thunder punctuated her words. "We need papers, information, I'll call the school, see what's required."

"What's the first thing to do?" Estelle asked.

"I'll stay home and work at my desk. I have a conference call at ten. Sophie can play in my office."

"I'll cancel my appointment, stay home with Sophie so you can go to work."

"Not necessary. We'll be fine."

"Well, if that's the way you feel." Estelle rustled

her newspaper in a manner that made Maggie want to escape the kitchen before she strangled her beloved grandmother.

She knew Rosa kept clothes, books, games and other items in the laundry room cabinets. Rosa had asked if she could use the basement room for storage. "Okay. Let's see what we can find for you to play with."

Maggie eased Sophie onto the floor, stood and took her hand. Walking downstairs to the laundry room, she realized that it had been awhile since she looked around her own basement. Rosa was an efficient housekeeper. There was no need. When Maggie opened the first cabinet, she saw stacks of neatly folded clothes for Sophie. A lower cabinet held art supplies, books, small boxes of Lego toys and a pink iPad she and Estelle had given Sophie for Christmas. Sophie loved to play by herself.

Rosa had been planning for this emergency! Damn! Blood coursed through Maggie's brain. She felt selfish and deceived at the same time. Rosa had taken advantage of her by not discussing her preparations. On the other hand, Maggie was flattered that Rosa knew in her heart that she, Maggie, would take care of Sophie. She couldn't help comparing this to how her own mother had provided for Maggie's safety when she purchased that gun.

CHAPTER 3

MAGGIE REMOVED her suit jacket, rolled her shirt sleeves, looped her hair behind her ears and searched through Sophie's clothing in the basement cabinet. What would she do if she couldn't find useful documents? Hiring someone to create a counterfeit birth certificate could jeopardize her career as an attorney. Was she willing to take that risk? Last week she'd noticed her neighbor down the street glaring at Sophie playing in Maggie's front yard. Would the old witch go so far as to report a Mexican child on her block who might be undocumented?

She had to enroll Sophie in school. Sophie had been home-schooled, but she needed the socialization and breadth of knowledge she'd get in a classroom. Maggie knelt to go through envelopes and stacks of clothing Rosa had left on the basement shelves. Under a neat pile of tee-shirts, she discovered a battered picture album featuring Sophie, Rosa and Carlos with other people at beaches and amusement parks, swimming and riding bikes.

Stuck in the back of the album was a stiff manila envelope. Written in caps on the front was "SOPHIE'S BIRTH CERTIFICATE." Opening the flap, Maggie discovered the treasure she'd been seeking. Eureka! She rejoiced at her good fortune. In her hands was a birth certificate for Sophie Maria Melendez, born October 10th, 2011 at five pounds seven ounces, signed by Elena Garcia, midwife, in Phoenix, Arizona. Attached was a detailed list of Sophie's immunizations.

But wait. The certificate had no official seal. The paper was faded and rumpled. Though Maggie didn't know exactly how a legal birth certificate should look, this piece of paper wouldn't convince anyone. It looked as if Sophie had created it in a day care art class.

Rosa had said she'd lived in California, Colorado and Arizona over the last twenty-five years. Sophie was only eight, nearing nine. She must have been born in the U.S. Had Rosa been too afraid of the authorities to register the birth? Had she created this document herself? Maggie knew she couldn't take this piece of paper to the school as a legal birth certificate. She also knew Sophie needed a Social Security Number.

Maggie turned to Sophie. "Are you documented? Do you know?"

Sophie searched her face, looking for the correct answer.

Maggie switched off her legal mind. "Do you know where you were born, honey?"

"Of course." Sophie relaxed. She could answer that question. "Phoenix, Arizona."

"Phoenix. That's a good start." Could it be that Sophie was an American citizen or had Rosa taught her to say that for her own protection?

"What do you want to play with?" Maggie would deal with Sophie's legal status later. She'd first check birth records on the Internet. With the information she had she could immediately tell if Sophie was registered as an American citizen. Then she'd try to track down Elena Garcia in Phoenix.

Sophie stuck her head into the cabinet, pushing aside the pink iPad Maggie and Estelle had given her last Christmas. She knew what she wanted and where they were stashed. Lifting out a folder of hand-made paper dolls, Sophie fished in a plastic bucket for a small pair of scissors.

Had Sophie and Rosa discussed the possibilities of separation? Maggie felt herself slipping into her own eight-year old out-of-sync heartbreak. She scanned Sophie's face for signs of sorrow or fear, amazed at how this special child handled her life of troubles. For Sophie's sake she laid the folder of paper dolls on top of the dryer and admired their clothing. Sophie was thrilled at the attention to her beloved paper dolls. Maggie had never been responsible for a child twenty-four/seven. Would she be able to sustain Sophie or would Sophie sustain her?

At the urging of her shrink, Maggie dated in high school only to become ensnared in a disastrous marriage in her twenties. The pain remained strong. She'd recently accepted that she'd never marry again or have a child. Now in her thirties, she knew women had healthy babies in their forties and early fifties, even if the risks were higher. The "law" was a jealous profession that left her little time for a social life. If asked, she would have admitted she enjoyed Sophie's presence in the house when Rosa came to clean. Or when Sophie occasionally stayed overnight to free up Rosa for another job, but....

Back upstairs in her office with time before her conference call, Maggie couldn't decide what to do first. She sat at her desk to make a list. Hiding Sophie's identity seemed the priority until Maggie could confirm her legal status. She had to get a birth certificate with a raised seal and a social security number for Sophie. School would start soon.

Estelle's ancestors were Greek. Maggie herself had dark hair and Mediterranean skin, despite the resplendent blue eyes inherited from her Irish father. Maybe she could pass Sophie off as a relative from Greece, a cousin's child whose mother had died. A child her aunt couldn't take care of. She had to explain her and she had to register her in school. She did not want to deal with suspicious questions about Sophie's presence, particularly with Rosa gone.

On TV people seemed to get fake documents all the time. How hard could it be? A detective who did some special work for her law firm was known to help immigrants. She hadn't met him, but his reputation was excellent. She would make inquiries. Sophie needed a new identity, yesterday. Would the neighbors recognize the difference between a Greek child and a Mexican child? How often had they seen Sophie at her house before today?

Sophie carefully placed the fat folder she'd carried up from the basement on an empty chair in the corner of Maggie's office. One by one she dressed the beautiful hand-made paper dolls in elaborate costumes and real-feathered hats, making a careful snip here or adjustment there before parading them around the floor, speaking softly in different voices.

Maggie opened the line to her conference call. Rosa must have spent hours creating those dolls, she thought, half listening. They were museum quality. When she finished the two-hour call, she disconnected, marveled at Sophie's patience and asked, "How about lunch? You must be starving."

Sophie beamed her glorious smile. "Si, señorita."

It was going to be harder to pull off the Greek deception than Maggie had thought.

CHAPTER 4

AFTER LUNCH Maggie glued herself to her desk and composed several new columns for *The Juniper Hills Gazette*. MISS CHLOE had deadlines to meet. Her brother, Josh, was owner and editor of the *Gazette*. When his advice columnist retired, Josh asked, no begged, Maggie to take over the column until he could find a replacement. A year later she was still writing the MISS CHLOE column in her meager spare time.

> Dear Miss Chloe, I suspect my 14-year-old-son is gay. He's always been sweet and different from other boys. Lately he's having trouble relating to his schoolmates and his grades are slipping. Should I bring up the subject with him or wait until he tells me? I can accept the knowledge.

I will always love him as I do now. I see him suffering and I would like to open the subject with him, but I don't want to upset him until he's ready to talk to me. *Stymied in Buckeye*

Dear Stymied: You seem like a loving sensible mom. Just blurt it out. "Would you like to talk to me about your sexual identity?" See what he says. Kids today are pretty savvy. He may be mum because he's worried about upsetting you. *Miss Chloe*

Josh told Maggie, when she first started writing the column, the newspaper was receiving hundreds of letters about the "new" MISS CHLOE. Half complained she was too blunt and uncaring while the other half was delighted that she didn't write mealy-mouth, sentimental responses. The newspaper's circulation actually increased and his editorial board thought it was because of the controversy. Josh received an offer to syndicate her column.

Maggie read and answered more letters, some silly and annoying, others heart breaking. She sighed and sat silently, watching Sophie arrange and rearrange her dolls while chatting in different voices. She was such a special child and deserved the very best Maggie could do for her, particularly now that people without documentation were being treated as less than human and their families were being ripped apart.

Tomorrow she must hire someone to help her find or create a "legal" birth certificate for Sophie, even if it affected Maggie's status as an attorney. She prayed the risk would be small.

Maggie scanned another letter. Shivering, she smoothed it flat on her desk and sat back, closing her eyes. The woman expressed being overwhelmed and frightened by her husband who'd recently returned from a tour in Afghanistan. She'd signed it Collateral Victim of PTSD.

Tears swelled in Maggie's eyes. These days there was at least one such letter in every batch of mail Josh sent over from the *Gazette*. Each brought Maggie memories she'd hoped never again to think about.

She knew Josh had offered the MISS CHLOE column to help her over her traumatic marriage to Hank Leonard, but sometimes it made things worse. Not wanting to upset Sophie, she wiped tears from her cheeks and blew her nose. Ever vigilant, Sophie looked up to see if she was okay. Maggie forced a smile at her small self-appointed protector.

After years as an abusive husband and five years of absence, Hank Leonard had recently appeared in Juniper Hills. Maggie's divorce lawyer told her that Hank, now a major in the Marine Corps, had retired and become a member of the Reserves. He hadn't contacted family or friends, if any were left, until a month ago when he appeared at his mother's house.

Maggie had been so shocked she considered pulling out of the law firm she had worked hard to establish and moving to Chicago to work at her cousin's firm. Estelle was not happy about a move but agreed to go. Maggie couldn't bear to live in the same small town with Hank Leonard if he decided to stay.

Josh and her law partners, Lisa and Gus, talked her out of a rash decision, reasoning Hank wouldn't hang around. He was not well liked. To her chagrin, he was still in Juniper Hills and hadn't tried to contact her, which was good and nerve-racking at the same time. He was a lost, damaged soul who refused to acknowledge he needed help. She'd never understand the horrors he'd experienced in Afghanistan, but she'd been willing to try. Hank locked her out of his life. He was scarred and scared. She lived with deep regrets but could never again trust and love him and probably not another man either.

They'd been high school sweethearts. Senior year, Hank was accepted at West Point Military Academy. Tall, muscular, dark-blond hair with striking blue eyes he'd been a good-looking young man in high school with a charming manner. Overnight, decked out in his West Point uniform with its complicated braids and glossy metals, he became a desirable attractive man. For the first time Maggie sensed streaks of jealousy from some of her long-time girlfriends. It didn't help that Hank strutted around obviously enjoying the increased female attention. She didn't know whether to be disgusted or amused. She'd never known him to have an outsized ego.

Maggie went to the University of Arizona in Tucson, planning, at Estelle's insistence, to apply to Law School. Immediately after their graduations, she and Hank married in the beautiful West Point Cadet Chapel on a breathtaking June day along the Hudson River in upstate New York. When Hank was deployed on his first tour to Afghanistan, they stayed close through Skype, texting, emailing and occasionally an old-fashioned love letter. He had been a nice guy. Tender and caring.

Hank's three tours in Afghanistan deranged him.

"Don't tell me what to do," he screamed one day when she suggested therapy.

"I'm only...." She continued setting the dinner table.

"It's none of your business. Do you realize what'd happen if the guys found out? I'd be laughed out of my unit."

"Nobody thinks like that anymore."

"Little you know." Hank stepped back and smashed his hand through a small kitchen window pane.

She gasped. "You're bleeding. Let me wash—"

"Stay away from me, bitch. Don't coddle me. You'll make me weak."

"I'm trying to help."

"Bullshit." He stomped out the back door.

She ate dinner by herself.

Before her eyes Hank became a monster, frustrated at the smallest problem, angry and violent. He broke a kitchen chair, slamming it against the refrigerator because she didn't buy his favorite beer, which hadn't been his favorite beer two days before. She threatened to leave if he didn't seek help.

He refused and started coming home in the early hours of dawn, smelling of alcohol and drug-store perfume. One night he grabbed her shoulders, shoved her against the wall, knocked her out and left town. The next day, suffering a fierce headache, she filed for divorce and applied to Stanford Law School in the same week. It took forever for her lawyer to find Hank and get a response from him. The process was painful. She didn't ask for anything from him. The marriage was beyond repair.

She set the letter from "Victim of PTSD" aside. She would need time to deal with it in a helpful way. She picked up another letter.

Dear Miss Chloe: Yesterday when I was in the supermarket with my ten-month old baby, an elderly woman stopped to tell me I should have socks on my child. My baby was wrapped in a light blanket and covered in a one-piece terry jumper with her feet bare. It was eighty-five degrees outside! I was tempted to tell the uninvited advice giver to mind her own business, but controlled myself. Why do seemingly sweet grandmotherly types always think they know everything about babies? *Supermarket Mom*

Dear Mom: You sound like a diligent caring mom. Please be patient with older women who want to tell you how they raised their babies. In time you, too, will be old. *Miss Chloe*

Some days Maggie wanted to string up Josh by his cojones for getting her involved in MISS CHLOE'S affairs. Other days she wished he'd asked her to become a reporter for the *Gazette*. The law no longer excited her. She'd lost a sense of purpose. It had become routine, too corporate. Perhaps it was time to think of a career change. She felt lost. She had come to a strange crossroad. A place she didn't recognize. Did she want to make more money? Did she want to help more people? Could she do both? She needed a cause. A reason to exist!

CHAPTER 5

MONDAY MORNING Maggie arrived at her law firm to find her partners, Lisa Pérez and Gus Palmer, huddled in the conference room, preparing to meet with the firm's real estate agent, Stephen Duval, to complete the purchase of their new office building.

Maggie joined them at the table and sank heavily into a leather chair. The news about the two Latino kids attacked by a white supremacist group hung heavy in her heart. "What've you heard about this hate gang attacking Latino kids? There was another article in the paper this morning. It's at least the third incident. Doesn't sound like our town."

"I don't know what to think," Lisa said. "Robbie was talking about it at breakfast. As a Latino he's on high alert to anything racist."

"Your husband's right," Maggie said, brushing a strand of her long dark hair out of her face.

"Aw, it's a bunch of rotten kids with nothing to do but bully other kids." Gus dismissed the discussion and steered the conversation back to the matter at hand ... moving. "We need to make decisions here, ladies." He flapped the plans for the new office on the table.

"No, Gus. I think you're wrong," Maggie said. "These attacks smell menacing. It's more than immigrants crossing the border. It's domestic terrorism. Antisocial extremism."

Gus shrugged. "I think you're over reacting." He went back to studying the plans.

Maggie didn't feel like fighting. Gus often drove her to wanting to pull out her hair or better yet his.

After a year of searching they'd found a larger, more suitable office in a recently renovated, beautiful Queen Anne Victorian house in the center of Juniper Hills. A pitched roof and scalloped fish-scale-shingles adorned the left front. Smooth river rocks covered the front right side, reflecting sunlight in different tones and shadows, depending on the time of day.

At first Maggie thought it looked like a storybook house, but Gus convinced her it'd be distinctive.

"People will say just look for the house with the pointed roof and wrap-around porch," Gus said.

"In San Francisco these houses are painted vivid colors with even brighter trim. They're called Painted Ladies," Lisa stood to refill her coffee cup.

"Well, I'm glad ours is gray with dignified maroon trim or we might get an unwanted reputation." Maggie giggled at her own joke that no one seemed to get and restacked a pile of documents on the table.

Thrilled at their good fortune, they hoped they weren't overstretching their budget with a big mortgage. Although business had been extraordinary the last few years, Maggie knew you could never count on the economy to go your way.

She waited with Gus and Lisa to sign the documents to close the deal. She had left Sophie with a delighted Estelle and promised to return for lunch. Removing her ivory-colored linen suit jacket, she hung it on the back of a chair and sat at the conference table. In a month they'd be in their new offices. She prayed Hank would've left town by then.

"Stephen called. He was running late, so we're relaxing here for a few," Lisa said, sipping her coffee. Aides and secretaries bustled in the outer offices, packing up for the move.

"I need the name of that detective you were so pleased with," Maggie said. "The one who testified in the Sanchez case."

"Aah. That detective!" Lisa lifted her blond hair off the back of her neck and fluttered green eyes that seemed as large as traffic lights. "Dan Clarke. What a honey and a gorgeous redhead. For the record, he's single." Lisa winked at Maggie, who shrugged and stuck out her tongue. "Said all the right things in his testimony. No way was the judge or the jury going to deport the father of five kids and a wife of twenty years." Lisa pointed her finger at Maggie. "The prosecution tried to prove that it was a marriage of convenience. Without Clarke's testimony, Sanchez would have been shipped back to Guatemala."

"Twenty years! Five children a convenience!" Maggie moved to the credenza and poured a cup of black coffee. Lisa wasn't taking enough credit for a job well done. Maggie knew how hard she had worked to save Enrico Sanchez.

"The prosecutor was on a roll. I can't believe he almost sounded reasonable. 'What if we let anybody walk across our border,' blah, blah, blah? You should have heard Clarke go on about ripping a loving family to shreds."

"Do you think he can help me get a birth certificate?" Maggie asked. "ICE picked up my housekeeper's husband. She's out searching for him. Her daughter, Sophie, is staying with me and Mom. I need to register the little one for school."

"Be careful, Maggie, it's nasty out there since SB1040. You can be arrested for hiring the child's mother as well as harboring an illegal if Sophie stays," Gus warned, as he adjusted his round tortoiseshell glasses.

Well over six feet, straight and thin as a post, he got up to close the window-blind shading the sun from their eyes. "ICE is now coming after immigrants who are more or less legal. People who have been in this country for twenty years, become teachers, built businesses, paid taxes. I don't get it. Why mess with something that isn't broken?"

"Call Dan Clarke. It's amazing what he can come up with." Lisa picked up her iPhone, scrolled through her contacts, found the number she was looking for and sent it in on to Maggie's phone. "That's his personal number."

Stephen Duval and his paralegal arrived as Maggie entered Clarke's number in her contacts list. The closing documents were discussed, signed, notarized and stamped. Maggie, Lisa, Gus and their employees would vacate the premises within two weeks. Fourteen days to clean out almost ten years of their law lives and make decisions: what they must legally keep, what they could toss, hundreds of small decisions. But foremost on Maggie's mind was Sophie and her predicament. She had to call Dan Clarke before tackling the job of moving.

She said good-bye to Duval and his paralegal, went into her office and called Detective Dan Clarke's number. A warm, clear-toned masculine voice told her he was not available but to leave a name and number and he would get back to her. For an emergency he left another number. Maggie didn't think her problem was his kind of emergency, so she gave her personal cell number, hung up and thought, is it possible to fall in love with a voice? She castigated herself for being silly. Men with lovely voices, plain voices or ugly voices, for God's sake, didn't attract her anymore. She said 'bye to Lisa and Gus and went home to have a peaceful lunch with Estelle and Sophie.

CHAPTER 6

MAGGIE LEFT HER CAR at the office and walked home. Last night's rain had washed the air. The summer sun felt soft on her skin. It would take ten minutes to climb the hill to her house and she welcomed the quiet time to think about plans for Sophie.

Approaching her house on Palisade Avenue, she saw Estelle's dark-gray Honda in the driveway with the back-passenger door open. One of the two wide garage door was rolled up. As Maggie moved closer, Estelle appeared at the kitchen doorway leading into the garage with Sophie at her shoulder, covered in a fuzzy pink blanket, a heavy white towel wrapped around her left leg. Blood oozed through the terry cloth.

Maggie yelled, "What happened?"

"Sophie heard the doorbell ring. Afraid it was ICE; she ran down the basement stairs like her parents taught her. She slipped and flew, slicing her leg on one of the blades of that old rusty lawnmower when she landed."

Estelle motioned for Maggie to hold the car door so she could lay Sophie on the back seat of the Honda. "Apparently she was told to run and hide if the doorbell rang unexpectantly. ... Oh, I said that. ... Get a pillow for her head," Estelle commanded as she settled the small body.

"I'll ride in back. My lap can be her pillow." Maggie carefully lifted Sophie's head and tried to catch her eyes. "Are you okay? Everything will be all right. We'll get you to the hospital in a jiffy."

Sophie giggled, mimicked, "jiffy" and moaned. Tears trickled down her checks.

Estelle slid under the steering wheel. "The hospital knows we're coming."

"Would you rather I drive?" Maggie offered.

"Close the door." Estelle already had the engine in gear. "Damn. I intended to give that old thing away last year." Estelle adjusted her rear-view mirror. "A blade gashed her calf. I cleaned it, but it was gushing. I thought her femoral artery may have been nicked. I used my belt for a tourniquet and called the ER and told them to prepare for an emergency."

"Oh, Mom. Thank God you studied to be an EMT. Please don't blame yourself."

"I feel better now that we're on the way to the hospital. I couldn't wait for an ambulance."

Maggie looked at Sophie's pale face. "Do you hurt, honey?"

"Not really. I'm just all bloody." Her breathing shallow, Sophie barely moved.

"We'll take care of that. Don't worry. When this is over, we'll buy you a pretty new outfit." Maggie held back her own tears and stroked Sophie's damp hair.

When Estelle drove up to the emergency entrance, two attendants with a gurney met them at the door. "We've been waiting for you. Surgery's been notified," one said.

The man and woman lifted Sophie to the gurney. Maggie continued to hold Sophie's hand as they moved into the hospital and down the hall. "She needs immediate attention."

"We'll take it from here," the male attendant said.

"I can't leave her. She's only eight." Maggie walked along with the gurney.

"Almost nine," Sophie mumbled.

"You'll have to sign her in," hollered the woman at the admitting desk, whose name tag on her large bosom, read Beatrice. "Are you her mother?"

Anticipating a problem, Maggie turned to the attendant who had stopped pushing the gurney. "No," she said in her most authoritative tone. "I'm her lawyer." Turning to Beatrice, she called, "I'll be back to sign her in and give my consent. I need to speak to the doctor first." The gurney attendant gave the woman at the admitting desk a wary nod, then rushed toward the double doors to Surgery.

Beatrice frowned and looked to see if anyone else was paying attention. She didn't want to get herself in trouble. No way was she going to start a fracas in the hallway with a lawyer while a child bled to death.

At that moment, down the hall came Detective Dan Clarke. He had brought in an older gentleman who'd fainted in front of his squad car as Dan was about to start the engine. It was almost a miracle he saw the man go down, or he might have run over the guy. The doctor said that the man's hip gave way, an old hip honeycombed with osteoporosis.

Dan had checked on Miguel and Luis while at the hospital and learned that Luis had been discharged but Miguel was not expected to make it. He tucked his grief behind his heart and headed for the door to go home.

At the end of the hallway, Dan spotted a dark-haired woman in a blood-stained ivory suit leaning over a child on a gurney. Did a double take: glowing skin, long perfect legs, insistent and bossy. "What was that about?" he asked Beatrice.

"You didn't hear this from me." Beatrice motioned Dan to lean closer. "An old woman called, said she was an Emergency Medical Tech, bringing in an injured child for surgery. Then this woman shows up and refuses to check her in or leave the child. Says she's her lawyer. That's a first for me. When people bring in children, they're often irrational, so we'll straighten out the details later. I'm so tired of haggling with patients."

"You do a great job, Beatrice. Don't be hard on yourself." Dan looked down the hall and watched as the elegant woman held the door for the attendant, completely in charge of the situation.

A bustling white-haired lady carrying a fuzzy pink blanket slammed into Dan as he walked through the automatic door to the parking lot with nary so much as an "excuse me, sir." He barely noticed, walking in deep thought. Insistent and bossy. Hmm.... Pretty woman.

Estelle stopped at the admitting desk. "My daughter brought in a little girl a few minutes ago. Where can I find them?"

"They've gone to surgery, ma'am. Can you give me information about the patient?"

"You'll have to ask my daughter."

"There's a waiting room down that hall to your left. I'll tell them you're there."

Estelle, clutching the blanket, walked down the hall, pleased with herself for having played dumb as to Sophie's name and information. Maggie would have to figure out what to say. Estelle put the fuzzy blanket on the arm of her chair and rested her head until she dozed off, exhausted by stress.

"Mom." Maggie's voice startled Estelle awake. "Poor dear. I'm sorry it took so long." Estelle blinked and opened her eyes "The doctors wanted to run tests and take x-rays to be sure Sophie had no other injuries.There's bruising on her hands and elbows. Fortunately, she didn't hit her head." Maggie brushed back her grandmother's tangled hair. "We need to get you home."

Behind Maggie, Sophie sat in a wheel chair with a smile on her face. Her left leg, supported by a metal bracket, swathed in heavy gauze bandages, no plaster cast.

"Mom," Sophie said to Estelle. "I asked to watch. Said I didn't want to be put to sleep. Gave me a shot they called a local."

"Oh, darlin', I'm so glad you're out of surgery." Estelle stood, bent over Sophie and planted a gentle kiss on her forehead.

"They only did ten tiny stitches inside. But I have forty-three on the outside!" Sophie took a huge breath. "The nurse said when I grow up, I'll hardly notice the scar. Oh, Mom thanks for getting me to the hospital so fast. I could have bled to death."

Estelle looked at Maggie.

Shaking her head as if to say not to worry, Maggie chuckled. "I think our patient is a little high. The doctor said a half-inch closer and the artery could have bled out. You were right to hurry here. They gave her a tetanus shot, a local anesthetic, antibiotics and pain pills."

"And what's with calling me Mom, Miss Sophie?"

"Maggie does."

"What's your mother going to think about that?"

"I call her Mama."

"I see. Okay. Kinda like it." Estelle turned to Maggie. "How did things go at the admitting desk?"

"I apologized to the agitated lady, Beatrice, and gave her my ID and insurance information. Told her the child's name was Sophie Melendez. Her parents were out of town and she was staying with us. I said our homeowners' insurance would pay for the accident of a guest, but if not, I gave her my personal info too. That was it. No other questions."

"Oh, thank God. I hope registering her in school goes as well."

"It will if we ever get a damn birth certificate!"

CHAPTER 7

ON THE WAY HOME from the hospital, they stopped at a medical supply shop where Maggie rented a child's electric wheelchair. Sophie begged for the red one. Maggie didn't have the heart to refuse, although it cost twice as much as a black chair.

The crescent moon beamed on the small rocks covering the driveway as they pulled into the garage. Maggie carried Sophie into the kitchen and settled her in a chair at the table. Estelle dragged the wheelchair into the kitchen, then put a pot of chicken vegetable soup, made the day before, on the burner to warm. Sophie, mildly agitated, continued to rattle on. The lush aroma of the soup created a calming atmosphere.

"Did the doctor give you anything for Sophie's future pain?" Estelle asked.

Maggie fished in her purse and pulled out a script. "It's for a mild painkiller. She may need it during the night. I'll push her into town to the drugstore while you get dinner ready. The fresh air will be good for us."

Maggie bundled Sophie back into the wheelchair. With Estelle's help, they bumped down the two narrow steps into the garage.

As they moved along, Sophie pointed and cried out a welcome when stars appeared in the darkening sky. "I think that one's a white dwarf," she said, stretching back her head as far as possible.

"How do you know about white dwarfs?"

"An astro ... phy ... si ... cist who lived in the apartments last year told me all about them." Sophie pronounced the word as if practicing for a spelling bee. "We have molecules in us that are the same as molecules in the stars. Think of that, Maggie, we're made of stars."

"Neat," Maggie said, almost afraid to ask for more info. Once or twice she let Sophie use the electric button and move the chair herself while Maggie trotted alongside, thinking the exercise would do her good.

She wheeled Sophie into the drugstore and handed over the prescription. The pharmacist said, "It'll be a few minutes. ... How did you hurt yourself, sweetheart?"

"I flew. It would have been fun if I didn't fall on a rusty lawnmower."

"Sorry you fell. Must have hurt."

"I'll be all right in a few days. The doctor said."

The pharmacist nodded at Maggie and took the prescription over to his lab. "Just take a sec."

Ten minutes later Maggie maneuvered Sophie's chair out onto the sidewalk. "Okay, baby-doll, we're going home for chicken soup and a good night's sleep."

While traveling along at a vigorous pace, Maggie heard leaves rustle behind her. Someone emerged from the shadows and brushed her shoulder. "Hello, Maggie." The words were pronounced with deliberation.

She turned and nearly ran the red wheelchair off the curb. "Hank!"

"What's with the little cripple?"

"I don't want to talk to you."

"Still holding a grudge?"

"Hank, please get out of our way. I have to get Sophie home. Estelle's waiting on us for dinner."

He didn't move. Maggie feared her heart would beat through her ribcage; her legs moved like jelly.

"Mr. Hank, please get out of the way. Maggie has to take me home."

Hank peered at Sophie as if noticing her for the first time. "Hi, sweet-pie. What's your name?"

"I can't talk to you **either**. We have to get home. Mom is making dinner for us."

Seeming confused and unsure, Hank moved off the sidewalk. Maggie rolled Sophie past him and headed up the hill without a word. That was the way she intended to behave until Hank left town. No sense attempting a rational dialogue. Their lives had moved beyond conversation. After their divorce, she'd spent two years in therapy, finally accepting that the Hank she had deeply loved and married no longer existed. She steered the red wheelchair down the street and let Sophie use the button to go the last block and turn into the driveway.

Estelle pulled open the kitchen door as soon as they entered the garage. "I've been thinking, we need to put a board over those steps to create a ramp. Sophie could go in and out by herself."

"She'd have to promise to stay close to the house."

Maggie sighed with relief, deciding to let Estelle make the rules. The chicken soup smelled divine. "I'm starved. How about you?" Maggie lifted Sophie from the wheelchair and carried her to a seat at the kitchen table.

"Si, I love soup. Bread and butter too. Mom, we met Mr. Hank on the sidewalk." She tugged one of her braids for emphasis.

"What?" Estelle looked at Maggie. "How did that go?"

"We didn't talk to him," Sophie said, "except to ask him to get off the sidewalk."

"I kept my promise," Maggie said, "not to speak to him. He makes me crazy. He twists everything around. My best hope for sanity is to say nothing. So that's what I'm going to do."

"He called me a cripple."

"He's being mean. He has no idea what he's talking about. I hope he didn't hurt your feelings?" Maggie looked over her shoulder at Estelle who busied herself at the sink.

"No," said Sophie, "I know cripples aren't bad people. Anyway, I'm going to be up and about in a short time."

"Who told you that?" Estelle asked.

"The nurse at the hospital said I'm very lucky."

"You are. Keep listening to the nurse and pay no attention to Hank."

"He's an angry man." Sophie yawned and stuffed the end of a braid in her mouth to suck on it.

"I think somebody is tired," Maggie looked at Estelle for confirmation.

"You are not only wise but correct, Miss Sophie. Now let's finish up dinner and go to bed." Estelle placed a puff of creamy custard in a light crust in front of Sophie. "Here's a special lemon tart for your dessert. The kind you like."

"Oh, Mom. You're the greatest." Sophie wolfed down the tart in three forkfuls.

"I think she's been watching too much TV," Maggie said to Estelle. "Come on, you little rascal. I'll help you wash and get in your pjs." She hoisted Sophie over her shoulder.

Maggie's cell rang. "Get that for me, Mom."

Estelle reached into Maggie's bag on the kitchen chair and turned to her. "For you. A man ... It might be that detective."

"I'll call back."

"No. Don't put it off. Give me Sophie. I'll take her to bed." She grasped the child's hand and handed over the phone.

"Hello." Maggie fumbled the phone to her ear.

"Hey, there." She recognized the voice before he introduced himself. "This is Dan Clarke. You called me?"

She explained who she was and that she had a legal problem but didn't want to discuss it over the phone.

"Could we meet somewhere tomorrow?"

"Your message sounded like it was important. How about right now? I can be at Rodney's Café in fifteen minutes."

Bone tired and blood-splattered, Maggie hesitated, but she needed his help. "How about eight o'clock?"

"Forty-five minutes. Sure thing."

"Rodney's is only a couple of blocks away."

"I know. I looked up your address."

"You did?"

"That's what I do. I'm a cop, remember."

"Oh, wait. I left my car at the office."

"I'll pick you up at your house."

CHAPTER 8

MAGGIE DASHED up the stairs, pulled off her blood-stained clothes, took a quick shower and ran a drier and comb over her wet hair. Should she pull it back with a fancy clip or let it hang loose? Squirming into a pair of jeans and a bright pink tee, she added a spritz of "Coco Chanel" for good luck. Her wavy dark hair hung free.

She stopped at Estelle's bedroom where her grandmother, propped up on pillows, was reading *Little Women* to a near comatose child. She'd seen Sophie pull the book from her bookshelf. Now she was insisting it be read to her.

"I told her she could sleep with me for one night." Estelle looked as if she'd been caught in an illegal act.

"She's had a rough day," Maggie said and bent down to kiss Sophie's cheek, wondering if Sophie understood a word of the plot.

"Every time I stop reading, she wakes, wanting more story," Estelle said.

"Pretend you're asleep. She'll forgive you, turn out the light and pull up your covers. She likes to take care of you, Mom. Right Sophie?"

Sophie nodded, barely able to hold her head up.

"So, you're going out with this detective. Is this a date?" Maggie knew Estelle couldn't help herself. She had to ask.

"You know I don't do dates. This is business."

"You have a certain anticipation in your eyes."

"Oh, Mom, ever the romantic." Maggie knew Estelle ached for her to meet a man she could love again.

"Do you have everything you need for the detective?"

"I have all I've got, which isn't much."

"Do your best."

By the time Maggie walked down the stairs, Dan Clarke was on her front porch about to ring the bell. When she opened the door, she saw what Lisa had called a "gorgeous redhead" in a blue cotton shirt with the sleeves rolled, khakis pants and gray sneakers standing before her. He was solidly built and well over six feet.

Dan Clarke scanned her face. "It's you," he said, looking rather foolish.

"Have we met?" Maggie smiled and studied his face. She noted he didn't have the pale, freckled skin that usually went with red hair. His complexion was smooth and tawny like *café au lait*. Neatly combed damp hair with a few cowlicks and a slightly chipped front tooth completed the picture. But those eyes, engaging and attentive, seemed to absorb her.

She watched him regain his composure and heard him say, "I saw you at the hospital this afternoon with a little girl."

"Sophie Melendez," Maggie said as they walked to his car, and he opened the door for her. "She fell and slashed her leg. We thought she'd severed an artery, but she only nicked it, bad enough to spurt blood all over the place and scare us to death. Sophie's the reason I want your help." She had to curl her long legs to fit in the bucket seat. "No black and white?"

"I'm off duty. You said you wanted to speak privately about something."

"Yes." She sighed. "I've brought a document I'd like you to look at." She held up the manila envelope she had on her lap. "Lisa Pérez, my law partner, told me that you help immigrants."

"I do what I can. Some of these new immigration laws are cruelty personified."

When they arrived at Rodney's Café, it was not crowded and they sat in a booth near the back of the bar where they could comfortably talk. "Would you like a beer?"

Maggie, who rarely drank, nodded to be polite, and Dan ordered two Sierra Nevada Pale Ales. The Café started to buzz. Groups of threes and fours were arriving. It was a warm place filled with laughter. Although she had only been here once or twice, Maggie knew that Rodney's Café, with its old-western décor, had been in

Juniper Hills as long as she could remember. It began as a sports bar and in time added a fine dining room that lived up to its reputation for the last twenty years. A few years ago, they'd expanded the bar and added music and dancing to attract a younger generation.

"I remember Lisa Pérez from the Sanchez case," Dan said. "That was a near disaster. She saved him from deportation to Guatemala."

"She said the same thing about you."

"Sometimes it does take a village."

Maggie found herself feeling easy and comfortable talking to Dan. Because of the escalating noise, she leaned in and told him about Rosa and Carlos Melendez. "She's looking for him. Not sure where though. My mom and I are taking care of her daughter, Sophie."

She related the details. He scanned her face.

"Rosa wants me to enroll Sophie in school." Maggie undid the clip on the manila envelope and pulled out the discolored birth certificate. "I found this with Sophie's vaccination records. Rosa takes good care of her, but this birth certificate looks so fake it's laughable." She slid the folded, faded paper across the table to Dan.

He took a pair of readers from his shirt pocket, picked up the document with two hands and carefully unfolded it. He smiled as he read through the words. "I've seen these before. It may be legal. Elena Garcia is or was a midwife in Phoenix. She writes these letters after she delivers a baby and tells the mother to register the birth with the City Records Department. Many mothers are too afraid of Immigration Officers to do so."

"I know Sophie's not registered. I checked the Phoenix birth records on the internet. I googled Elena Garcia, but I couldn't find any reference to her."

"May I take this?"

"It's the original, but I made a copy."

He folded the certificate and carefully put it in his pocket. "Tomorrow I'm going to Phoenix and testify for a man ICE is about to deport to Mexico. Guy worked as a janitor for thirty years at our City Hall. Something's goin' on in this town that is seriously wrong. A young boy named Miguel just died, victim of an attack by a hate group that's recently been showing up here in town. Please be careful not to say anything. We don't want the gang to know we are after them for homicide."

"Of course." She liked that he felt comfortable confiding in her.

"I'll stop and talk to Elena. She had a record book of babies she'd delivered. I haven't seen her in years. I'm not sure she's still in business."

"I can't believe this will be that simple."

"Let's not celebrate yet. Anything can happen in these cases, but we now have tangible information. I'll have Elena verify this so we can register Sophie and you can enroll her in school. ... How about another beer?"

Maggie hesitated, tipped up her beer bottle, surprised to find the bottle empty. This was beginning to feel like a date. Dates were not her thing. Excited, she had forgotten to be suspicious of this man. Now she felt vulnerable. Was he trustworthy? Should she go home? While having a good time, "sure," popped out of her mouth before she could close it. "How did you get so involved with immigration issues?"

"To make a long story very short, Dad was a Scotsman. I was big for my age. Mom, being Mexican, wanted to live near her friends and family in Arizona. I was always beating away the bullies who came into the neighborhood to pick on the little Latino kids."

"And you're still chasing those bullies?"

"It would seem so."

Lisa was right. Dan Clarke turned out to be charming, which made Maggie more nervous. When the beer came, she reached across the table and accidentally knocked over his bottle, spilling it into Dan's lap.

"Oh! Sorry!" She hurried over to the barista for a cloth, came back and handed it to Dan. "I'm so clumsy, so mortified. The waitress is coming."

"Don't be. At least you didn't throw it in my face." He laughed, wiping his pants, the bench and the table.

"Has a woman done that to you?"

"Not recently."

"I would never do that." She sat down.

Dan wiped his face with the back of his hand. "Only kidding," he said and stood.

She'd missed the joke. What had happened to her sense of humor? Maybe she lived on another planet. Maybe she was dying of embarrassment.

A waitress arrived with a large cloth and began swishing it around the table, spewing a spray of beer in both their directions. Maggie brushed a strand of hair out of her eye and giggled.

"You look exhausted. It's been a long day." Dan helped her crawl out of the booth, took her hand and guided her to his car. "We have a scent of hops about us."

Maggie giggled again. "Hops and Cops!" What a way to say we stink of beer, she thought.

When they arrived at her house, he walked her to the front door. "I enjoyed meeting you. I'll try to help with Sophie." He stepped back and held her at arm's length. "If this were a date, I'd ask to kiss you good night."

He leaned in to open the door knob and she kissed him on the cheek thinking he was going to kiss her. Surprised he smiled and lightly placed a warm kiss on her cheek.

"I'll call as soon as I have news."

Embarrassed, again, she stood in front of the grand oak door. She stroked her cheek and watched him leave. His lips were soft, gentle. It felt like a date. It was as if she'd been sprinkled with stardust or Ecstasy or whatever was the latest drug of choice. She was so out of the dating scene, so turned off by men. But that kiss on her cheek....

She sighed, closed the door, went up to her room, washed her face and collapsed on top of the spread. Then she remembered. She'd forgotten to ask Dan to drive her to her car, parked at the office.

CHAPTER 9

MAGGIE BOUNDED out of bed the next morning. Memories of the previous evening tumbling around in her brain. Darkness still coated her windows. The August days were getting shorter and the nights cooler. She looked at the alarm clock, shocked to see it registered four a.m. What was she doing up and ready to go at this ungodly hour? Too late to go back to bed. She showered and dressed for work in a tailored black suit and white silk blouse.

Shuffling into the kitchen, to make a pot of coffee, still in her bedroom slippers, she heard movement on the back porch. OMG, she thought. What now? Hank? Gang members? Rattling at the porch door made her nervous.

She took a deep breath and came down to reality.

"That damn raccoon is back," she said to herself. Switching on the porch light she saw a figure, shivering, bundled in an old fake fur coat of Estelle's, huddled on the doorstep.

"Rosa!" Maggie untoggled the chains and locks on the door and Rosa fell into her arms. "You feel like a chunk of ice. How long have you been out there?"

"An hour or so. I travel at night. Less police on the road. I hope you don't mind. I pulled this coat out of bag at the curb for the Salvation Army."

"Oh, Rosa. We'd have given you that coat."

"Didn't know I'd need it or I would've asked."

"You shouldn't have to go through this misery." Maggie wrapped her small housekeeper in her arms. "Sit. Let's have coffee. How about oatmeal or bacon and eggs? Something nourishing?"

"Don't fuss. Coffee is fine. I'm on my way to New Mexico."

"New Mexico! What for?"

Rosa had learned from a friend of a friend that Carlos was transferred by bus to a new immigration detention facility prior to being deported to Mexico. There was no room for him in the one at the Nogales border. "Carlos needs me. His back is tricky. Most times it's fine, but other times it collapses. Really bad."

"How can I get you to New Mexico? Buy a ticket? Plane? Train?"

"No. I'm driving my car with Lupita who is also legal. Even so we're afraid. I don't want to make trouble for you. I have a license, but police ask for proof of our citizenship because we're two Latinas. Even when

I show my papers, they harass me. I drive carefully. If I see a police car, I turn off the road. You are helping by taking care of Sophie."

"We're getting her birth certificate registered so we can enroll her in school."

"Thank you for that." Rosa sipped her coffee slowly.

"Do you want me to wake her?"

"It's not good to say goodbye twice. But maybe I will peek in? I don't know when I'll be back."

"You have a cell phone. I've seen Sophie playing with it. Can you text a message on that?"

"Carlos taught me how. Oh, but I don't know. The government traces calls."

"Wait. If you don't feel safe directly contacting me, let's use the MISS CHLOE column to communicate. Josh told me it's being syndicated in several papers across the country. Call or text MISS CHLOE at the *Gazette* and I'll respond. Send a message to my column at the newspaper."

"I'm not sure. ... Don't want to get you in trouble. Let me think on it."

"You need a code name. Use a man's name. Not many men write to MISS CHLOE or even read her column."

"It scares me." Rosa drained her coffee cup. Maggie refilled it and set a pumpkin muffin and a crock of strawberry jam in front of her.

"ICE is not going to pay attention to a self-help column. Always use 'Mr.' and I'll always respond to 'Mr.' even if it's not the same name ... Let's see. How about we start with Adam? Yes, that's a good strong name for a beginning. Use any last name. Whenever I get a message from a Mr. Adam something, I will know it's from you or one of your friends and I'll respond in a MISS CHLOE's column. I'll always respond to 'Mr.' even if I don't quite understand the message, I'll pass on the information to whomever you want to contact."

Rosa listened, but didn't reply.

"Ask me anything. Tell your friends. As MISS CHLOE I can be part of an underground network for immigrants to contact one another."

"We could try. ... See how it works."

"Good. Give me your phone and I'll type in MISS CHLOE'S address."

Rosa rummaged in the bag she carried on her shoulder. She handed her phone to Maggie who entered her address at the newspaper. "There. We're all set. Now let's take a look at Sophie before you go."

They tip-toed up the stairs and opened Sophie's bedroom door. Estelle had finally tucked a sleeping Sophie into her own bed late the night before. Eerie slits of light played through the drawn window slats. After Sophie's fall, Maggie had given her a filigreed bottle of rosewater body-splash which she applied lavishly throughout the day. The smell of rosewater permeated the bedroom air.

The minute they'd looked in, Sophie popped up from under the covers. "Oh, Maggie, I had the strangest dream. I heard ... MAMA." She threw herself into Rosa's arms as Rosa sat on the bed. "Mama, I heard your voice. I thought I was dreaming. You're home."

Rosa looked ruefully at Maggie. "It's hard to get anything past this one."

"You don't have to tell me," Maggie replied.

Sophie wrapped her sleep-tousled hair and arms around Rosa and they both fell back on the bed. "I miss you, Mama."

"Listen to me, Sophie. I have to go to Papa." The early morning shadows exaggerated the dark circles of concern under Rosa's eyes.

"I'll come too."

"No. It's not possible. You stay with Maggie and go to school. I'll be back soon."

Sophie started to cry. "I wanna come."

"Don't make Maggie feel like you're not happy here."

"I love Maggie. But I want to come with you."

It had been a mistake to peek in. Maggie should have known Sophie would sense her mother's presence in the house.

Estelle appeared in the bedroom doorway. "What's going on here so early in the morning? Hi, Rosa, has Sophie shown you her big bandage or her little red wheelchair?"

Rosa looked confused and mumbled. "Not yet."

"Show Mama."

Sophie pulled up her wide pajama leg, displayed her enormously bandaged leg and laid it on Rosa's lap. Then Sophie dried her tears with the bed sheet and crawled to the top of the stairs, dragging her left leg. "Come downstairs, Mama."

Sophie bumped down the staircase on her butt, seated herself in the wheelchair at the bottom of the stairs, pressed the start button and began to spin around the living room.

Maggie, Rosa and Estelle followed her downstairs and stood in the front hall. "What happened?" Rosa asked Estelle. Worry contorted her face. Rosa rubbed her hand across her brow and looked unsure as to whether she should stay or leave.

"She slipped on the basement stairs and slashed her leg on that old lawnmower. We had to get her stitches. Doctor says she'll be fine." Estelle wrapped her arm around Rosa's shoulders.

"Look at me. I have a horse," Sophie sang. "Give me land, lots of land." She twirled an imaginary lasso over her shoulders.

"I appreciate your taking care of her. She's such a tom-boy. I'm always afraid she'll hurt herself. It's hard to slow her down."

"We'll be extra careful," Estelle said, hugging Rosa.

"I know you will. Thank you. My friend is waiting. I must go."

"Sophie, come kiss Mama good bye," Maggie said, relieved that Estelle had distracted Sophie from Rosa's departure.

Sophie rolled her wheelchair over to Rosa and gave her a hard hug and big kiss. "You come back soon."

"I will, my sweetheart. I will." Rosa hugged Estelle, said thanks again and hugged Maggie. "I will send a message when I get to New Mexico."

Rosa left by the front door, stood on the porch for a moment, turned and waved.

Sophie drove her chair over to Estelle and began to cry again. "I know Mama has to find Papa. I'll wait for her here."

Maggie walked into the kitchen to find a tissue. Her eyes brimmed over with tears. They were all trying to be brave. Estelle asked Sophie if she was ready for breakfast.

"After I exercise my horse," Sophie replied.

Realizing it was much too early to head out to work, Maggie went into her office and picked up the letter from the wife who claimed to be collateral damage to her husband's PTSD. She reread it. Her tears dropped on the paper. She knew that trauma made people afraid, afraid to know what they know and feel what they feel. Her heart ached for the letter writer, but she wasn't ready to tackle her problem. When she did, she wanted her response to be thoughtful and helpful. She pulled out another letter and wrote a quick note.

Dear Miss Chloe: There's a homeless man who spends his days on the corner of our block. I do not know where he goes at night but he sits on the corner from nine until five. He has a dog that patiently sits next to him for those long hours. I can't say that he mistreats the dog. I've never seen him do anything but stroke the dog in a kind way. The dog is tied with an old rope and the man keeps a bowl of water close by. The dog looks old so maybe he is content not to move around too much, but still I feel the animal is leading a "dog's life." Should I report the homeless man to the ASPCA? *Animal Lover*

Dear Animal Lover: I think you are misreading this situation. The homeless man sounds as if he is taking good care of his pet. It's probably his only friend and he loves him very much. The dog must love his homeless friend because he spends all day quietly sitting on the sidewalk with him. Why would you want to break up these two lovers? Buy the dog some doggie treats and a new leash. *Miss Chloe*

CHAPTER 10

IN THE HIGH COUNTRY, Juniper Hills remained a gold and copper mining town years after Arizona lost its status as a territory and became the forty-eighth state of the Union. Despite twenty-first century upgrades, the town retained a genuine atmosphere of the Old West. Hitching rails to tie up horses still dotted the streets, although closely parked cars prevented access to someone who might ride their horse into town.

Mountains soared in every direction, with miles of trails and ancient ponderosas. Shimmering blue lakes and running creeks in the rainy season reflected perennial blue skies. Now it had become an artists' and musicians' mecca and a retirement destination. Twenty-five years ago, a popular national magazine rated it as The Number One Retirement Place in the United States. The population nearly doubled. Expensive new houses appeared. A huge mall put small merchants out of business. Real estate agents, doctors, dentists and lawyers reaped lucrative rewards from the larger population.

Maggie, Lisa and Gus officially closed their offices for three days after they remodeled their Queen Anne Victorian in the middle of town. Still, the phone rang and rang. Maggie told her secretary and the staff to take messages and not to disturb the attorneys unless it was unavoidable. She didn't say "important" because everyone who called thought their matter important. Gus had a court case on Friday, so he spent hours doing double duty, preparing his brief and cleaning out his office space. They'd agreed to close their present offices and compress the job of moving into three days if they were to save their sanity and be available for their clients.

After weeks of discussion they decided to keep their new building's original style on the outside but to modernize the inside. No heavy velvet drapes or rococo molding. They'd go for a pristine contemporary look: simple blinds that pulled up from the bottom for privacy but allowed the light and sunshine in at the top. They put in a new heating and air-conditioning unit that cost a fortune, hoping it would last a long time. The natural wood floors had been sanded and stained a warm honey color. They didn't want anything walnut and dark. The Victorians would've had a fit, but this was now and the lawyers wanted the offices to reflect their own tastes.

A month earlier, Lisa had said, "I don't want a dingy old basement beneath us." So, they had the basement scrubbed and painted when the new heating unit was put in. The carpenters cut out low round windows for more light and the landscape crew planted flowering asters and lemon lilies in front of those windows.

Lisa had been poking around in the basement for days and decided that she and her husband, Robbie, would tile the floor with Italian limestone. They'd tiled their condo, and it had made an amazing difference. Robbie was a perfectionist, according to Lisa. His full name was Roberto Pérez. Maggie had met him once when he came to pick up Lisa. He was a good-looking young Latino man with a warm smile, dark wavy hair and a genuine handshake.

"Are you sure you want to take on that huge basement?" Gus had asked her.

"Absolutely," Lisa said.

Maggie knew Robbie taught Political Science at the local college during the day. "I guess it's good to get out of your head once in a while."

"That's what he says," Lisa said. "We can do it at night. Robbie loves to work with his hands. He finds it relaxing. I can help and keep him company. It'll make a great storage place for our files. We could even have our grand opening party down there."

"There's an idea," Gus said.

Maggie stood. "We should do it. A party is a perfect idea. We can invite all our friends and clients."

"Enemies too. Let them drool."

"Gus, we don't have enemies, only opponents." Maggie wished that were true.

The basement floor was almost completely tiled, and a party would be held two weeks from Saturday night. They'd contracted a caterer and a band but remained undecided about a theme. Lisa suggested "Autumn" with lots of colorful leaves. Gus pushed for "Good Bye to Summer" with lots of margaritas. Maggie had yet to offer her two cents.

Pulling into her driveway after work that night, Maggie saw a police car parked at the curb. Dan? She walked over and leaned into his window. "Hi, there. Am I being followed? Want to sample Estelle's cooking?"

"Come sit a minute. I have good news." He stretched over, released the passenger door lock and pushed it open.

"I'm so glad." She climbed into the front seat.

"I had a hard time locating Elena Garcia. She retired a few years back. That's why you couldn't find her. She sold her business to another midwife." Dan turned off the engine, rested his hands on the steering wheel and faced her. "ICE is cracking down on midwives now. Afraid they'll forge birth certificates, I guess."

"Do they think up these things to harass the Latinos?"

"I managed to track down the new owner. She had all Elena's records. She gave me a fresh notarized copy of Sophie's birth certificate. She's a notary! Can you believe that? Told me it's good for her business and keeps the authorities from asking questions of the babies' parents. I took the old and the new versions to City Hall." He gave her a foxy-grin. "Miss Sophie is not only registered as a U.S. citizen, but she now has her own Social Security number."

"Oh, Dan!" Maggie leaned over and flung her arms around his shoulders. He hugged her back, his hands splayed across her spine. He felt soft and solid at the same time. "How can I thank you?" Realizing he was very much into holding her and that she was still hugging him, she withdrew her arms and clicked open the side door. "Come tell Sophie and Estelle."

She sensed he was reluctant to release her. He leaned away and said, "I've got to check on a fire down on Route 69. It's the third one this month. That gang's attacks on our Latinos are getting more ruthless. I'll come another time. You'll be getting the formal documents in a week or so in the mail."

"What time are you off duty?" Maggie asked. "Do you want to meet for beer at Rodney's later?"

"Is ten too late?

"No, that's fine. We can meet there."

"I'll pick you up."

Walking up the steps, she couldn't believe she had asked a man she barely knew out for a drink. Excited, she couldn't wait to tell Sophie and Estelle the good news about the birth certificate.

When she entered the kitchen, Sophie was sitting in her wheelchair pushed up to the kitchen table. Estelle stood at the range turning over chicken cutlets in a fry pan. "Sophie saw you drive up and talk to that detective, so I knew you'd be in soon. Dinner will be ready momentarily."

Maggie washed her hands at the sink, kissed Estelle on the cheek and hugged Sophie. "I have excellent news."

"Mama's coming home?" Sophie looked overjoyed.

"Not that good, but almost better for now. Detective Clarke found your birth certificate and we can enroll you next week, in plenty of time for the first day of school."

Sophie got out of the wheelchair and hopped on one foot over to Maggie for a hug, then twisted to embrace Estelle. "Oh, Maggie and Mom, this is the happiest day of my life. At least until Mama and Papa come home."

"We're excited for you. How would you like to go out for lunch tomorrow and celebrate?" Maggie dried her hands on a kitchen towel.

"A real lunch party for me! Oh, Mom and Maggie, that would be so cool."

Maggie and Estelle smiled.

"You must be pleased." Estelle said as she studied Maggie's face whose cheeks were flushed.

Maggie, for a moment, felt like she had left the room and forgotten her body.

"Yes. Dan found the record of the original midwife who delivered Sophie, had it authenticated, notarized and filed. A certified copy will be sent to us by next week. We'll be good to go."

"It's Dan now, is it?" Estelle teased. "What happen to the woman who didn't do dates?"

"It's not a date. He's helped us a lot. I'm buying him a drink to show our appreciation."

"So, I'm hearing."

"MOM!" She couldn't take any more comments from her beloved grandmother because she wasn't sure how she felt. She needed time to absorb this new man into her life.

CHAPTER 11

TWO WEEKS LATER, Maggie and Dan gravitated to the booth they'd occupied the last three times they were in Rodney's Café. It felt familiar and private. She loved the rustic smell of the place. Maggie had piled her long dark hair on the back of her head and fastened it with a tortoiseshell clip. It made her feel free and light to have her neck bare. She had chosen a silk shirt to wear with her jeans. Her mirror had shown that the blue of the shirt electrified her blue eyes. Dan had changed his black leather jacket to a grey lightweight sweater. The night was balmy, most likely one of the last of the summer.

"I'm concerned about the latest fire I came from," he said. It seems different than that miserable group's previous attacks we've been dealing with, more vicious."

"What do you think it means?"

"Bigger troubles." A waitress appeared at their table with the beers in ceramic mugs Dan had ordered at the bar tap when they walked in. He nodded to Maggie as he held up his mug and took a big swig. "A small hair salon was burned to the ground and the owner, Sylvie Vassallo, was raped. It'll be in the papers tomorrow. Not her name, of course."

"Gang raped?" Maggie sat back in the booth and fiddled with her mug, not ready to take another sip.

"Only by one goon, but bad enough." Dan took another gulp of beer. "Sylvie's furious. She swears she won't let them destroy the rest of her life. She's a strong lady." Dan turned his face to the wall, away from Maggie.

She saw tears on his cheek. ... "Damn that gang," she grumbled.

Dan got up to hand the barista his mug for a refill, then walked around the table and slid into the booth next to Maggie. He let out a long sigh.

"You knew Sylvie, didn't you?" Maggie asked.

"She was a friend of my mom's. Did her hair."

"One thing I love about Latinos is that they stick together, take care of each other, like a big family."

"Don't idealize them. They can be pains in the butt sometimes."

"Consider yourself lucky to have a lot of close relatives," Maggie said. "When I was twelve, an old friend of my mother's asked me what I was. Confused I said American. When I asked Estelle, she said the woman wanted to know my heritage."

Estelle had told Maggie that her great-great-grandparents were Greeks and there were some Irish ancestors in her father's family, but nobody ever talked about them. Now everyone was dead.

"So much for my family. It's me, Josh and Estelle," Maggie's voice cracked.

"Oh, Maggie." Dan reached for her hand and warmed it in both of his. "It's not only the twelfth Latino connected crime we've had in four months, but the senseless brutality that haunts me." Dan stared into his beer.

"I'm still sick about those two young boys mauled by that vicious group."

"I'm freaked out about that attack."

Dan reminded Maggie about the young boy, Miguel, who had been brutally beaten and killed. "We don't want that gang to know we're after them for murder. Luis Gonzales and his family have moved back to Denver. They didn't feel safe here. ... Our town used to be so peaceful."

"I'm sorry to hear that." Maggie took a swift gulp of beer and then another.

"I need to keep some things quiet," Dan said, "but the paper reported that it's a hate group from our southern border. Some are not much older than teens, maybe early twenties. They brandish small swords and knives. They've been stirring up trouble here for months. We can't seem to get specific details about any of them. They strike and move back into the shadows."

Maggie put her arm around Dan's shoulder. "Is it always at night?" She worried about him. He was obviously upset.

"It seems so."

"How did the paper know they were from our southern border?"

"According to the *Gazette*, after the fire, somebody in Juniper Hills got a license plate number from Leonardo, a small border town, and called our police. The plate turned out to be stolen. ... One thing that's nags at me is they don't claim credit."

"Why does that disturb you?" Maggie asked.

"Because they don't brag online. They want to play cat and mouse. They want to stay out of sight, off the radar."

"You make it sound so planned, so sinister."

"I'm positive it's not spontaneous. I don't understand why Chief Strunk doesn't take this seriously. He and the Mayor act like it will go away of its own accord. They're ridiculous!"

"Is it a large group?"

"Witnesses have given different stories. They wear all black and half masks. They shout despicable things, hateful remarks. I don't get it. They target regular people like you and me. The thugs aren't attacking people who rally to protect the undocumented. They're going after law-abiding, quiet illegals and legals. Why pick on good guys who've made a success of their lives?"

Maggie fiddled with her mug. "So many people are hurting. They work three jobs and still can't make ends meet."

"I think there's more to it than that. These are angry, ugly, hate filled young adults. Someone thought one or two may be older." Dan ran his fingers through his hair.

Maggie sipped from her mug. "Where does all this hate come from? What do they get out of it?" she slouched back in her seat.

"Status, power, money. It's as if they've sold their souls to the devil."

"It doesn't seem worth it."

"It does if they had nothing before."

"That kind of hate is learned early. It becomes a defense against reality, closes down your mind, cuts you off from anyone different."

"And they have reason to hate because they think immigrants compete with them for low paying jobs." Dan stabbed a chip into a spicy sauce and sighed.

Maggie tugged at the beads around her neck. "That's the fault of big corporations. They moved jobs out of the country. But people's jobs aren't taken by Mexicans, more likely by microchips."

"I can't argue with that. Those kids are so frustrated they don't know where to place their rage."

"We let the immigrants come in for years and years and now we round them up and ship them to places they've never lived and know nothing about. People don't realize what horrors some immigrants suffered in their home countries." Maggie tapped her fingers on the table.

Dan unbuttoned his sweater. "But murder and mayhem aren't the answer."

"We're not going to solve this problem tonight."

"Want to dance?"

Maggie thought he was joking but realized for the first time that soft music played in the background.

Other couples were moving around on the small dance floor. She studied his face. "Are you okay?"

"If I only focus on the dark, I'll go crazy. I need to feel something other than anger." He stood, pulled Maggie into his arms and held her close.

She felt a moment of her old caution then leaned into him and closed her eyes. It had been a lifetime since a man held her in his arms.

CHAPTER 12

"WE HAVE TO SERVE Jimmy Buffet margaritas," Gus declared. Twenty members of the firm sat around a metal picnic table in the renovated basement of their new office building. After one month they had finally settled into their former routines.

"That's dumb," a paralegal said.

"Can't offer just one kind," another shouted.

"We need to give people a choice," Lisa said. "So many other kinds: pomegranate, honey vanilla, cranberry kiss."

Maggie smiled. Everybody was getting into the spirit of their Grand Opening Mexican Fiesta. "Why don't we have a Margarita Bar and let people choose?"

"Perfect. Robbie can bartend," Lisa said. "He considers himself an expert on margaritas."

"Wonderful. That's settled. Now for the menu." Maggie picked up a clipboard and read off suggestions. "How about a buffet table with lava crocks of homemade guacamole and chips?"

"That's a good start. We need chicken and fish tostadas and enchiladas and burritos and empanadas too." Lisa said.

"Don't forget chiles rellenos," Gus's secretary said. "They're the best."

"Listen up, team. We've only invited a hundred people. Not the entire town. I'll speak to the caterer." Maggie stood to indicate they needed to get back to work.

"For dessert we must have sopapilla cheese squares with chocolate sauce and Mexican brownies." Someone shouted from across the room.

"Good suggestions. The caterer will provide tables and chairs. I've also hired mariachis."

The group clapped and hooted as they gathered their notes and pens.

"Thanks everyone. You're a great team." Maggie headed for the stairs.

Saturday night arrived. Maggie wore a long blue silk dress with velvet trim on the bodice; it accentuated her blue eyes and her long dark hair. She and Estelle had bought Sophie a frilly yellow party dress with matching sandals. Estelle donned a shimmery silver dress she swore was forty years old but looked purchased last week."

"I'm packing a small bag with jeans and a tee." Maggie spoke as she rummaged through her dresser drawers looking for socks and lingerie. "There'll be some clean-up work to do in that basement after everyone leaves."

"May I wear the orange scarf you gave me after I slashed my leg?" Sophie asked Estelle.

"Sure," Estelle answered, "If you wanna look like a citrus grove."

"Oh. Mom, lemons and oranges are complementary."

Sophie's use of words awed Maggie. Carlos had been an excellent teacher. Her adjectives and verbs were adult and colorful, choices a writer might make. She seemed to understand metaphors and similes. Rosa had said Sophie had no formal schooling. Sophie was an original. Nothing much was lost on her.

Maggie, Estelle and Sophie, out of her wheelchair for two weeks, entered the new offices and headed down the stairs. Lisa and Robbie had hung crepe paper strips in autumn colors everywhere. It was truly an end-of-summer affair. Strategically placed open lanterns highlighted the margarita and taco bar. A large piñata shaped like either a cow or a teddy bear, Maggie wasn't sure, hung from the ceiling in the corner.

When Lisa walked over to her, Maggie said, "I'm stunned. What you and Robbie have done is beautiful and fun. We should never take any of this down." She raised her arms to encompass the walls. "A permanent party-room."

The mariachi band arrived and began setting up. Sophie's eyes grew huge as if she didn't know where to look first. Sitting on the floor, she studied the band members. "I know the names of those instruments," she told Estelle. "Papa has a book."

"Let me find you a chair. You'll get your pretty new dress dirty." Estelle walked off to locate one. When she returned with a folding chair, Sophie was on the lap of a band member who wore a jumbo sombrero. "Mom, come meet Manuel. He plays the vihuela."

"Hola, Miss Mom. Sophie told me about you."

"I hope she isn't bothering you." Estelle held out her hands for Sophie to come to her.

"I'm fine, Mom. Manuel lived at the apartments before ICE came. We're friends. His wife Terry taught me to read and write English."

"But he can't play his music with you on his lap."

Sophie slid down to the floor. "We'll catch up later, Mannie."

Manuel stood and held out his hand to Estelle. "We all thank you, Señora, for what you and Maggie are doing for Rosa and Sophie and Carlos. There was no one left at the apartments to help them."

"Oh, please," Estelle said as she shook his hand. "We love Rosa and Carlos and Sophie." She noticed that Mannie had no accent. Terry must be one hell-of-a good teacher. They moved the chair against the wall and walked over to the taco bar.

"This is the best party **ever**," Sophie said as she piled cheese slices, shredded lettuce and shrimp onto a taco shell and added salsa. "Can I make one for you, Mom?"

"Not right now, honey. I'll eat later."

When Dan arrived a little before eight, Maggie's heart skipped around in her chest when she saw him. They kissed and hugged. "Where've you been? Not another fire?"

"No. Break-in at Walmart, though I definitely smelled gasoline. We think the gang was interrupted by the night watchman and ran off. Not sure if it was the hooligans from down south or copycat locals. Forensics is working on it. What bothers me is that the manager is Latino. This gang has me paranoid." He brushed his fingers through his hair and looked around. "Nice party! Your new offices are stunning. You three did a great job."

"Have you met Robbie? He's Lisa's husband. What a gem. He can do many things: teach political science, tile a floor, make a fantastic margarita. Come to the bar."

"I'd like a beer." Dan put his arm around her waist and slid it along her hip. "You feel so soft in that dress. ... Okay, I'll try a cranberry kiss, thinking of one of yours later tonight."

Maggie gave his shoulder a light punch. "You won't be disappointed. Robbie's been practicing new concoctions for two weeks. ... Oh, there's the mayor. I suppose I should say hello. Get your drink and come over."

"Thanks for coming," Maggie greeted Mayor Giles Buchanan, never one of her favorite people, although she'd worked well with his wife. Large and lumpy, he had always been a little too stiff, for Maggie's taste. Clean-shaven, with dark hair fringed with grey, he gave her a cartoon-like smile which stretched his thick skin and, God save us, she thought, he actually bowed. His eyes narrowed to slits. His face so red he could've had high blood pressure or a bad sunburn. A bow tie pulled up to his Adam's apple was so tight his jowls hung down over his shirt collar. He'd once lied to her about an important zoning matter that created months of needless work and still irked her. Jackass, she thought.

"Hello, Maggie. Have you met my wife?"

"Yes. Charlene and I are on a couple town committees together. ... Hi, Char." They embraced carefully so as not to crush the large pink rose pinned on the front of Charlene's dress.

While the women wore their finest party dresses and the mayor wore his usual Tux, most of the other men were in dark suits or sports jackets and khakis. Maggie said a few chatty words to Charlene about the renovations at their lovely Federalist-style Court House in the middle of town.

"Yes, they're cleaning that wonderful granite," Charlene replied as a chubby woman approached and stroked Charlene's arm insisting to be recognized.

Maggie turned as a colleague walked by, smiled and nodded to welcome another lawyer from a competing firm. She felt a hand on her shoulder. Expecting Dan, she almost dropped her margarita when she saw ... Hank!

He looked desolate, like he'd slept in his clothes, hadn't washed or combed his hair in weeks. "You shouldn't be here." She folded her arms as if to protect her heart.

A trace of thin mustache showed on his upper lip. She wondered where that was going. She could imagine him with a stash and waxed tips, a Victorian villain.

"Holy shit, the whole town is here," Hank spat out.

"They were invited. You weren't."

"Can't we bury the hatchet and talk?"

"We've tried that. Last time you ran away for five years."

His face flashed scarlet "People change, you know." His fists clenched.

"I could never get back with you."

"It's that cop, isn't it? I saw how he groped you."

"Please leave. We've nothing to discuss."

"You'll be sorry."

Maggie was tempted to ask what that meant, but she didn't want to continue the conversation. Every word he said upset her. Every word he said hammered into her skull.

Hank scanned the basement, searched unsuccessfully for someone to talk with, then walked up the back stairs.

Dan appeared at her side with an impish grin. "As I engaged in a spirited conversation with Sophie and Estelle, I saw you talking to a man. Sophie said it was your ex. You were holding your own so I didn't come to your rescue. Something's odd about that guy. Sophie said he looks ready to explode."

"I'm thinking I should report him to his commanding officer or his doctor or his mother. Gloria, must see something is wrong. I can't call her. I'm not high on her favorites list. He's a sick man."

"Would Gloria listen to Estelle?"

"Not sure. They used to be friends, but ... I'll talk to Estelle tomorrow. Maybe we can come up with a plan."

"How long were you married?"

"A few years. We dated through high school. During most of our marriage he was back and forth to

Afghanistan. A bad, sad time. You were married. You have an ex. How's that going for you?"

"I met Dolores when I was at the Pentagon. We held it together for three years and then divorced." Dan told her his friends tagged Dolores as a gold digger. He thought of her as insatiable. He'd been lonely and didn't care about the money. "She thought I was wealthy. When she discovered I was a cowpoke from the west she took off and filed for divorce. ... Now let's dance."

They clung together the rest of the evening. Estelle took a sleepy Sophie home without much resistance. Only a few guests remained when the band announced their last song at midnight.

"Let's go to my place," Dan said to Maggie. "I need a beer."

"Good. I need to get out of here."

"Would you drop Robbie and me off at our condo?" Lisa asked Maggie. "It was such a beautiful night we walked over, but we're too tired to hike back."

"Of course. You guys have been terrific support. Your drinks made the evening, Robbie."

"It was my pleasure. I like to concoct new experiences." He had a broad smile, jet black hair, the lean body of a long-distance runner and deep brown eyes that attracted a second look. "I'm glad people had a good time."

"We hired a cleanup crew for early tomorrow morning. There's not much we can do now. Let's make sure those open lanterns are blown out and everything else is turned off."

Somehow the four crammed into Dan's sports car and they were off. "What a wonderful night," Lisa said. "I could live in that office. I love the drapes and paneling, and windows and private spaces. It already feels like home."

"The party's a perfect christening for a long life," Robbie said. "Speaking of births and christening, have you told them about us?"

"I was going to wait another month, but I guess you just blew it." Lisa pretended to scowl at Robbie. "We're having a baby in early June."

"That's wonderful, you guys! I'm so happy for you," Maggie said. "We can set up a bassinette in your new office. It's big enough."

"That's what I was thinking." Lisa cuddled into Robbie's arms. He looked quite proud of himself.

Dan pulled up in front of their condo. Robbie and Lisa untangled themselves, emerged from the car and waved good bye.

Maggie and Dan headed for Dan's house.

CHAPTER 13

THE DRIVE to Dan's place took fifteen minutes. Maggie had stopped by on business several times, always in midafternoon. His house was an all stone structure built in the 1900's that Dan had gutted and renovated. She had been surprised at how neat he was and what fine taste he had. This evening the first thing she noticed was the moonlight playing on his Scandinavian furniture in the darkness.

His house was on the side of a mountain overlooking Juniper Hills Valley, allowing her to imagine being in a small hill town in Italy. When he went to click the light switch on, she put her hand over his. "Not yet. It's so lovely in the moonlight."

The south wall was glass. Stars highlighting the sky, forming a celestial mural on the wall. They moved through the shadows into the bedroom. Maggie felt nervous, amazed how a couple of margaritas could undo her. It had been so long.

Dan found the tag at her back and gently pulled down the zipper until the velvet dress dropped to the carpet in a dark blue halo. She stepped out of it and their remaining clothes scattered themselves, making a trail to the king-sized bed.

She lay naked. He knelt on one knee beside her on the mattress. They touched each other with curiosity. His gaze lingered on her face and body. He slid his hands tenderly and slowly over her breasts and down her hips. His whisper felt warm in her ear. His mouth tasted of peppermint. When did he pop a mint? She held her breath against surging sensations. Pleasure bathed her as Dan hovered and kissed her. He removed a condom from the nightstand, ripped open the foil with his teeth and slipped it on. She trembled, moist with anticipation, as he moved into her. They clutched and cuddled, her arm caught between their bodies. They exchanged mild elbow jabs, their knees knocking each other's. "I'm feeling clumsy," she mumbled.

"We'll find our rhythm," Dan said. And they did.

She felt exquisite sensations her body had forgotten or maybe had never before experienced. They rested a bit, made easy sensuous love again and lay side by side, dog-tired.

In an attempt to gain control and perspective, she pushed herself up on the pillows and changed the mood. The door to his clothes closet stood half open. A dim light from within the closet allowed her to see two formal dress uniforms from his Pentagon days, side by side, arranged on hangers. She recalled he had spent six years in the Marines and shivered. She hated everything to do with the military.

"Whatever made you decide to become a cop?" She'd wanted to know the answer to that question since they met.

You really want to hear the story?"

"I wouldn't have asked, if...."

"I joined the ROTC at Michigan to help with expenses. I thought I'd apply to law school after my military duty. But the Marines pulled me out of the service and set me up in The Pentagon doing investigative work. I was there for six years." He joined her, upright on the pillows. Maggie absorbed his natural beauty as moonlight rippled over his bare body. "I liked the work."

His voice softened as he explained that when he came home for good, he found his mom sicker than she'd let on. He caressed Maggie's arm.

"Dad had died five years earlier. I barely made it back from D. C. for his funeral. Then when Mom died, I learned I had a substantial inheritance." His dad had worked hard and died suddenly, he added. "Mom never told me Dad had a generous life insurance policy she was saving for me."

He put his arms around Maggie and continued. His voice broke. "I wish she'd spent more on herself."

"Sounds like she did what she wanted."

"I have to be thankful. I bought and fixed up this house. My old buddy from high school, Charlie Wright, was Chief of Police at the time. He was looking for a detective and asked me to apply. I had to take a few courses to get certified. I miss old Charlie. He died three years ago of a ruptured aneurism. They say I'm a good techie and investigator, so here I am, except now I have to deal with Chief Gene Strunk."

"We've never met. What's wrong with him?"

"We're not living in a similar reality."

"Interesting. I can't wait to hear about that." Maggie sat up to study his face.

"I spent the war years in D.C. Please don't think about PTSD and me in the same sentence."

She slipped into a fast-moving stream of warmth again. The crosscurrents swept her into the secrets of his life. How easy it was to talk to him. She kissed him tenderly. "I'll try."

"Don't let Hank color your thinking. He refused help, remember."

"It's a damn shame. Too many vets are coming home messed up, some violent and dangerous to themselves and others." Maggie moved closer to Dan, seeking his warmth.

"Movies and TV shows don't help. It's true some vets are scarred and need help, but they don't want pity. They want medical care and jobs."

"I agree. But we do lose some like Hank."

"Lady, do you know I'm falling in love with you?" The full moon had slid out of range of the window but left an afterglow on the glass wall.

She knew, but she wasn't ready to return his words. Her feelings confused and frightened her. Those uniforms made her think of Hank and Afghanistan and war and.... She would need more time to get her heart and head in harmony.

They fell asleep in each other's arms. At exactly 4:10 a.m. both their cells rang. Dan answered his while Maggie searched in her purse.

"There's another fire!" He grabbed his clothes.

Finally putting her phone to her ear, Maggie shrieked, "Holy Hell! It's the Painted Lady."

CHAPTER 14

AS THEY SPED to the center of town, Maggie realized Dan would have to park blocks away. The main street as well as the side streets had been cordoned off. The air, smoggy and mustard-yellow, smelling like burning chemicals, irritated their eyes and clogged their noses. Juniper Hills' fire engines were stacked in the streets along with three rigs from nearby towns.

"We'll have to walk," Dan said.

"Run!" Maggie was out of the car racing toward the fire before Dan pulled his key from the ignition. Glad she had brought jeans to Dan's house the night before or she'd be running around in her blue velvet gown at four in the morning. A cop stopped her. She had to wait until Dan caught up, showed his badge and explained she was one of the three owners of the burning building.

They walked as near to the fire as they dared. "Don't move any closer." Dan squeezed her hand. "I won't be long." He went to talk to the Fire Chief.

She stood on the opposite corner from the burning house. Flames spiked through the roof like giant yellow arrows. Small explosions punctured the air. Intense heat burned her face like a high fever. She should move back but felt rooted.

Lisa came up beside her, terrified. "Robbie's in there."

"ROBBIE? How could that be?" Maggie shouted above the din, and feared she would wet her pants.

"He woke early this morning. He'd left his margarita booklet on the bar. Afraid the cleaning crew would toss it, he took an early morning run over here, and … I haven't seen him since. … I thought he'd stopped someplace for coffee. I'm only here because Chief Strunk's office called me." Maggie's heart filled with sorrow as Lisa struggled to get her words out.

Maggie took Lisa in her arms. Tears washed over their faces. "Let's think positively."

"I wish I could."

Maggie felt sure the worst had happened. Lisa had lost her husband. If Robbie were alive, he would have called by now. Nothing could change that feeling.

Dan came back with Gus, who had also been called by the Police Chief's office. "You three should find a place to wait. Watching won't make you feel better. The police are beginning to move the crowds back."

"I can't leave," Lisa said, "Robbie's in there!"

"Nobody could survive that fire," Gus blurted.

"Thanks, Gus, just what we needed to hear." Maggie scowled at him. Lisa broke into uncontrollable sobs.

"Let's walk to Nancy's Deli across the street. I saw the lights come on. We can watch from there."

Lisa stood resolute. "I can't."

"The heat's beastly. We can see everything through the deli windows. Pretty soon this'll be an inferno and the police will chase us away." Maggie put her arm around Lisa's shoulders.

Dan stepped closer to Lisa. "I'll notify the Fire Chief about Robbie. As soon as I know anything, good or bad, I'll come to the deli. I'll tell Strunk where we'll be." He crossed the street to confer with three soaked firemen taking a break, sitting on the back fender of a truck.

Gus joined Maggie and put his arms around Lisa's shoulders. The three walked at a funereal pace to the deli. They sat in a booth by the window and ordered coffees, barely touching the cups.

"Maybe we can move back into our old offices until we rebuild," Gus said, trying for an upbeat moment. "The realtor may not have sold the place yet."

"Duval thought he had a possible buyer," Maggie said. "Do you remember how much insurance we took out on our new building?"

Lisa sat in a trance. Maggie saw she wasn't taking in the conversation. Words probably faded in her brain.

"How do you think the fire started?" Maggie asked Gus. "I remember we checked and doused those open lanterns."

"We'll probably never know. These things just happen." Gus took a quick sip and yelped, "Hot!" ... For half an hour they sat talking about insurance. "At the time it seemed like more than enough coverage, but I didn't expect—"

"A debacle." Dan squeezed into the booth next to Maggie. "I'm sorry, guys. The house will burn to the basement. The Fire Chief says it can't be saved. They think it was arson, but they have to wait for the state inspector's confirmation. There's a heavy smell of gasoline. They're saying someone broke those new small windows behind the flowers and poured gasoline into the basement. They must have soaked the floor, somehow ignited it and run."

"The gang from down by the border?" Maggie asked.

"Well, it's the MO used at Theresa's hair salon and two other fires. The dumb asses tossed away the same brand of gasoline cans. It's like they want us to know."

"That fits," Maggie said. "We had a Mexican Fiesta. This hate group is anti-Latinos."

"Our fiesta may have goaded them into vengeance," Gus proposed. "The fire burned in the basement before anyone saw flames. The first call came in at three-fifty. By then the flames were coming through the roof."

Lisa momentarily emerged from her trance. "Robbie left at four."

"You don't think he'd run into that inferno to rescue his margarita recipes?" Gus struggled to hide his exasperation.

"He was proud of that booklet. He even drew pictures of the drinks. He intended to publish it." Lisa covered her face with her hands and stifled gulping sobs.

Maggie felt like punching Gus in the face, although she knew he was as upset as she and Lisa.

"Searching for victims is the first action the crew takes. There's no report of a body yet." Dan got up to pour himself a glass of water.

"Then, where is he?" Lisa wiped at the tears pouring from her eyes.

"Have you called home? Of course, you have." Gus reached for her hand across the table.

"Every five frantic minutes. I'm ... I'm going to be a widow with an infant before I'm married a year."

A young uniformed man rolled his bike into the deli and approached their table. "I'm Officer Tim Haggerty." He nodded to Dan. "I'm looking for Lisa Pérez."

Lisa raised her hand, then buried her face in Maggie's chest. No words came from her mouth.

"I'm sorry to tell you, we found Roberto Pérez in the back yard. He had ID and a picture of you in his wallet."

Lisa burrowed deeper into Maggie's arms as if searching for deafness. Maggie knew she didn't want to hear.

Officer Haggerty continued, "He must have run in and out of the fire saving things. We found three laptops and folders on the ground near him. It appears he died of smoke inhalation before the firemen arrived."

"Damn. He died saving our files." Maggie stroked Lisa's hair.

"The area is marked off as a crime scene and the Medical Examiner is there now," Haggerty explained as he steadied his bicycle with one hand. "Shortly they'll move your husband's body to the county morgue. They'll call when they're ready for you to identify the body." The young cop looked from one to the other in the booth, bowed his head, turned his bike and left, plainly relieved to have delivered his sad message.

"I want you to come home with me, Lisa," Maggie said. "You can't stay alone. We have to notify your families."

"I only have my parents and a sister, but Robbie has three brothers in Mexico and dozens of relatives."

"Let's get out of here." Maggie gathered their jackets. "We have to deal with Robbie's death. Then we must move quickly before we lose our business, if we haven't already."

Dan dropped the three of them at Maggie's house and headed for the station to gather more information. "I'll call when they're ready to release Robbie's body. You'll have to decide on a funeral home."

Estelle was standing in front of the large oak door as they came up the walk. "I heard the news on the radio. I've been sick at heart, watching the flames on TV. Sophie's still asleep. Come in the kitchen."

They silently moved into the room and slumped into the padded chairs around the table. "Would you like anything, Lisa?" Estelle asked, reaching for her hand. "Soup, coffee...."

"A glass of water, please." Lisa, ghastly white, could barely get words out. Her Robbie was gone.

"Me too," Maggie said. "I'm parched from just thinking about the fire."

"I'll have some coffee," Gus said, "but only if it's already made. We don't want to be any trouble."

"Today is nothing but troubles," Estelle answered from the sink.

"We have to make plans." Maggie picked up a pencil and scrambled around for a piece of paper. "Lisa first. Second, Robbie's funeral. Then save our firm."

Estelle handed her a clipboard with a blank pad.

"I insist you stay here, Lisa," Maggie said. "We can help. How do you want to notify the families?"

Lisa stood to find a tissue. "My parents are too frail to travel from Texas without help. Robbie has three brothers in Hermosillo who own a huge restaurant."

"Do you want to call them or shall I?"

"I'll do it. Maybe my sister can pick up Mom and Dad." Lisa let out a sigh, then a loud sob. "It'll help to keep busy. I have to go home and get phone numbers." She dabbed at her eyes with the fresh tissue.

"I'll drive and you can pack a bag for a few days. We need to choose a funeral home so we can notify the Medical Examiner's office."

"How can I thank you?" Lisa hugged Maggie. "I'm just not able to think."

"No need. We all care about you, Lisa." Maggie turned to Estelle. "Can you recommend a funeral home?"

"Of course. At my age I've had lots of experience and know the good ones."

"We also need to find temporary rental space," Maggie said. "I'll stop at the real estate agency. Gus, you call our insurance companies and see how we stand with this complete loss. We have health insurance on all our employees. Get a list of their names so we can contact everyone. Some of the associates, secretaries and paralegals can recreate the client list. They all have to be notified. Tell everybody we intend to open in two weeks."

"Are you crazy? Be realistic." Gus sat frozen with a glassy stare and looked like he needed a kick in the pants.

"Get busy." Maggie told him. "Go. Use the phone in my office. ... Mom, can I ask you to make the funeral arrangements with Lisa and Robbie's brothers when we contact them?"

Estelle put her arm around Lisa. "When you come back, we'll get you settled. You need rest. You have to think about your growing child." Lisa broke into loud sobs. Maggie realized that Estelle never missed the slightest subtlety in a conversation. She'd only mentioned Lisa's baby once.

A sleepy Sophie shuffled into the kitchen in her pajamas, carrying her pink fuzzy blanket. "Are we having another party?"

"No sweetheart, this is a sad day," Maggie said. "Robbie Pérez has died,"

Sophie limped over to Lisa who was only inches taller and wrapped her arms around her. "My heart is broken for you." Lisa's tears poured over Sophie's hair and fuzzy blanket, but Sophie never let Lisa go. "We're all here to help," Sophie added. "Everything will come up roses."

Maggie and Estelle looked at each other, turned away with tears brimming in their own eyes and hoped they could live up to Sophie's expectations. Lisa hadn't seemed to hear.

CHAPTER 15

STEPHEN DUVAL stood at an open window smoking a skinny brown cigar when Maggie walked into the real estate office at noon. A healthy, good-looking, man with a blond crew cut, he reminded Maggie of a California surfer. She was surprised to see him smoking. Not wanting to leave Lisa alone, Maggie had begged her to come along though Lisa had refused to get out of the car. Finally accepting Lisa's fragility, she promised she wouldn't be long, but didn't want to rush the conversation she was about to have with their agent.

"I'm sorry about your loss. I figured I'd hear from you today. I've been looking through my listings for temporary digs for your office." Duval blew a final stream of noxious smoke out the window and snuffed his cigar in a small clay pot.

"Have our old offices been rented?" Maggie dreaded the ensuing hassle she could feel in the recesses of the room.

"Sold! The afternoon you moved out. Very desirable space, you knew that."

"Any chance of a negotiation?"

"I doubt it. He's an old codger and his kid's a nasty son-of-a-bitch," Duval said. "Not nice people to deal with."

"What are their plans?"

"A single occupancy hotel. They figured twenty rooms. It's a big building," he said.

"What about zoning?"

"I checked. It's legal."

"Damn. That's a dead end. What have you got for rent? We figure we can rebuild the Queen Anne in a year. If all goes well."

"I have an empty furniture store on Donner Street that you could convert into offices with moveable partitions. It's not fancy, but plenty big. Three stories high. Been vacant for over two years. Owner will probably be happy to rent it for a reasonable amount."

"Can you show it now?" Maggie asked.

"Sure. It's empty."

"I'll follow you over. Lisa is with me."

Maggie knew Lisa was in no condition to make a decision but thought the idea of fresh space might offer some diversion from her grief.

"Impossible," Lisa said as they walked around the huge empty space. "How are we going to fill all this area?'

"We'll go to a used-furniture place and get cheap desks, chairs, and credenzas and put up movable partitions. We'll be in business. We can put the conference room upstairs. It'll be workable. ... You have a terrific sense of design; I'm counting on you, Lisa. We need you."

Maggie hoped she wasn't pushing too hard. Grief was paralyzing. She wanted to spare Lisa as much as she could. "I've always thought it sounded romantic to be a store-front lawyer and have down-on-their-luck, people walk in off the street and we'd make them millionaires. Well, here we are."

"Do you have anything else, Steve?" Lisa whispered.

"There are offices in the Bright Building on the second floor. But it's pretty dreary over there."

"We should take this, Maggie. It does have possibilities." Lisa was showing interest. "We can also look into renting furniture." She looped her blonde hair behind her ears in a gesture that said, "Let's get down to business."

"There is even a small kitchenette and bath on the second floor," Stephen said. "Want to take a look?"

"We believe you," Maggie said, in a hurry to make a decision.

"It will be fun decorating. The conference room will need a large table and ten chairs. I'm thinking that we should hit antique shops and get something special to move over to the new offices when they're rebuilt." Lisa's big green eyes momentarily danced.

Maggie feared a meltdown was not far behind.

"We'll have to get Gus' agreement." Lisa added, "Unfortunately." They both knew how crabby and difficult he could be.

"He's in my office at the house checking on our insurance," Maggie said. "Let's go! ... I'm calling Richard Harvey. He's the best carpenter in town, does excellent work. If he's not too busy, maybe he can start tomorrow."

"I'll bet he could get you in here in a couple weeks," Duval said.

"Two weeks," Maggie repeated, hoping Lisa could keep it together and Gus would agree. "Okay. Draw up the papers and bring them over to my house later."

Back at her house, Maggie heard that after several attempts, Gus had reached the emergency number of their insurance company and learned they were adequately covered for the complete loss of their building and its contents.

"Thank God you got that Rolls Royce policy." Gus pranced around the kitchen as if in a Hamlet soliloquy.

"The problem is that we have no back-up documents because the temporary record room was destroyed in the fire." Lisa sank into a chair at the large kitchen table.

"The agent has a record of our investments, and our credit card companies will have proof of our purchases," Gus said as he plunked down next to Lisa. "We can move ahead knowing our basic losses will be covered."

"Our client's records are another matter." Lisa put her head down on her arms at the table. "What can we do about them?"

"That situation could take years to solve." Gus shrieked from the refrigerator where he had gone for ice in his glass of water.

Maggie strove for calm and hoped most of their clients had kept copies of their cases as she always advised.

They were fully aware that they could never be compensated for the care and love they had poured into their almost hundred-year-old Painted Lady.

Later that night at her house, Estelle finally persuaded Lisa to go to bed after they had signed the rental agreement and Duval had left. Maggie thought the guest room across the hall from Sophie would be the most comfortable and allow easy access for Sophie to entertain their new guest.

Lisa, on the brink of a nervous breakdown, talked fast, hysterically fast. At least three times she'd said, "We have to have a new sign. A brass plaque. SWEENEY, PEREZ & PALMER. We'll be in business again."

Maggie still anticipated Lisa's breakdown, but Estelle came to the rescue with homemade calming tea that she kept for emergencies. Maggie wondered about the age and potency of the brew, but Lisa seemed to be sleeping peacefully. Sophie had positioned herself at the side of Lisa's bed, constructing a tall Victorian house out of Legos.

Dan called early Sunday and told Maggie to bring Lisa and meet him at the morgue in half an hour. They needed Lisa to identify Robbie's body. The Medical Examiner would complete the autopsy and release his body to their funeral home of choice. He'd tried to make the experience as easy as possible. "This is a special favor to me because they don't usually work on Sundays," Dan said, "It will be quiet and less traumatic."

"You're a godsend. We really appreciate your running interference for us," Maggie said. "Lisa can use tranquility. We'll be there as soon as we can."

Twenty minutes later, Maggie held Lisa's hand as they entered the county morgue. She was surprised that it seemed like a clean bright lab or hospital clinic. No antiseptic death smells or sweet flowery odors. She had been expecting squeaky gurneys and masked attendants, a dour place. Lisa remained calm, stoically holding herself together.

Dan was already there and greeted both with warm hugs. "The Examiner has Robbie's body ready." He led them into a pleasant side room that looked like a typical living room where the body, half covered with a white sheet, was laid out on a steel table. Lisa walked over and put her hand on Robbie's chalky-blue chest. "It is my husband," she said softly and turned away. "I'd rather not remember him like this. I like to think of him as full of life."

Maggie put her arm around Lisa and was about to lead her to the door when the Pathologist said, "This was in your husband's shirt pocket." He held out Robbie's illustrated margarita booklet. Lisa took it and said, "thank you" in a soft voice, clutching it to her breast. What he loved, she loved.

"Was he an artist? The pictures were something special," the doctor said, handing over a small plastic bag of Robbie's clothing.

"Yes. Thank you," Lisa repeated. Her grief had gone too deep to say more.

Maggie gave the Medical Examiner a sheet of paper with the address of the Funeral Home Estelle had chosen. She, Dan and Lisa left with the small plastic bag hanging from Lisa's hand.

CHAPTER 16

ROBBIE'S FUNERAL was scheduled for Thursday to give the families time to make travel arrangements. Lisa's sister, Betty, agreed to pick up their parents in Texas. They would stay in Lisa's condo. Robbie's three brothers were driving up from Mexico with wives, children, aunts and uncles as soon as they could get everybody together. Would Maggie make reservations for them at a local motel? They would probably need six rooms. Maggie agreed and said she still had two empty bedrooms and a couple of sofas. Anyone was welcome to stay there.

Early Monday morning Maggie rode her bicycle to Richard Harvey's carpenter workshop behind his house and pleaded her case. He was dressed in his usual coveralls, crisp, white and ironed. His wife once told

Maggie that he had seven pairs at her insistence so he'd change every day. She had embroidered one day of the week on the pocket of each. Sometimes he mixed up the days, but at least he changed his clothes. He was in his late seventies, a broad, tall man with a beach-ball-belly and longish white hair brushed back to reveal pink cheeks. This Monday he was in his Wednesday coveralls.

"I guess you heard about the fire." Maggie pushed down her kickstand.

"Is there anybody within five hundred miles who hasn't? The word is going around that your ex is saying it's your fault."

"Hank?"

"Yeah, says you deserved it. God is punishing you for abandoning him."

"God! Richard, you don't believe in a vengeful deity, do you? The police think it's a hate group from near the border who want to stick it to successful Mexicans. Our Mexican Fiesta Grand Opening set them off."

"There're a lot of strange things goin' around in this town lately. It's like Mayor Buchanan and Chief Strunk are out to lunch." Richard pulled a large, perfectly pressed linen hankie from his pocket, unfolded it and blew his nose.

"What?"

"Why haven't they formed a special committee to deal with these attacks against our Latino community, our community?"

"I hadn't thought of it that way. But you're right, it *is* our community," Maggie said. "You don't think Hank set fire to The Painted Lady?"

"I don't know what to say, but that ex of yours is acting mighty strange since he's been home. I see him sitting around most mornings with that uppity Horace Grundy and his gun-totin' group at the Crystal Diner. Just because he's loaded with dough, Grundy thinks he and his son, Ron, can do anything they dream up. Buchanan and Strunk hang there at the diner and Hank goes right along with them."

Maggie stood mystified, not knowing how to respond.

"My neighbor on the next block told me Grundy killed his friend's cat with poisoned water. They couldn't prove it, but the vet verified that their cat was poisoned. Antifreeze. And my friend saw Hank setting out a pan of water in Grundy's side yard. Neighbors complained the cat howled a lot."

"No more, Richard. I can't bear to hear about Hank. How busy are you? Can you work on that empty furniture store on Donner Street for us? We'd like to get in there in two weeks."

"Well, you're lucky. With the beginning of school, not many people are looking for a carpenter. And you know I'd always come to your rescue. Remember the time I saved you from being run over by a train?"

At the time she'd been eight months old but had heard the story so often she knew it by heart. She believed he and Estelle had at one time been in love, although no one ever confirmed it for her. She also knew Richard beamed when she herself related the events. "Estelle was baby-sitting when her heel got caught in the tracks; you came along, dislodged her shoe and pushed my carriage under the crossbar just in time. How could I forget?" She never let on to Richard that Estelle said the train was miles away.

"I have two small jobs I can postpone. Where do I go?"

"Stephen Duval can give you a key. Two weeks, Richard. Please. One other thing. Do you think we should use Merton Builders for the reconstruction of the Painted Lady?"

"They have a cool reputation. On the expensive side, but probably not too busy either these days."

"I'll talk to them. For you we've drawn up a sketch of how many offices we'll need." Maggie handed over a single paper with a pencil drawing of offices and hallways mapped out. "Two weeks, Richard. You can even overcharge us."

Maggie got back on her bicycle and rode away, but thoughts of what Richard had said about Mayor Buchanan and Chief Strunk refused to quiet down in her brain.

Robbie's High Mass and burial had been perfectly arranged by the Ignatius Funeral Home. Still, it was sad with much wailing and hugging. The front pews of Sacred Heart were hung with white flower wreaths to indicate where the immediate family would sit. Music with a soft Latino beat flowed from the church speakers. Lisa was amazingly calm, gone to another level of grief, holding it together for the sake of her family. Maggie let Sophie come because she begged and promised to tell Estelle if it was too sad for her to deal with. Pablo and Joseph arrived from Hermosillo with four cars full of relatives. Each brother looked like a Robbie clone with jet back hair and the bodies of long-distance runners.

"Jesús was stopped at the border. His visa expired," Pablo told them. "We explained we were on our way to our brother's funeral, but they wouldn't let him pass. Jesús told us to go ahead. He has a good friend he thought might be able to smuggle him across in the dark." Now it was two days later and he hadn't shown up. Pablo's face was dark with worry and he gripped the funeral program tightly.

Maggie and Dan sat close together near the back of the church. Dan was on duty and kept his cell in his hand turned to vibrate.

After the service and trip to the cemetery, they went back to Maggie's for an elaborate breakfast. Estelle had been collecting and organizing casseroles and pies and cakes that neighbors were dropping off. There was enough food for the entire city of Hermosillo. She wanted the Pérezes to take most of the food home. They planned to stay another day or two and explore Juniper Hills because they'd never had a chance to visit Robbie's town. Lisa and Robbie had been married in Hermosillo.

Sitting in Maggie's living room the second night, Pablo answered his cell. He listened, then burst out, "*Por el amor de Dios*! Jesús is in jail. The patrol caught him trying to cross. He slipped into a canal along the border and they pulled him out. Not gently, I'm sure. He has a broken shoulder. The police took him to the jail hospital to have it set."

"Jesús will never learn not to fight," Irena, his cousin, said.

"We leave at first light in the morning. He's mad. He'll get himself in more trouble before we get him out of that pit," Joseph said.

"If you don't have a disease when you go in, you come out with one." Pablo squinted his eyes. "We're not ready to leave just yet. Running off tomorrow makes me feel disrespectful of Robbie's memory."

"Well, you and your family stay," Joseph said. "We're going tomorrow to save Jesús who fortunately is still alive."

Lisa stayed calm, but Maggie was worried, waiting for her to crash again. Sophie sat on Lisa's lap with her arms around her neck, staring down at her hands. Maggie noticed how, easily Sophie alternated between English and Spanish. The Pérez brothers were obviously well educated. Their English was near perfect. Their thinking careful. All afternoon Estelle brewed more of her homemade tea for Lisa.

Early the next morning half the Pérez family filled Estelle's kitchen, sipping coffee, munching donuts and thanking her. Sophie cried and hugged everyone, said she would miss them in English and Spanish. Lisa sat quietly and made Joseph promise to call when they got Jesús released. Maggie invited them to come back. They were welcome any time of day or night. They left with six casseroles in thermal bags.

Maggie, Lisa and Gus spent the rest of the day with the Merton Builders, some time in their temporary offices and other time in front of their beloved Queen Anne's ashes. The lot had been leveled and the fiesta basement loomed as a black hole in the ground. Estelle hadn't wanted Lisa to go, but Lisa reiterated for the tenth time that keeping busy made her feel less sad.

"I think we can finish this project in a little over a year," James Merton said, looking at the plans the three had brought him.

"We have some sepia photographs of the original house," Gus said. "Thank God I took them home after

I found them when I cleaned out the attic." He handed over a folder to the builder.

"They will give us a good idea of where we want to go," Gary Merton said, examining the old photos.

The three left, feeling the day had ended well for a change.

Four days later they all said a tearful good-bye to Pablo and his family in a repeat kitchen scene of their farewell to Joseph and his family.

CHAPTER 17

DEAR MISS CHLOE: I'm writing because I don't know where else to turn. Maybe you or your readers can help. My husband of thirteen years after three tours in Afghanistan has become a monster. He's lost three jobs because of his temper, beats up on our two kids for almost nothing (like spilling a glass of milk), pushes me around and even slapped his own mother. We have little money and no family to help us. I tried to make an appointment at our local VA hospital, but they can't see him for three months. He's always sorry after an incident and promises never to do it again, but then he does. I've called the cops several times. They talk to him and tell me to be patient because he's a veteran. I'm at my wits end. *Victim of PTSD and collateral victim of this gruesome war.*

Dear Wife and Mother: Please do not think of yourself as a victim. You are a strong, resourceful woman, collateral damage of an endless war. IMMEDIATELY call your doctor or take your husband to a local hospital. The United States Government will pay for his treatment if he can't be seen at a VA hospital in a reasonable amount of time. Your husband is a very sick man and a walking time bomb. You and your family need help ASAP. Do not delay. Accept no new apologies. Call the police or an ambulance if necessary and have him evaluated. He is a danger to himself and others. *Miss Chloe*

Maggie stared at the walls of her home office. She was pleased she had chosen the beige rice paper for its sophisticated look. To her it meant business, serious business, no nonsense, which was the way she ran her law firm. It was how she thought of The Painted Lady when they were renovating and how she hoped to rebuild the new structure and furnish it. She closed her computer and leaned back in her ergonomic chair. Her neck ached and exhaustion was about to overcome her spirit. Over the years she had thought her troubles with Hank were off the charts. Here was a woman caught in the flames of Hell. Maggie's heart ached for her. For the first time writing as MISS CHLOE, she felt unsure of her response. Did she say too much or too little? Thinking about anything to do with war and Hank made her feel sick to her stomach. She and Hank had at one time been deeply in love. She now felt guilty because she had no feelings for him, neither pity nor hatred. All that remained was numbness, leaving her hollow when in his presence. She was beginning to think she never **ever**, as Sophie would say, wanted to date another man, until she met Dan.

Therapy after her divorce had helped her see her weaknesses and strengths and deal with the changes in her life. Now, since Hank had come home, she wondered if she should schedule more sessions with her therapist. In many ways she felt totally confident for the first time in her life. Hank's unexpected appearance had put her off balance. Maggie was up to renovating the store-front office and even rebuilding their Queen Anne office, but nagging concerns about Hank's presence in Juniper Hills clattered in her head. Why didn't he leave as he said he would? Why did he tell Richard Harvey's friend she deserved their offices to burn down? Could Hank have had anything to do with the fire and Robbie's death? She would speak to Dan. Why risk slipping back into that dungeon of darkness.

She left her office and walked into the kitchen where Estelle was busy sorting the remaining casseroles, trying to decide what they might eat and what to give to the Food Kitchen at Open Door. Lisa had taken Sophie to her condo to say good-bye to her sister and parents.

"The Pérezes and our neighbors took all they could and I have no more room in the freezer. I don't want this good food to spoil." Estelle had the phone propped on her shoulder beneath her ear as she talked to her Russian friend, Irina, who lived next door.

Maggie made herself a cup of herbal tea and sat at the kitchen table waiting for Estelle. "What can I do to help?" she asked when Estelle hung up.

"Do you want to drop off a box at the Food Pantry?"

"Sure. I'm not exactly busy at the non-existent office."

"You will be soon. Don't despair.... I'm concerned that we haven't heard from Joseph or Pablo. It's been days and they planned to drive right through the night. They should have news about Jesús by now."

"I've been thinking the same thing."

As they spoke, the kitchen door burst open. Maggie's brother, Josh, walked in. His short-sleeved tee and khaki shorts displaying a well-toned, well-tanned body glowing with sun-blessed health.

"Hi, you busy bees. Fun Mexican Festival, devastating fire, meaningful funeral. Any other exciting events planned? I'm sorry Fran and I, lounging on the beaches in Costa Rica, missed it all."

"Don't be cruel, Josh." Estelle swatted him with a dish towel.

"I know, Mom. Just trying for a light touch." He placed a small bulging gunny sack of letters on the table. "Your devoted readers are increasing, Sis. We were inspired when we syndicated the MISS CHLOE column. The two kids in the mail room want a raise."

"Thanks. I'll get started on this batch while I have extra time until the new offices are ready. Meantime please start looking for my replacement while I have the time to train her."

They talked for a while. Estelle told Josh he looked as handsome as ever with a deep tan. When she was in middle school studying Greek culture, Maggie thought Josh looked like several of the Greek Gods, dark hair, beautiful body, in her history book. She couldn't remember which Gods, always meant to look it up, but over the years it didn't seem to matter. She was glad to have him and hoped people could see how much they loved and resembled each other, even if she had Irish blue and he dark Greek eyes.

"You should see Fran," he said. "She avoids the sun because of her delicate skin. Looks like a ghost. People will think we took separate vacations. How the tongues will wag!"

"Like you care what people think," Estelle quipped.

Maggie picked up the box Estelle had prepared for the Food Pantry, kissed Estelle good-bye and hugged Josh. "You two enjoy each other. I have a mission of mercy to accomplish." She headed for her car. Those two would joke around for the next hour. She usually relished her brother's humor, but today she wasn't in the mood for comedy.

She dropped the food at Open Door and drove around town, hoping she might see Dan's squad car and have a moment with him. She stopped at the Donner Street store-front and was pleasantly surprised at how quickly Richard Harvey and three assistants were creating their new offices out of empty space. They had placed the hall partitions and were about to define the various offices. The brass plaque Lisa had requested was ordered. Maggie hoped it arrived in time for their opening.

When she was sure Josh would have left, she went home, anxious to check out the new batch of letters to see if there was one from Rosa pretending to be a man. She took the sack into her office, opened it and created piles on the floor, looking for letters from men. She shuffled through nearly thirty envelopes when she came

across a letter with the return address from Mr. Adam
Jones. She set it aside and searched through the other
stacks. There was a letter from Mr. John Gonzales and
another from Mr. Fred Smith. She put those aside and
finished going through the rest of the mail.

Picking up the three envelopes she sat at her desk.
Using a sterling silver opener Josh had given her when
she became MISS CHLOE, she slit open the envelopes
one at a time and pulled out the contents. The first one,
from Mr. Smith, was a screed complaining about his
nagging wife. She dropped it in the waste paper basket.
He thinks he has problems, she thought. The one from
Mr. Gonzales asked if she could put him in touch with
Rosa Melendez as he had a new apartment for her. Rosa
had given him MISS CHLOE'S address as a reference.

The third letter was from Rosa, aka Mr. Adam Jones.
She was in Roswell, New Mexico. When she arrived,
Carlos was being moved to a new detention facility
back in Phoenix on his way to deportation. She had
come to visit him, but was forced to watch as they
dragged him into a van. He could hardly move. His
eyes and face twisted in pain, she wrote. Something
was very wrong with his back. They had injured him
in some way. He was always in good health. Although
he complained about back pain, he was never crippled
by it. She asked if Maggie had any way to get him to a
hospital. She also asked to borrow a small amount of
money to return to Arizona.

"This is getting dangerously bad," Maggie said to
her office walls.

CHAPTER 18

MAGGIE PLANNED to go to Phoenix when she heard from Rosa, but first she had to assemble some people with clout. She wired five hundred dollars to Rosa via the Roswell, New Mexico Western Union and called Dr. Peter Burke, an orthopedist she knew at St. Joseph's Hospital in Phoenix. He graciously promised to be available if and when they arrived.

Then she asked Dan to get an order to transfer Carlos to St. Joseph's for health reasons. She also asked him to go with her to the Phoenix detention facility, hoping the transfer order and Carlo's replaced passport card and citizenship certificate that Rosa possessed would be enough to get Carlos released to a hospital and prevent his deportation.

Dan said, "No problem. I can switch days with Whitey. He owes me. I'll get old Judge Gerald

Lynch to issue me an order of transfer. Carlos needs immediate care."

Maggie sat down to think about the best way to deal with Rosa's situation. She composed two letters for the next day's edition of the *Gazette* and wondered how Rosa would contact her.

Dear Miss Chloe: I'm stranded in Roswell, New Mexico without money or help. Could you please print this letter and ask my daughter to send help? I've tried to contact her, but her phone's been disconnected. I know she reads your column every day so I'm hoping she will see this letter. *Desperate*

Dear Desperate: Your daughter read your letter and contacted me. Go to the nearest Western Union, 63 Main Street, Roswell and tell them you are expecting a check from your daughter. Show them your driver's license ID. A money order will be waiting for you. She will meet you in Phoenix at St. Joseph's hospital front lobby. Call when you arrive. *Miss Chloe*

She had no idea what to do about Mr. John Gonzalez with the available apartment but would ask Rosa when she got a chance. She was afraid for Rosa and Carlos now. Phoenix was a dangerous and unfriendly city for immigrants, illegal or legal.

A week later, Estelle and Maggie watched the Friday night "News Hour" on their new Sony TV in the den.

The dark green velvet curtains were drawn against the night's chill. Sophie was upstairs in bed with Lisa reading to her. Sophie turned out to be the best medicine for Lisa's grief. As a pledge drive for the PBS station came on the TV, Maggie's cell rang. At the same time their landline jangled and Estelle moved to answer. There was an unfamiliar number on Maggie's screen and all she heard was, "I'm here. See you tomorrow noon at St. Joe's." Before the click that ended the call, Maggie knew it was Rosa. She called the number back and it rang and rang until a young male voice answered, "Hey."

Maggie took a deep breath and said, "Would you please tell me what number I've called?"

"Yo, Lady, I'm passing by and pick up the ringing phone from under a bush. This is Scottsdale, Arizona."

"Thanks," Maggie said and hung up. Rosa had arrived, purchased a throw-away phone and called. She wished Rosa wasn't so terrified of the telephone and the police. She would have liked to talk to her.

Meanwhile a plan formed in Maggie's mind. She'd make a copy of Sophie's birth certificate, change the date of birth, recopy it and bring Sophie's social security card in case Rosa needed more documentation. Maggie had heard too many stories of documented immigrants being plucked off the street in Phoenix.

Estelle was still on their landline, giving directions to their house. A few minutes passed, she hung up and said, "We're getting a visitor. That was Jesús Pérez. He'll be here soon."

"No!"

"He escaped from the Mexican jail hospital, crossed the border with a friend and hitchhiked to Juniper Hills. He thought his brothers were still here."

"I have to call Dan. Rosa is going to meet us at St. Joe's Hospital tomorrow. Can you handle Jesús by yourself? Lisa and Sophie can help."

"Of course, I can handle Jesús. I've been tear-gassed, hit in the shoulder with a rubber hose and jailed. Have I turned feeble overnight?"

"We can't let him go outside until we get a feel for his safety."

Thirty minutes later there was a knock on the front door. "Didn't want to ring the bell. Thought I'd slip in quietly, without fanfare." Jesús, looking like a taller Robbie, entered the house. "Been sneakin' around for three days, avoiding people and hiding in alleys and back yards." His hair, oily and unwashed, hung limp about his ears. When he removed his jacket, which appeared to be something he grabbed out of a dumpster and was three sizes too big for him, his left arm and shoulder were wrapped in a soft cast. "I had to get out of that hospital jail or I would have died from some exotic disease."

"Are they looking for you?" Maggie asked, noticing that he spoke English without an accent.

"I doubt they even know I'm gone. One less mouth to feed."

Lisa and Sophie came running down the stairs. Sophie cried out, "Robbie, you're back! ... No. I know that's not so. You must be his brother." She hugged him anyway.

"Smart little girl," Jesús said, patting the top of Sophie's head. He hugged Lisa. "Hi, Sis, I'm so sorry. I missed the service and the gang. Robbie was a special man."

He clung tightly to Lisa. "Maybe tomorrow you can show me the cemetery?" he asked Maggie who was still trying to take in his likeness to Robbie.

"Come and sit in the den." Estelle gently took his right arm and led him to a soft sofa. "You must be starving? Can I get you something to eat?"

"Tea, if it isn't too much trouble? I stopped for a sandwich at a place called Subway."

Lisa, as if coming out of a coma, sat next to Jesús. "I'm sad you missed Robbie's funeral. It was lovely. Your brothers and family all said wonderful things about him. He was so loved."

"Here and at home," Jesús said.

"I have to go to Phoenix tomorrow." Maggie felt she had to take control. "Jesús, I'd like you to stay out of sight until we're sure no one is following you. Then we can give you a tour of town and take you to Robbie's grave. Lisa might have some of Robbie's clothes that will fit you."

"I do," Lisa said. "I've been putting off giving them away."

"They'll be too short." Jesus made a mischievous gesture halfway up his leg.

"I can take care of that," Estelle said, imitating someone sewing.

"Great." Maggie was in executive mode. "Sophie, maybe you and Estelle could put sheets on one of the beds in the other guest room for Jesús? While he showers, Lisa and I will run over to her condo and bring him clothes. Dan is picking me up at six in the morning. I'd like to get us settled tonight."

Once in the car, Maggie told Lisa that Rosa was back from New Mexico and she and Dan were meeting her in Scottsdale to get Carlos out of the detention center in Phoenix and into the hospital. Rosa was afraid he had a fractured spine. She didn't want Sophie to know. "Sophie already carries too heavy a burden for a little kid."

"Don't worry about Jesús. Estelle and Sophie and I will take good care of hiding him. Sophie will entertain him with her toys. You know how engaging she can be. She's so naturally smart. It's hard to believe she's never been to school."

"Speaking of school, Robbie as well as his brothers all seem well educated."

"Yes. Their Dad insisted they go to UNAM, the University of Mexico." Lisa explained that Pablo was a lawyer, Joseph a tax accountant and Robbie had a teaching degree. Jesús went to the university art school. "But in the end, they decided to combine their talents and create what has become the most popular restaurant in the State of Sonora. I'd like to take you there one day. The walls are covered with murals that Jesús has been working on for years."

"I'm getting the feeling that Sophie has been surrounded by a rich cultural life. Remember Mannie. He was a member of the Mariachi ensemble that played at our Grand Opening."

"You mean our Grand Closing?" Lisa rolled up the car window.

"A good way to put it. I spoke briefly with Mannie. He doesn't have the slightest accent either." Maggie told Lisa how his wife tutored Sophie. "There were three or four families at the apartments where Sophie lived. She's a sponge. If one of the families was Chinese, she'd be speaking several versions of Chinese by now. She's remarkable."

Lisa rolled her window down. "I can't decide if I'm hot or cold."

"It's your hormones. Having a baby makes them run wild."

"Do you think you can get Carlos released tomorrow?"

"Let's pray."

CHAPTER 19

MAGGIE AND DAN left before the sun rose over the
ponderosas. To avoid the heavy traffic into Phoenix,
they took a back road that Dan had known as a boy.
"This was an Indian trail before it was paved. It ran
along the old railroad. When they dug up the tracks
most people forgot about this area and as you can see
the weeds took over. It's mostly a dirt trail, but spots
of it are still paved. We'll go as far as we can. It'll be a
bit bumpy, but save us time."

Maggie, as she jostled around in her seat, kept a
cautious eye on the road, hoping they didn't end up
with a flat. "I'm worried about Carlos. I hope we can
move him from that detention center. I've alerted Peter
Burke, an old friend and orthopedic surgeon, that we
were trying to get Carlos to the hospital in Scottsdale

today, so he's expecting us. Not sure how she did it, but Rosa got a look at Carlos in New Mexico. He's in bad shape."

"Judge Gerald Lynch gave me an order to remove him to a hospital, but he didn't sound too confident that it would be honored in Phoenix."

"This is a city unto itself when it comes to immigrants. Did you know that Carlos lived in Denver for twenty years before he met Rosa and they moved to Juniper Hills? He's quite educated. Two university degrees and teaching jobs, which may help explain Sophie's smarts."

"I love that kid."

"I don't want to get us into any trouble, but I made a copy of Sophie's birth certificate and changed the date of birth and recopied it. I thought it would give Rosa some extra protection in Phoenix if she's asked for her documents. I even brought Sophie's Social Security card. My concern is that she may faint if approached by a law officer and forget to say her name is Sophie. Uniforms make Rosa tremble."

"What's she going to do when she sees me in this full-police dress gear I borrowed from Whitey?"

"Say hello, I hope. Thanks for coming to rescue Carlos. Was it difficult to take the squad car without an explanation?"

"I said I had to pick up an immigrant in Phoenix and nobody wanted to hear about it. Most cops around here don't want to get involved in family immigration problems. They want to catch criminals and keep order. This ripping children from their mothers and fathers, from their families disgusts me and many officers I know."

After a two-hour drive, Dan pulled the squad car into the St. Joseph's Hospital short term parking lot and said, "I'll stay here 'til you find Rosa."

Maggie hopped out. "I can't wait to get her out of this city." She pushed open the front door and looked around. The woman at the courtesy desk asked if she could help. "I'm meeting a friend here," Maggie said hoping there were no more questions. She sat in a chair where she could watch the front door.

Ten minutes passed before a woman swathed in a blue scarf appeared from a hallway, sat next to her and whispered, "It's me."

"Oh, my God! Where did you come from? I never recognized you." Maggie and Rosa stood to hug each other.

"I stand in the parking lot. Watch you pull up in cop car."

"It's okay. That's Dan. He's going to help. Let's get out of here. I'll explain everything in the car." They moved toward the front door.

"Glad you found your friend," the woman at the desk trilled.

"We'll be back." Maggie spoke over her shoulder. She grabbed Rosa and eased her into the back seat of the squad car. She walked around the other side of the car and slid in beside a tense Rosa.

"This is Dan Clarke. He found Sophie's original birth certificate. He also registered her for a Social Security card." ... Maggie paused for emphasis.

"Gracias," Rosa said, as she unwrapped her scarf and clasped Maggie's hand.

Dan turned around and smiled. "Just to be sure. You do have Carlos' citizenship papers and replacement passport card with you?"

"Oh, *si*. I carry them all over the country."

Maggie could see Rosa visibly relax. "Here's our plan." She turned to Rosa. "I've altered a copy of Sophie's birth certificate to the year you were born and I have her Social Security card. For the rest of our time in Phoenix you are Sophie Melendez, if anyone asks. Put these in your purse. I'm hoping you won't have to show them. It's just a precaution. I don't want anyone questioning your refugee status."

"You'll have to show ID at the detention center. Try not to seem nervous," Dan said. "It's routine."

"Which ID should I use? Sophie's or mine?"

"Use Sophie's," Maggie said. "It's more definitive, easier to understand."

"How is Sophie? I miss her so much."

"I'm not sure Estelle will want to give her back." Maggie stroked Rosa's arm.

"She is something special," Dan said.

"I know," Rosa said, wiping a tear from her cheek.

Maggie put her arm around Rosa's shoulder. "Dr. Peter Burke is waiting for us at St. Joe's. He's a highly trained orthopedist and will exam Carlos' back as soon as we can transfer him to the hospital."

They quieted down for the ride to the private detention center a few miles outside the city. "Where is Lupita?" Maggie asked, thinking small talk would be good for all of them.

"She liked Roswell and decided to stay. Nobody there cares if you have papers. It's not like here."

Maggie was glad Rosa had a good experience in New Mexico and hoped that today would be a good experience in Arizona.

Three miles down the road in front of them appeared the diamond-shaped mesh of a chain-link fence with razor wire on top. At the guardhouse Dan showed his transfer orders from Judge Lynch to the security official, who seemed bored and disinterested. "We're here to move an immigrant to the hospital," Dan said. They had decided the best approach was to tell the simple truth as often as possible. They were passed through, parked close to the low adobe-brick building and walked to the front entrance.

Once inside they were asked who they wished to see and given forms to fill out. Rosa/Sophie said she was Carlos' wife, Maggie said she was his lawyer and Dan wrote down Security for himself. They were taken to a small room with a few chairs and a wobbly round table. The walls were dreary institutional beige and the room smelled musty as if it hadn't been cleaned in a while. Cobwebs hung from the ceiling corners. Rosa mentioned that the floor needed a good scrubbing.

After waiting forty minutes a tall thin man with round black-framed glasses entered the room. "I'm Mathew Unger. I understand you're here to visit Carlos Melendez." He spoke to Dan as if the two women were not present in the room.

"Yes. I have a court order signed by Judge Gerald Lynch. We believe Carlos Melendez needs medical care beyond what is available here at your facility." Dan handed the order to Unger who acted as if it was full of fleas.

"May I ask on what you are basing that judgement?" Unger asked, definitely not happy with the request.

"Mr. Melendez has spinal problems which he described to his wife, Mrs. Melendez," Dan indicated Rosa, "as worsening in New Mexico. We'd like to see him."

"I'll make a call and be right back," Unger said.

Dan followed him out into the hall and returned in a few minutes. "When Unger went into his office to call the judge, I walked to the end of the hall. Through a glass door I could see bunk beds in a room that was constructed to house a hundred men filled with more like five hundred lying around, some on thin mats."

"What do you think," Maggie asked.

"I'm afraid to think anything yet." Dan stared out the window.

Rosa looked ghastly. She had developed a blue tinge to her face and her hands were shaking. She held them behind her back to keep them out of sight.

"Let's not panic until we see what happens," Dan said.

In twenty minutes, two guards supporting Carlos between them walked into the room. Carlos was obviously drugged. Rosa ran to him. "I'm so glad to see you."

"Rosa, how did you ...?"

"Carlos," she quickly corrected. "It's Sophie. Rosa is our daughter. How do you feel?"

"Better since you're here."

"You know Maggie Sweeney, our lawyer."

Carlos, as if coming up from the deepest recesses of the ocean answered, "Of course. Miss Sweeney."

"And this is Officer Clarke." Rosa stroked Carlos' arm. "He has a court order for you to be transferred to St. Joseph's Hospital. We need to check your back, *rapido*."

Maggie held her breath. Dan asked the two security guards who were still supporting Carlos, to help Mr. Melendez into the squad car. Dan left to bring the car around to the front door. The guards appeared uncertain as to what to do.

CHAPTER 20

WHEN MATHEW UNGER returned, the guards supporting Carlos' slumped over body looked to him for confirmation. Maggie noticed that Unger seemed unsettled by Judge Lynch's order. She and Rosa moved toward the front door of the detection facility. Dan arrived in the squad car at the entrance and the guards plunked a wincing Carlos in the back seat so roughly that Maggie cringed. Rosa crawled in beside him.

As Maggie climbed into the front passenger seat she heard: "Wait!" Her heart threw a fit in her chest.

Unger came over to Dan's window. "Officer, you forgot to sign this release." Dan took the clipboard from Unger, scribbled his signature on the proffered sheet, nodded goodbye, and drove through the open gate down the road to Scottsdale and the hospital.

"What do you suppose Judge Lynch said to Unger?" Maggie asked Dan.

"Knowing old Gerry, he probably threatened to send a reporter for a newspaper interview and a picture of Carlos unable to stand. He read him the riot act about having his name in the paper and his private facility being closed, in the kindest way, of course. That's why I wanted that order from Lynch. Just his name commands respect, particularly with someone who doesn't know the fine points of the law."

"I am soaked with sweat," Carlos said, collapsing into Rosa's lap and falling asleep.

"They drug him out of his mind," Rosa said.

"We'll have him evaluated at St. Joe's by Dr. Burke and then take him to Juniper Hills. I'm afraid to leave him in the Phoenix area." She leaned over and squeezed Dan's arm. "I feel like a character in *Mission Impossible*."

"Me too." Rosa let out a sigh from the back seat and put her hand on Carlos' chest where she could feel his steady breathing.

Dan sped up to the emergency entrance of St. Joseph's; Maggie got out and told the officer stationed at the door that Dr. Peter Burke was expecting them. "We think the man in the car has a fractured spine." Then she told the full-white-bearded gentleman at the admitting desk the same story.

"I'll call the trauma team." The Santa look-a-like picked up his phone and began making calls. "Dr. Peter to emergency..." screeched over the intercom. Three white clad attendants, two men and a woman appeared within minutes, pushing a wheeled stretcher topped with bracing equipment. The woman gently asked Rosa to move out of the car and they began to work on Carlos who was still unconscious. They laid him out on the back seat. The woman put a brace around his neck and the two men lifted him at the hips to slip another brace under his back and secure it on his abdomen. They then moved Carlos to the stretcher. Maggie wondered if it wasn't too late for that kind of attention but hoped it would at least prevent more pain and damage.

Peter Burke arrived. Tall, slightly graying hair, sweet smile, rimless glasses, a Hollywood model of a physician. He gave Maggie a hearty hug and a quick kiss on the cheek. He then acknowledged Dan and Rosa. "I'll take Carlos up to the OR and do what I do. Where shall I contact you?" he asked Maggie. "This might take some time. Have Rosa sign a consent form at the admitting desk in case surgery is necessary."

Maggie looked from Rosa to Dan. "I think we should find a place to stay overnight." She then said to Peter, "You have my cell. Rosa will register Carlos and sign whatever needs to be signed."

Peter turned to follow the stretcher.

"I'll call the station," Dan told Maggie. "Tell Whitey we've run into complications. Ask him to relay the message and cover for me tomorrow. Let's get Rosa settled and something to eat. It's almost seven and I'm sure she's ready to collapse. Burke will call when he has something to say. There's no need to wait around here. Rosa looks unsure and exhausted."

Maggie took both Rosa's hands in hers. "Carlos will need X-rays and an MRI and maybe surgery. It might take hours. You need to rest. Let's check Carlos in, find a place to stay and wait there for them to call us."

Rosa followed with great reluctance. Leaving Carlos was not to her liking. She had put her and Carlos' lives in Maggie and Dan's hands. "Not sure it safe for me to stay in a hotel. Some front desk people report Hispanics to authorities."

"I believe you'll be okay with me and Dan. He's the law."

Rosa laughed and Maggie hugged her and laughed too.

They registered Carlos at the admitting desk and drove to a nearby hotel on the hospital campus that served patients and their families. Rosa sank into a large soft chair in the lobby, "I can't wait to see Sophie."

"Sophie talks about you all the time." Maggie told Rosa she'd be right back and followed Dan to the check-in desk.

He had arranged for three rooms, one for Rosa and adjoining rooms for Maggie and himself. "Just to be discreet; I want to protect your reputation."

"I can't believe you'd think of sleeping with me at a time like this."

"This is the time. Love-making is good for stress."

"You're bad." Smiling, Maggie walked back to Rosa and helped her up from the chair. "You look whipped. Let me take you to your room. I've registered you as Sophie Melendez. Do you have anything but that big purse you've been toting around?"

"I left my things with Lupita. She can use them. I put what was left in storage in your basement before I went to look for Carlos."

Maggie escorted Rosa to her room, opened the door with the key card and picked up the room service menu. "You must have something to eat. You've got to stay healthy for Carlos' sake as well as yourself." Looking around the room, Maggie almost laughed out loud. The hotel designer must have been a dancer. The walls were covered with large Edgar Degas posters. Ballerinas leapt and floated around the walls in pastel colors and graceful movements. At least it wasn't depressing.

Rosa flopped on the bed. "Okay. Some soup, please. Any kind but split-pea. I hate it."

Maggie dialed room service. "We'll have a bowl of chicken noodle soup, two rolls with butter and a dish of coconut ice-cream. As soon as possible, please." She called Peter's office and told his secretary where they were staying.

"You remembered I like ice cream," Rosa said, sitting on the side of the bed.

"How could I forget? Estelle buys the coconut by the gallon for you and Sophie. ... Room service should be here any minute. Have the soup and ice cream. ... Maybe you should have the ice cream first, depends if you like your soup hotter than your ice cream colder." Maggie was struggling to keep the conversation light. "Take a shower and go to sleep. I'll call the minute I hear from Dr. Burke, though it may not be till morning." Maggie opened the small bag she had brought from home and laid a silky folded nightgown on the end of the desk. "This will help you sleep more comfortably. Good night, Rosa. If you need anything call room 406."

Rosa hesitated. "Don't try to fool me, señorita. I know you too well. Dan is a nice man, Have a pleasant evening."

Maggie closed the door as a smile burst across her face.

CHAPTER 21

PETER BURKE called Maggie's room at five-thirty the next morning after a few minutes of confusion. There was a question as to which room or rooms they occupied. Dan, at Maggie's insistence, had canceled the third room as an unnecessary extravagance. This, of course, was a bogus excuse as she did want to sleep with him, even if the walls of their room were covered with large stylized sunflowers and vines that made her feel like Thumbelina.

Peter reported he'd been with Carlos almost all night. He sounded tired but confident. Could they meet him in his office? He was spent and ready to go home.

Maggie hopes soared. They would meet him in twenty minutes. She called Rosa who picked up the phone on the first ring. "I'm coming to get you in ten minutes. Dr. Burke will give us a full report on Carlos."

Dan was showered, dressed and half out the door by the time she finished the two calls and hung up the phone. "I'll meet you and Rosa in Burke's office after I make new arrangements at the station with Whitey. I like to talk from the squad car."

Peter Burke told Maggie and Rosa that the MRI, X-rays and tests revealed damage by violent blows or falls. Dislocation of several vertebrae caused bone fragments to pinch spinal nerves. He held up an X-ray and indicated small, sharp-looking white spots. "If his condition had continued, Carlos' spinal cord could have been severed and he'd be in a wheelchair for the rest of his life. That New Mexico private detention center and Unger's in Phoenix would both be subject to a huge lawsuit."

Rosa stood confused. Her voice shook as she spoke. *"Caramba!* How is he now?"

"I believe we retrieved all the bone fragments. We have him heavily sedated because the pain is intense. I don't know how the poor soul survived until now. The surgery took six hours, but I think Carlos will mend well. He's sleeping, but you can look in on him."

Remembering, in the past, how tender he was with his patients, Maggie gripped his upper arm. "How can we ever thank you, Peter?"

"Just keep working on the immigration problems in this ridiculous state. I'm embarrassed to say I live in Arizona. I'm going to report that detention center as soon as I figure out who will listen to me," Peter looked at her with those intense brown eyes she remembered well.

"When can we move Carlos? I'm afraid to leave him in the Phoenix area. Even though he's a legal citizen, he's still a Mexican. Phoenix is a harsh place for Mexicans."

"If all goes well today," Peter said, "I could arrange to have him transported to Jupiter Hills tonight. They have an excellent orthopedic unit in the hospital up there. He's going to need intensive care for at least another week and afterward lots of physical therapy. ... We'll brace him and he'll have to be moved carefully. I'll have my secretary arrange a for private transport."

"Dan and I will pay for that."

"No charge for my services. It was great to see you again. I'm sorry it was under these conditions." He took Maggie in his arms, hesitated, then gave her an ardent hug as if he'd finally decided how to say a proper good bye.

"Maybe we'll meet at my reunion?" Maggie offered a tired smile. She had forgotten how attractive Peter was. She wondered if he still cheated on his wife.

"Are you ten years out already?"

"Next year, Doctor." She gave Peter a gentle punch in the arm before he left and walked back to Rosa who was shuffling her feet, anxious to see Carlos.

Dan came through the door and walked over to them. "You and Dr. Burke seem pretty chummy," he teased, putting his arm around her shoulder.

"We were friends for a while at Stanford. I was at the Law school when he was doing a Post Doc; he still teaches a class now and then at the med school. Jealous?"

"Should I be?" Dan asked.

"Not of Peter Burke."

CHAPTER 22

BY ELEVEN P.M. that same night Carlos was settled into a private care room at Juniper Hills Hospital, arranged by Peter Burke.

"I will stay," Rosa said.

She and Maggie were sitting in creaky plastic chairs next to the bed where Carlos slept in a jungle of tubes. Dan had left to return the squad car and check his schedule at the station.

Maggie waited for Dan to pick her up but felt uncomfortable leaving Rosa alone. "I'll be back." Maggie walked into the hall and spoke to an aide. When she returned, she told Rosa, "I've arranged for you to have a sleeping-chair. The nurses are happy to have extra hands at night." Maggie cautioned Rosa to keep the fake birth certificate and the copy of Sophie's

Social Security card available in case anyone should question her. Authorities often didn't understand her refugee status.

"We've come too far to blow your cover. As soon as Carlos comes around, tell him to call you Sophie. If he slips do what you did in front of Mathew Unger at the Detention Center. Act as if Carlos is confused. That was perfect."

Maggie thought of all she wanted to tell Rosa, the destruction of the Painted Lady, the death of Robbie, the family funeral, the arrival of Jesús ... but decided that Rosa had enough on her mind. It also occurred to her that she hadn't as yet registered Sophie in school. The one thing Rosa had asked of her. She would do that tomorrow morning, come monsoons, floods or fires.

Trying to stay positive, Maggie said, "A Mr. John Gonzales wrote to MISS CHLOE and said he had a new apartment in Juniper Hills for you."

Rosa smiled. "That's Juan, my nephew. He promised to look around for a place after the apartments were raided. He said it's not a good idea for Latinos to live together in one place. Makes sweep too easy for ICE."

"Sounds smart."

Dan arrived to take them home.

"Rosa is going to stay here for the night," Maggie said to Dan then turned and asked Rosa, who looked as if she didn't plan to leave Carlos' bedside. "What do you want me to do tomorrow? I think you should let me or Estelle stay with Carlos while you get yourself organized. How do you feel about seeing Sophie?"

"She gets too excited. It might be more sensible to wait. Maybe 'til Carlos is feeling better."

"I agree. I'll ask Lisa to take her to a Disney movie. Okay, so we have a plan." Maggie hugged Rosa and urged her to rest as much as she was able to.

Dan kissed Rosa on the forehead. "You're a real hero, lady. Don't let anybody tell you different." Rosa blushed and tucked her face under her raised bent arm.

Maggie and Dan left the hospital, holding hands, and walked to his car in the parking lot. "Where to?" he asked in his most seductive voice as he opened the passenger door. She sank into the bucket seat, knowing exactly where he wanted to go. Deep in her heart she felt the same pull, but....

"I think I'd better go home and check on Estelle and Sophie and Lisa and, come to think of it, Jesús. ... I'm feeling guilty. The one thing Rosa asked me to do was register Sophie for school. With everything else going on, I forgot."

"You've helped Rosa a lot. I'm sure she'll forgive you."

"I'll do it tomorrow. School must start soon."

They sat in front of Maggie's house in the silvery dark, kissing and caressing, feeling like teenagers on the lookout for parents. "Do you want to hop in the back seat?" Dan challenged her, mischief in his eyes.

"We're not midgets, you know?" Maggie giggled, despite herself. "There're too many situations." She had a new office to open, plus a million other decisions to make.

It was after two a.m. when she entered the shadows in the quiet house. She went directly to her bedroom. Rushing to take a quick shower, she dropped the soap in the tub. It landed with such a loud thud she felt sure everyone would wake up, but there wasn't a sound in the sleeping house.

Maggie woke to the smell of fresh brewing coffee. The morning light washed over her bedroom; the room Estelle had allowed her to decorate in pink by herself when she was thirteen. Not much had changed. It had been repainted several times, discarded and new pictures hung. The drapes and bedding were more sophisticated, but the furniture unchanged. She checked the clock on her dresser, shocked to see it was nine. She was a morning person, not used to rising in what seemed like mid-day. She pulled on a light robe, went down to the kitchen and found Estelle washing up breakfast dishes. "Where is everyone?"

"Lisa walked to school with Sophie. Jesús is weeding the vegetable garden." Estelle looked out of the window over the kitchen sink.

"He's a good worker and can do most anything. Yesterday he fixed the drip in the laundry room faucet."

"Sophie started school?"

"You were so busy and preoccupied after the funeral and fire. One morning Lisa and I took Sophie, her birth certificate and Social Security card over to Lincoln School and registered her. A piece of sponge cake. We were a month late, but I used Sophie's accident as an excuse. They gave her a couple of tests and said she should be in third grade. We left. Sophie skipped down the school steps and if I wasn't so damn stiff, I would've followed."

"Thanks for doing that."

"Last night Sophie sat at the table and did homework."

"Do they really give third graders homework?"

"Beats me. She said she was writing an essay, but wouldn't let me look at it. Said I would see it at the proper time. Whatever that means."

"Carlos is in the hospital for at least a week and then a rehab facility. His prognosis is good. Peter is taking care of his expenses." Maggie poured herself a cup of coffee. "Rosa's nephew found her an apartment. She has things in our basement that she wants to come and get, but doesn't want to see Sophie until she can tell her Carlos is well. She also doesn't want to leave Carlos alone in the hospital. I told her you and I would take turns relieving her while she gets her new apartment set up."

"Aren't we bossy. Thanks for offering my services."

"Don't give me that look. You love to help. I know you. ... What are we going to do about Jesús?" Maggie rubbed Estelle's back.

"Nothing for a while. His shoulder is still mending. He's very handy around the house. He's afraid to call his brothers and tell them he's okay. He doesn't want to make trouble for them or us. We don't even know if the authorities are looking for him."

"We could send a message in the MISS CHLOE column."

"That might work. How do we tell them to look for it?"

"Let me think about it." Maggie went upstairs to dress.

Two hours later, driving Estelle to the hospital, Maggie said, "I'm going to send a copy of the *Juniper Hills Gazette* to Robbie's brothers, Joseph and Pablo, at their restaurant in Hermosillo. I'll tell them to read the MISS CHLOE column. I'll slip in a coded message so they know Jesús is safe with us."

"That's good."

"I'll include a message telling them that Robbie would want them to read about his adopted town. He and Lisa especially enjoyed MISS CHLOE'S advice column. Maybe they would like a six-month subscription?"

"Will they get the message?" Estelle asked as she rolled down the window. "I can't stand being cooped up in here with the AC. I like the natural breezes."

"It's over ninety degrees out there." Maggie looked at her grandmother's determined face and decided not to create a civil war over air. "Excellent idea."

"Jesús doesn't want us to get in trouble if they have the restaurant phone or his brothers' cell phones tapped." Estelle adjusted her side view mirror so she could check that they weren't being followed by a suspicious car.

"For a long time, I couldn't wait to have my own cell to call anyone anywhere in the world. Now I can't risk using it." Maggie flicked on her turn signal. "We don't even know if ICE is aware Jesús escaped from that jail hospital in Mexico."

"They should be focusing on the drug cartels and the gun runners."

"Righto." Maggie looked at Estelle with patience and respect, wishing it was that simple.

When they entered Carlos' hospital room, Rosa's eyes were blazing and her smile electrified.

"He's awake. Look." She pointed to a grinning Carlos despite the clear plastic oxygen mask that covered his mouth and nose. "They say he must walk down the hall tomorrow. Tomorrow! Can you imagine? Dr. Burke gave orders."

Maggie hugged Rosa and gave Carlos a kiss on his forehead. "Estelle will sit with you while I take Rosa and get your new apartment ready."

Beneath his oxygen mask, Carlos smiled like a pale-yellow emoji.

CHAPTER 23

NEWS ANCHOR: "Until 1848 Mexicans lived in Texas, Arizona, and New Mexico. Parts of California, Nevada, Utah, Colorado, and Wyoming were the northern provinces of Mexico. After the Mexican-American War, Mexico was forced to cede almost half of its national territory to the United States."

Guest: "I've heard Mexicans say they didn't cross the border, the border crossed them."

Anchor: "A lot of people don't know this. Latinos have been a legal part of the United States for a very long time. They founded some of our first cities. They fought in the Revolutionary War. Hispanic women even donated their jewelry to help the patriots."

Guest: "Up until the last twenty years, Latinos cycled back and forth across our borders almost casually, some stayed, others went back. If you made it across the border you were usually safe and not deported unless you committed a horrendous crime. That's why eleven million undocumented immigrants live in the U.S. today."

Anchor: "In the last few years the issue of immigration has been politicized and conflated with our drug problems. Even people in Washington who had been supporters turned against a welcoming policy."

Guest: "The situation is out of hand. All we talk about is walls."

Maggie switched off the NPR discussion on the car radio thinking, Rosa riding shotgun didn't need to hear....

"Don't turn it off," Rosa said.

"You don't want to think about that all day."

"I think about it all the time."

"How is Carlos feeling today?"

"Not bad. He thought he'd wake up in Mexico when they moved him to that Scottsdale detention facility."

"He's safe for now. We'll do everything we can to keep you both here."

"We still have to watch over our shoulders. We will work hard until Sophie graduates from high school, even though we continue to live in a state of anxiety. *Dios esté con nosotros.* Then we'll see. We're not feeling welcomed here."

"That makes me so sad. You know we will always love you and Carlos and Sophie. And there are many others who see the gifts you bring from your culture."

"And many who don't," Rosa mumbled.

Maggie marveled at Rosa's strength as she drove first to her house. Rosa called her nephew, Juan, and he promised to meet them in an hour at the apartment he had found for her. It was within walking distance of Maggie's house. Rosa packed up two huge plastic bags of items from Maggie's basement.

"I discovered Sophie's things were here, but I had no idea all these other items were stashed in the basement," Maggie said.

"I didn't want you to worry."

"What if something had happened to you? I may not have found them for years."

"Emergency I planned for came fast. I was scared."

"Please, Rosa, don't do that again. You know I'll always help."

"I know. I'm sorry."

They hugged and each dragged a huge plastic bag up to the kitchen and into the garage where Jesús was arranging rakes and other tools on a cork board with one hand, his shoulder and left arm wrapped in a clean sling.

"Hola!" he said, removing his garden gloves and coming over to greet them.

Maggie, realizing that she hadn't told Rosa of Robbie's death, said, "You remember Lisa Pérez, my law partner. This is her brother-in-law from Hermosillo. He's staying with us for a while."

Jesús held out his free hand and Rosa shook it. "We always need an extra hand around here, even only one," she said.

They laughed. Jesús helped them put the two huge sacks in the back of the car and they were off.

Driving along, Maggie said, "I have things to tell you." She went through the litany of calamities that had occurred since Rosa left.

Rosa was heartsick about Robbie's death even though she couldn't remember ever meeting him.

"I'm going to contact the Pérez brothers using the MISS CHLOE column because we don't know if the Federales or ICE are looking for Jesús." Maggie pulled up in front of Rosa's new apartment.

"I'm sad to hear that," Rosa said.

A week later Dan picked Maggie up for a date at Rodney's Café. When she got in the car, he said, "An hour ago I got a call from someone who said he had information about the fires. It was a young voice, almost child-like. He asked to meet at Hassayampa Park. I said, no. Someplace more occupied. You stand in front of the movie theater and I'll come by with my assistant and pick you up. No cop car, he says. I said I have a black sports car. We'll take a ride. No one will see you."

"Do you believe he's for real?"

"I asked, how will I know you. He tells me, I'm black. I said, everyone wears black, No, no, he says, I **am** black, but I look white. Oh, I said." Dan ran his fingers through his copper curls and turned to Maggie. "Juniper Hills is pretty pale so I guess he thinks he wouldn't be obvious in front of the theatre. I asked if he had a colorful scarf. Yeah, he says. Yellow one. I said wear that."

"Do you think he'll be there?"

"We'll soon see." He turned into the movie theatre parking lot.

Maggie searched the groups of people gathered in front of the theatre for a yellow scarf. It was a cool September Saturday evening and the teens were bundled up against unusual fall winds. "I see him. Over there at the end of the sidewalk."

Dan veered alongside the curb. Maggie hopped out and motioned for the young man in the yellow scarf to get in the front seat while she crawled into the back.

"Hi, son," Dan said, "What's your name."

"Alan Johnson." He lowered his head and pulled the colorful scarf up over his chin and mouth.

"I'm glad you called."

"I've been feeling like shit." He turned to Maggie. "Sorry for that, Miss. My mother would kill me."

"Listen, Alan, you're brave to call me." Dan drove away from the center of town. "What can you tell me?"

"I'm new to Leonardo. Drove there in our RV with my mom from Oklahoma. She makes jewelry and is crazy about the gem market there." He pulled the scarf off his face and folded it on his lap.

"I've heard about that gem market down by the Mexican border," Maggie said. "It's supposed to be breathtaking. ... Sorry. I didn't mean to interrupt."

"I met some members of this gang because, I don't know ... wanted to belong, I guess. It never occurred to them that I was anything but white. At first we were just foolin' around scarin' kids for the fun of it." Alan wiped sweat from his forehead with the end of his scarf. "Then ... not quite sure why, they decided to move north to Juniper Hills. I heard they got a call from somebody who'd pay them to make trouble. They said Phoenix and Tucson had too many armored cars and stuff. They thought they'd be harder to identify in a small town. They started those fires to scare Latinos. Like at the hair salon. But when Jimmy raped that nice lady I'd had enough. I'd stayed a couple of weeks and left. Two weeks too long. I'm ashamed of myself."

"I don't mean to be insensitive but I thought this gang hates non-whites. How come they accepted you?" Dan looked over at Alan who was passably light-skinned.

"My father was white. My color never came up. Go figure."

"How old are you, Alan?"

"Old enough to know better ... twenty-one next June."

"Do you have a job?"

"I'm a chamber maid, head of housekeeping, at the Hyatt Regency resort in Scottsdale. Don't laugh. The salary is awesome. I'm taking classes at ASU."

"How did you get here?"

"My Harley, yesterday. Slept in the park. Walked around half the day to get up my mojo to call."

"Were you part of an attack in a field west of downtown a while ago? Miguel Castro, that twelve-year-old boy your gang beat up, died in the hospital."

"No way, man. Oh, God, I didn't know. I heard them talk about it. They were two little kids."

"Help us catch the gang leaders and I can help you," Dan said as he parked the car in a quiet corner of the parking lot.

"What brought me to Juniper Hills was this girl ... Jennifer. We met at school. She was the one who told me about you. She said you helped Latinos without documents. I thought you might help me. I needed to report this gang."

"I'm sure I can, but I need information from you. Do your parents know you're up here?"

"My dad is dead. I told my mom I was spending a few days with a friend who might have a job for me."

"Is that true?"

"Not exactly. I think I'd like to be a lawyer or a social worker. I want to do something for other people. I like this town. I thought I would ask around. But mainly I wanted to talk to you."

"Where's your bike?"

"Locked at the park by the lake."

"What are your plans for tonight?"

"The park bench again, I guess."

"What can you tell me about the fire at the Victorian house in the center of town?" Maggie asked from the back seat.

"Nothing. I read about it. The gang was in Tempe at a ballgame that night. As a group they didn't start that fire as far as I know."

"No?" Maggie could hardly believe her ears. Her old suspicions surfaced as they had when she heard Richard Harvey talk about her ex, Hank, saying she deserved the fire.

CHAPTER 24

DAN DROVE Alan to his bike and told him to follow so they could buy him dinner. When Maggie and he were alone in the car, Dan said, "I was afraid that fire at your office was a copy-cat incident. The way the gasoline tanks were so obviously left on the property." He turned to Maggie. "You think it was Hank?"

"He hates me and he's so irrational."

"Would he go so far as to hire someone? Does he have friends that would help him?" Dan turned his eyes from the road to look at Maggie for a moment.

"I don't think he has any friends, except maybe Ron Grundy."

When Dan had discovered that Alan hadn't eaten all day, he insisted they stop at Rodney's Café and have a quick sandwich and soup and whatever Maggie wanted. By that time, she had lost her appetite. Tension caused by thinking about Hank tightened her throat. Dan ordered two beers and looked to Alan who said he'd have a Coke.

They sat in the bar and Maggie studied Alan's face. It was open and pleasant with a sincere luster in his eyes, although now they were veiled with sadness. How had a kid like this gotten mixed up with such a vicious gang even for a couple of weeks? There didn't seem to be anything fake or manipulative about him. *Earnest* was the word that came to her mind. She would have picked him for a jury without a second thought. He reminded her of a young Denzel Washington, only he looked white. If this was an act it deserved three curtain calls.

"Please excuse me," Alan said. "I have to clean up and use the restroom."

"What do you think?" Dan asked when Alan was gone.

"Seems like a good kid to me," Maggie said and took a swig of her beer. I trust my ability to read people. He can stay at my house tonight?"

"I'm not comfortable with that. We don't know much about him."

"I can tell he's a good kid."

"I'd take him to my house, but I want to keep him out of the limelight. Cops drop by all the time. I don't know who I can trust at the station anymore." Dan drained his beer glass. "Would you feel safe with Alan in the house with Lisa, Estelle and Sophie?"

"Are you kiddin'? Does he look like an abuser to you? Sophie spends most of her time in Lisa's room, anyhow. I could take down that pipsqueak with an uppercut."

"I didn't realize you had pugilistic skills." He chuckled.

Maggie laughed. "Estelle had me take a self-defense course when I was in middle school. Thought it would give me peace of mind and confidence after the trouble with my father."

"Did it work?"

"Try something, pal, and find out."

Dan put his arm around her and smiled. "You do keep me on my toes. Have you an extra room at your house?"

"For Alan?

"Yeah. He is a good kid." Dan said. "I agree with you even though he was a gang member for two weeks."

Feeling quite sure of herself, Maggie said, "I've lost track, to tell the truth, but we can find a safe place to stash him." She did like Alan. Thinking about Alan had little to do with her experience of her father.

Maggie could hear faint romantic music from the dining room and thought selfishly for a moment that it had been some days since she and Dan had quiet time alone. She made herself concentrate on the attacks and fires, the mayhem that gang had brought to Jupiter Hills.

When Alan returned, Dan asked, "Can you give me names and addresses?"

"Of the gang leaders? Yeah," Alan answered. "There are four major leaders and another five to fifteen who come in and out of the operations. Maybe once or twice and never show up again. Like me."

"Will you write down the names of the leaders? Dan handed Alan a folded piece of lined-paper and a pen.

Alan began to scribble. "I'm not sure of house numbers, but I pretty much know the roads where they live."

When Alan was finished Dan took the list and said, "Thanks. Now I'd like you to call your mom and explain that you'll be here for a few days. I want to keep your presence quiet until I check out these names and see if these guys have other charges against them. It would be helpful if we could round them up at the same time. I don't want to create any suspicions."

"Will they come looking for you if you're not around?" Maggie asked.

"I doubt it. I haven't been hanging out with them for months. Nobody's called me. They probably said adios. I never really fit in." Alan handed back Dan's pen, pulled out his cell and stood to make the call to his mom.

"I don't want your mom to start asking questions about you, so tell her you've found a place to stay and have several interviews for a job."

Maggie said, "We may be able to help you with that."

"That's a good beginning," Dan said.

Maggie called Estelle on her cell and asked if she could bring home a young man who needed shelter for a few nights. "Could he bunk with Jesús?"

Estelle said, "I'm thinking of opening a boarding house. Actually, with six or seven bedrooms I'll have a good start. They both might be more comfortable if your young man sleeps in the maid's quarter off the kitchen. Not much in there but storage boxes."

"I'll take that as a yes," Maggie said, thinking of the stuff in the rooms off the kitchen that hadn't been used in years—a lovely mahogany bed, an artificial Christmas tree wrapped in plastic that they put up one year and never used again, after deciding they all wanted a natural tree, a couple of chifforobes with seasonal clothes and formal dresses, several pairs of skis and poles standing in a corner. It did have a full bath.

Alan finished talking to his mother, stuck his cell in his back pocket and sat back in the booth. He beamed a satisfied grin and wiped his mouth with one of the checked cloth napkins.

"We'll take you to Maggie's house for tonight," Dan said. "Do you feel okay eventually returning to Leonardo? Will you feel safe there?"

"How will this come down?' Alan asked. "Can you really arrest the four leaders at the same time? If one or two of them gets away, I could be toast. They might suspect I ratted them out."

"Maybe you should plan to stay here until I decide what's best to do first?" Dan said.

They left Rodney's and drove to Maggie's house, Alan following on his cycle. Estelle was in the kitchen taking a peach cobbler out of the oven. The aroma of baking fruit hung deliciously in the air.

"Mom. This is Alan Johnson. He's going to be staying with us for a few days."

"Welcome, Alan. Sit down." Estelle motioned toward the table. "How about a piece of pie?"

"It smells great, but we just ate."

"A small piece, perhaps?" Estelle knew her young men.

Alan smiled and opened his hands as if to receive the plate of pie.

"Okay." Estelle cut a good-sized piece and placed it in front of him. "You two want anything?" She queried Maggie and Dan.

"Not right now, Mom. Thanks. We have some business in my office."

"Official, I presume?" Estelle leaned into the fridge looking for the whipped cream.

"Easy, Mom." She and Dan left the room and went into her office.

Dan closed the door with his foot and leaned Maggie up against the wall. "I'm missing you."

"Me too. Missing you that is."

They kissed and hugged until Maggie gently pushed Dan away. "We have to make some quick decisions. If Hank's about to take off, we may never find him. Last time he disappeared for five years."

"You're right." Dan stepped back. "If that gang discovers Alan's here in Juniper Hills talking to us, his life will be in danger."

"What are we going to do about Hank?" she asked. "And more to the point, how are we going to do it?"

"Smudged finger prints were found on those gasoline cans left at your office building. That's the first thing I'll recheck. If we can make a decent match, Hank will be charged with arson and second-degree manslaughter. I think he belongs in a psych ward, so we need to proceed carefully in building our case."

"I already have a restraining order against him." Maggie looked out the back window into the dark yard.

"Good. If we could get him to violate the order, we could bring him in for questioning."

"He's supposedly leaving town. We better act fast. I'll get Estelle to call his mother, Gloria, and see what she can find out. I've been meaning to do that for weeks, but other things keep coming up."

"Ask Estelle to call Gloria tomorrow to get info about her son's plans without creating suspicion. I'll work on the forensics at the crime scene and see if we can find some way to link Hank to the arson."

"Estelle's pretty good at getting information out of someone before they even know what they're revealing. My granddad used to say she was the best litigator in Berkeley, California."

"Do you remember those days?" Dan moved closer.

"I was young. My granddad died. Estelle, my mother and father, Josh and I moved here several years later. The civil rights struggle was ongoing and she was exhausted."

"She's some lady."

"You don't have to tell me. As you know, when I was eight my mother shot my father to protect me from him. Estelle stepped up and took Josh and me into her life without a second thought. When my mother was in jail, Estelle used to make a Sunday picnic and take us to visit. My mother only lasted a couple of months before she died. I have sketchy memories of those days. Estelle was always positive and made a party out of the jailhouse visits."

"I'm sorry. It must have been hellish."

"I had a good therapist and I had Estelle. They never made me feel like a victim, as if I had done anything wrong. For a long time, it was hard to keep my mind on what I was doing." Eventually she emerged from numbness as a life-saving necessity. It left her cautious and suspicious of all men for a long time. Hank slipped under her protective nature in high school.

"Estelle is an amazing woman. I've seen that in her many times since I've met her." Dan put his arms around Maggie.

"We'd better get a plan together soon."

"I'll get my techs to gather all the facts they can about the four names Alan gave me. I'm not sure why, but I don't want Chief Strunk in on this until I have more info."

"Good. I feel as if we know where we're going, at least for now. Let's get back to the kitchen. Estelle will be thinking we're making out in here on the floor."

"Let's."

Maggie opened the door. "You're bad."

Dan put his arm around her shoulder and they walked into the kitchen. "Don't forget that," he whispered.

CHAPTER 25

GUS NAILED the brass plaque: SWEENEY, PEREZ and PALMER, above the front door of their new storefront offices. "We are now officially open." He turned to the staff jostling around their makeshift lobby.

It was nine o'clock in the morning, the first week in October. The Painted Lady had burned to the ground eight weeks earlier. Maggie wondered how long it would have taken if she hadn't said "two weeks." Not a single employee had been lost. Everyone seemed joyous to be back in business. All were astounded at what Maggie had been able to accomplish and gave her a standing ovation at ten after nine when she hustled through the door.

"Thanks guys. I had a lot of help from Lisa and Gus." They gave a big hand for Lisa even though she wasn't there. "It's great to be back in business. Now let's get to work," she said and went into her neatly partitioned office.

Gus followed her in, "How's Lisa?"

"Amazing. I insisted she take at least two more weeks. She keeps saying she feels less sad when she's busy, but there's plenty at the house to keep her occupied. She doesn't need to think about other people's legal troubles just yet. Do we know if we've lost any clients?"

"Can't tell. The paralegals and secretaries have been keeping in touch. I've contacted all our major ones while you and Lisa were occupied with Rosa and Carlos and Robbie's death."

Maggie searched Gus's face for signs of cynicism or annoyance, but saw none. He was sincere in his comments. She thought the trauma of the fire had changed each of them in a different way.

Her secretary walked in with her day schedule. Maggie was happy to see five clients on the list. The first was an old friend who needed Maggie to arrange several loans for a Laundromat franchise he intended to buy.

After her four o'clock client, Maggie relaxed, waiting for her five-thirty when Estelle called.

"I talked with Gloria. She actually seemed happy to speak with me. She's very worried about Hank. The other day he sat on their back patio for hours polishing his guns."

"Guns?"

"Yes. She said he has five. She told him to put them away or she'd pack them up and take the whole lot to the police station. He sat there and grinned at her like a demented imbecile, she said."

"Damn!" Maggie sat back in her chair.

Estelle continued. "Gloria called Hank's dad, who said not to bother him. Hank belonged in a looney bin."

"The poor woman. Hank's dad has never been interested in the family. The situation is worse than I thought. Is there any way we can help her?"

"I asked and she sounded like she'd given up," Estelle said. "I told her he should be in a psych hospital."

"I'll be home by seven." Maggie finished up with her last client, made three phone calls and left her office.

When she arrived home, Lisa, Jesús, Sophie and Alan were hovered over a thousand-piece puzzle of what looked like a large aquarium laid out on a jig board in the living room. "How's it going?" Maggie asked. No one said a word. "Sounds like it's a good puzzle." As she walked away, she heard Sophie say, "Here's a little piece of the yellow fin."

Once in the kitchen Maggie stood close to Estelle at the sink. "I'm expecting Hank to bring over copies of our personal and divorce documents at eight-thirty. I want you, Lisa and Sophie to sleep at Lisa's apartment tonight. Jesús and Alan can hide upstairs. I'm going to excuse myself while Hank is here, call the police station where Dan will take my call, and report that Hank is violating my restraining order."

"This is making me nervous. I'm thinking entrapment." Estelle plunked two plates into the dishwasher.

"Don't get too lawyerly on me. Dan has to be at the station tonight. He is arranging for two friendlies to be conveniently across the street from our house. They will immediately pick up Hank and take him to the station for questioning. When the officers arrive with Hank, Dan will confront him with the fingerprints on the gasoline cans from the fire. We expect Hank to go ballistic. Dan will have him taken to the hospital under restrains for observation if necessary."

"It's pretty crude. But it may work. What if he asks for a lawyer?"

"Dan will make feeble attempts to contact Hank's lawyer. They may have to put Hank in a straitjacket if he's too unruly. When Dan finally reaches Hank's lawyer, he'll suggests he wait until the morning as they've just got Hank sedated and under control."

"You two should be in a television show."

"Meanwhile Dan will call Gloria and suggest that she ask to have Hank's sanity evaluated at the VA hospital because of his erratic behavior and all the guns he plays with."

"I'm overwhelmed. Did you arrange all this after I spoke with you?" Estelle dried her hands on a small towel.

"Yes, Ma'am. A little after-hours work. Dan also has a witness who thinks she may have seen a figure near our offices the night of the fire, and Gloria found a pile of gasoline-soaked clothing in the garbage can in her garage the day after the fire."

"What you have is circumstantial evidence that can be explained away, but with his mental condition so iffy you may be able to keep him in custody for a short period."

"At least he can't run or do more harm. I'll explain to Jesús and Alan. Lisa and I will take Sophie for a sleepover at Lisa's. Sophie will have probing questions, but we'll be gone." Estelle wiped her forehead with the dish towel she held in her hand.

"Thanks, Mom. I hope this works out for everyone's safety."

By eight o'clock Estelle, Lisa and Sophie were in the car with Sophie clutching her pink fuzzy blanket and Miss Kitty sleeping bag. Maggie closed the car door as Sophie said, "I wish you were coming for the sleepover, Maggie."

"I do too, honey, but I have important work to do. I'll see you in the morning."

Maggie went back into the house and called upstairs. "Everything okay up there?"

"We're in the back bedroom. I'm going to teach Alan how to play pinochle. You won't know we're here."

"Thanks guys. I hope this goes smoothly." The scene was set. Maggie with all her heart hoped it would be as simple as she had planned.

CHAPTER 26

MAGGIE WAS FLUFFING CUSHIONS on the living room sofa when the door chimes startled her, although she'd been on high alert waiting for Hank for the last fifteen minutes. She checked her hair in the hall mirror and opened the door.

"Thanks for coming. Were you able to bring all our records? I told you everything was destroyed in the fire. I don't have copies of our divorce agreement or even my birth certificate. Come in and sit down. Would you like tea or coffee?" She hesitated to offer alcohol. She knew she was rattling on.

"Why are you being so nice to me?" Hank sat in a chair by the fireplace and studied her face. His buzz cut was still damp from a shower. He wore a starched red-striped short-sleeve summer shirt. He had put on weight and seemed to overflow the green velvet chair. She'd almost forgotten how tall and broad he was.

She sat on the edge of the sofa. "When have I not been nice to you?" The words were hardly out of her mouth before she realized she had fed him an invitation to spout recriminations.

"What do you really want? Money, property, what?" He put his knuckles under his nose and squeezed his eyes shut.

"I've never asked you for anything. All I want now is copies of the records of our life together because everything I had was destroyed in the fire. Did you bring them?"

"I don't believe you. Somehow I feel you're about to screw me."

"They're all public records. It's easier for me to get copies from you than to run all over town. I'm going to put them in a safe deposit box at the bank."

Hank stood and dropped the folder he had been holding on the coffee table. He walked to her. Before she could rise from the sofa, he pushed her back, hands around her neck. "What are you up to, bitch? Tell me the truth."

Maggie grabbed his hands to loosen his grip. "Let go of me! ... Call 911," she managed to scream.

Jesús came crashing down the stairs followed by Alan, punching his cell.

"Let her go," Jesús threatened.

"The police are on their way," Alan said. They pulled at Hank's arms and tried to take him to the floor. He fought them off and stumbled toward the door.

"Are you taking in lovers now?" Hank yelled at Maggie, pulled a gun from his waist band and aimed it at Alan. With a stylized twist and turn, Alan kicked the gun from Hanks hand. "What was that? Karate? You punk kid!"

Alan chopped Hank in the neck. When Hank fell to the floor, Jesús straddled him, pushing his body into the rug. Stunned, Hank barely fought back.

Police sirens shrieked outside their door and two fully-armed officers blasted through the door. "POLICE. What's going on?"

They tugged Jesús up and pulled Hank to his feet, keeping a tight grip on each arm. "Whose gun is this?" the robust blond cop asked. He picked up the Smith & Wesson pistol, not touching the handle, from under the coffee table.

Alan and Jesús both pointed to Hank. "He came in with it," Alan said.

Maggie rubbed her neck. It hurt to speak. "This is my ex-husband. He came here against a restraining order and tried to choke me to death. My two-house guests heard me call. They subdued him. I want to file charges. Get him out of here!"

"We'll do the paper work later at the station." The good-looking black cop winked at Maggie.

Hank pushed and pulled at the officers as they attempted to yank his hands behind his back, screaming he'd been set up. "You'll all be sorry for this" The cops left with Hank in handcuffs.

Maggie called Dan. "Your officers were perfect. Our plan worked except Hank almost choked the life out of me." They spoke briefly and she clicked off her cell.

Alan and Jesús sprawled on the living room sofa.

"YOU PLANNED THIS?" Alan asked in utter disbelief.

"Not the choking part," Maggie said. "We have to get him to a hospital before he does more harm to himself or someone else."

"He's a psycho," Jesús said. "Sophie told me about him."

To relax, the three worked on the aquarium puzzle for another hour. Maggie and Jesús had a glass of red wine and Alan a coke. "I can't believe this is ever going to come together," Alan said, as Maggie massaged her neck and laid down a piece of bright blue water.

"This is the second puzzle the family has attempted. The first was a zoo with forty different animals. Sophie and Lisa are great, although Estelle is pretty good too. Jesús is learning fast. Stick around, Alan, and you'll become a puzzle master by learning from the best."

The door chimes rang and Maggie moved to answer. Dan stood on the porch and slid his eyes over her from head to shoes, "Are you okay?"

Maggie collapsed into his arms. He hugged her tightly and kissed her on the lips. "I so sorry. I never thought you'd be in such danger."

"I'm okay, surprised you're here so soon. What's going on at the station?"

"We have Hank sedated. Gloria is asking them to put him in the hospital under observation instead of in jail."

"Something else is wrong. I can tell by your face."

"The fingerprints on the gasoline cans are not Hank's."

"No! Could he have hired someone else to burn down our offices?"

"We don't know. He's not talking. Gloria contacted their lawyer again. He'll show up in the morning when Hank wakes up. We can keep him for carrying an unlicensed gun, assaulting you and violating your restraining order, but that's all we have on him."

"Damn," Maggie said massaging her neck. "He hurt me."

Dan bent down and kissed her neck. "Gloria is afraid of him, but she may not be able to commit him for treatment to a psych department at the VA. It's so crowded."

"What about our local hospital? Aren't they supposed to step up if the Vets can't find room for him? He's dangerous to himself and others." Maggie sat back down on the sofa.

"The problem is we can't yet prove he's an arsonist. But Gloria thinks she can get him into the hospital for PTSD observation."

Alan and Jesús stood in the background, listening.

"Alan, you think anyone in your old gang could have been hired to set the fire at the Victorian house? They were after Mexicans and we did have a Mexican fiesta," Maggie asked.

"I never heard anything, but I wouldn't be surprised at what they'd do."

"Tell me more about these leaders." Dan asked Maggie for a yellow legal pad and pencil and settled himself on the sofa. He unfolded the paper on which Alan had originally written the four names. "I haven't had a chance to discuss these with my tech guys."

Alan flopped into the chair by the fireplace. "I'll tell you what I know, but it isn't much."

Maggie returned with a pad and pencil and handed them to Dan. She and Jesús sat at the jig table staring at the aquarium pieces in front of them.

"Every little bit helps," Dan said, looking at Alan.

"Okay. There's Terry White. He's an auto mechanic. Got a neat red Nissan, pretty new. He's always working under the hood. Has a bad, ugly temper. Nobody dares to cross him. I've heard someone say he's 'raw-boned skinny', whatever that means. He's really strong, works out at the gym."

"Does he have a job?" Dan wrote as fast as he could.

"On and off at the Texaco Station in town. I think his uncle owns it. He does odd jobs for people. He might have agreed to set the fire."

"Who's next?"

"Jimmy Laker. He's into landscaping. I've seen some of his jobs and they're bad ass dope. He's short and stocky and mean ... really mean. He'd just as soon slice you with a pick axe as say hello. He's a sicko. He cares about colorful little flowers, but he's the one who raped that nice hair salon lady. He rides in a truck that says 'Lakes by Laker'. He has a bumper sticker on it: 'This truck is protected by a pit bull with AIDS.'"

"Definitely sick," Jesús said.

"What about this Joe?" Dan asked, reading from Alan's notes.

"Joe Santorini is an airplane mechanic. An orphan. No family. He works over at Sky Harbor Airport. He's a mystery. Quiet. Big muscles. I never trusted him. Can't tell what he's thinking.

"Zig Tipton is a plumber. Does work for the town. I've never known any of the guys to do anything really bad by themselves. They feed off each other. Zig's the smartest and ugliest. A lone wolf kinda guy. Looks like a dirty sewer rat. Never combs his hair, but can fix anything. A wild man. He might do something like burn down that beautiful house, particularly if someone paid him."

"Do they often do jobs for money?" Maggie asked.

"I don't know. But I wouldn't be surprised if someone from this town hired them to create trouble. They'd think they'd be safe because they don't live near Juniper Hills. They're not the sharpest tacks in the box. And they're often drugged up on coke and now Fentanyl. Laker's father supposedly has his own lab out at the ranch."

"Attractive bunch." Maggie got up to go to the kitchen. "Anyone want anything?"

Nobody spoke up.

CHAPTER 27

MAGGIE MADE UP three letters for her column and had them printed in the *Gazette* before she sent a copy of the newspaper to Joseph and Pablo Pérez at their restaurant in Hermosillo.

> Dear Miss Chloe: One of my sons died in a fire and the other has run off without leaving a contact number. I was hoping my son would see this letter and get in touch with me? I have been to the hospital, the police and even the mayor's office. No one has a record of his arrest. I had four amazing sons in Sonora State. One is dead and one has disappeared. I miss both dreadfully. Can you help me? *Grieving Mom in Mexico*

Dear Mexican Mom; Grieve no more. I posted
your letter and received this response with a
request to print it in my column. *Miss Chloe*

Dear Mom: I believe I am the missing son
you are looking for. I have been taken in and
cared for by a wonderful family. My shoulder
is mending and I hope to see you and my two
brothers soon. Please do not worry about me.
Your loving son

She'd included a note about Robbie, reminding them
how much Robbie and Lisa enjoyed MISS CHLOE'S
column. Hoping they would understand the message
and read her column, she attempted to soothe
their concerns that Jesús was well and safe without
revealing information that might cause trouble with
the authorities.

Under Jesús' expert direction, Lisa and Alan worked
for hours each day in the garden. Estelle's yards had never
looked so elegant. Almost everyone in Juniper Hills had
a vegetable garden. They were all into eating locally and
gladly swapping their produce with each other.

The flowers seemed extra-healthy and the vegetables
were producing small versions of wonderful things folks
would eventually eat. "We should be able to harvest
before Thanksgiving," Jesús told them.

He found some milkweed plugs in the back of the
garage and showed Lisa how to plant them in the yard
near the dry creek. "You can create a monarch butterfly
station to encourage more beauty around the grounds
in the spring."

Dan walked into the garden one afternoon and called Jesús to sit on the back-porch steps next to him. "How's it going? I see the cast is off."

"Almost back to normal. Lisa has me doing physical therapy with a friend of hers. It's really helping."

"I'm glad to hear that. I don't know what your plans are, but I'm asking you not to attempt crossing the border for a while. You have no I.D. It's chaos down there now."

"I've heard. They're tear-gassing the women and children."

"The President has ordered thousands of military men and women to the border. They're installing concertina wire, ignoring our historical role of accepting refugees fleeing from violence and persecution. I'm disgusted." Dan stood. "Sorry. I'm on my soap box again. This border mess makes me crazy. Now a migrant caravan of refugees escaping the violence in Central America, is headed for our southern states."

"Your President likes to scare your people," Jesús said. "Then he tells Americans that he and he alone can keep citizens safe."

"You're right. These refugees are families, women, children, old people." Dan sat back down next to Jesús. They're not gonna hurt anyone."

"He tweets that drug dealers, rapists and gangsters are hiding among the families. I think what he says are lies." Jesus brushed dirt from his shoulder.

"If you're caught without a visa, they may put you back in jail."

"I know." Jesús pulled off one of his garden gloves and rubbed his nose with his knuckle. "I had two

Mexican friends jailed in Texas for six months for trying to get to their day jobs."

"It's worse now." Dan stood.

"The border patrol is not accepting immigrants, just shunting them into facilities. Separating kids from their parents. Putting them in what we can only call cages. Little children under two. It's horrible." Jesús buried his face in his hands.

"I think it will be safer after our elections. Give it more time." Dan put his hands on Jesús' shoulders.

Jesús thanked Dan, stood and pulled on his gloves and went back to his vegetables.

Dan walked up the steps and into the kitchen where Estelle and Maggie were having lunch.

"Soup, Sandwich, Salad?" Estelle asked.

"I'm fine, thanks." Dan sat at the table. "I have to leave in a minute." He told Maggie he had his techs collecting information about the four gang leaders from down south. They had already discovered, only God knows how, that Zig Tipton was not at the Sun Devils football game with the other three gang leaders in Tempe the night of the fire at the Painted Lady.

"We have smudged fingerprints from the gasoline cans at your office fire and some pretty good prints from Theresa's hair salon," he said. "I'm determined to pick up these four at the same time. I don't want any one of them to slip through our nets, so we have to be thorough and sure."

Rosa had been adamant about Sophie not seeing Carlos in the hospital or even knowing he was home. She spent most of her days with Carlos helping him relearn to walk up and down the hospital hallways. The rest of her time she prepared the new apartment for when Carlos and Sophie would come home and be together.

A week later, early in the morning, Rosa, Jesús and Lisa brought Carlos home to their new apartment. Rosa made a special dinner party and invited only Sophie. The biggest surprise was when Sophie saw Carlos sitting in a wheelchair in the dining room. "Papa," she screamed. "I've missed you. I've so much to tell you." She climbed on his lap. "I had a wheelchair, a red one, after I flew down the stairs at Maggie's and slashed my calf. ... What happened to you? Are you hurt? Does your chair have an automatic button?"

"Sophie, Papa had an operation on his back and he must be quiet for a while. Try not to move around and be so excited. We're all glad to see each other."

"Oh. Yes. I understand. I remember when I first slashed my leg. I was very tired and needed to rest a lot."

"What is this slashing business?" Carlos studied Rosa's face.

"She fell, landed on a rusty lawnmower in the cellar. She's fine now."

"I'll show you my scar. Forty-three stitches. "Sophie tugged up her pants and laid her left leg across Carlos' lap. A thin pink thread of scar tissue ran down her calf. "The doctor and nurse said when I grow up, I won't even see the scar. They put a few stitches inside that melted away."

"I'm so glad." Carlos winked at Rosa and raised Sophie's leg to plant a smoochy kiss on it. "I'll be up and out of this wheelchair in a couple of weeks. We can hike on the trails and have ice cream."

"You know coconut is my favorite," she said and hopped off Carlos' lap.

CHAPTER 28

Two weeks later on Halloween evening Sophie appeared at Estelle's door in a long, soft, light-blue shawl and a silver mask as Our Lady of Guadalupe. She carried a rose-colored pillowcase filled with candies. She and Rosa had been trick-or-treating for over an hour and had come to Estelle and Maggie's house to say good-bye to Alan who was leaving that night.

Rosa remained off to the side so Sophie could ring the bell by herself. As they all stood in the open doorway, she told them she had wanted Sophie to be a fairy godmother with a wand, but Sophie said fairy godmothers were "passé."

"This child," Rosa said in a voice of pride overlaid with exasperation. "Next week she'll be speaking French. There's a new girl from France in her class."

Rosa had come back as Maggie's housekeeper. Sophie walked between the two houses every day. Carlos was in physical therapy five mornings a week.

"Where are Lisa and Jesús?" Sophie asked as they entered the house.

"Lisa took Jesús to see 'The Rocky Horror Picture Show,'" Maggie said. "I can't believe he's never seen it."

"What is it?" Sophie removed her shawl and carefully folded it on the kitchen table.

"Movie for adults," Rosa said. "Maybe when you get older, I'll take you." Rosa spoke softly, the usual slight lilt in her voice.

Maggie had arranged for ice cream and tea, as if Sophie needed more sweets, but she wanted everyone to say good bye to Alan, who had decided it was time to go home and back to work.

Dan was still speaking with Alan as they entered the kitchen. "It's a safe time for you to leave. The gang doesn't have any idea you've talked to me and I don't want you to lose your job at the Resort. You've given me a lot of information. We're dealing with a violent racist gang, so I'm looking for a young officer from another area to infiltrate the gang and report back to me. It would be my pleasure to catch all four of them at one of their next rampages."

"What about me?" Alan asked. "If they don't know I contacted you, I'll be safe. I could hang around with them again and report to you."

"No. That's too dangerous. These guys are killers, Alan. We need a trained officer who can go undercover."

Alan looked sad; his eyes were puffing up with tears. "I want to make up for getting involved with those goons in the first place."

"That's not necessary. You've told me more than I ever expected to know. When we capture these guys, it'll be because of you."

"Okay. I guess I'll go then. If I pick up on anything, I'll get in touch with you."

"Don't call me at the station." Dan ran his fingers through his rust-colored hair. A bad habit he had picked up at the Pentagon from his supervisor. They used to tease each other.

"Call me," Maggie said. "The gang won't know who I am."

"We're not sure what the gang knows." Dan looked concerned. "You had a large sign outside the Painted Lady with your complete name along with Lisa's and Gus' on it."

"And we're not sure ICE doesn't have us connected to Jesús," Estelle said." He's afraid for us to use the phones."

"You can contact MISS CHLOE at the *Gazette*," Maggie said to Alan. "I get those messages daily. Do you have access at the Resort to a computer?" Maggie wrote the email address on a post-it and Alan put it in his pocket.

"My Mom uses a computer," Alan said. "But I don't want her to get in trouble."

"MISS CHLOE is the safest way. Nobody would suspect wrongdoing from an advice columnist."

Alan shook hands with Dan, hugged Maggie and Estelle and kissed Sophie on the cheek. "Hurry up, Beautiful, and grow up. I'd like to take you dancing." He slipped on his backpack and closed the screen door behind him. They heard his Harley kick into gear and he was gone.

"I wish he would wait until morning when it's light," Estelle said, scooping five dishes of ice cream.

"He says it's easier and quicker to ride at night, more peaceful and lighter traffic." Dan again ran his fingers through his hair. "He's such a gentle kid. I'm sick that he's mixed up in this."

"I hope he comes back soon," Sophie said. "I want to learn to dance."

CHAPTER 29

LISA AND JESÚS worked in the garden daily, talking and talking. One afternoon, through the kitchen window above the sink, Estelle saw them kissing under the rose covered arbor. Oh, Lord, it's too soon! Maggie is going to lose a partner or Jesús will have to find himself a new art studio, she thought. In another month it would be cold and they'd have to come in from the garden. She worried they were moving too fast. She promised herself to talk to Lisa or have Maggie bring up the subject, no matter how difficult.

That night after dinner, Lisa and Maggie sat in the den, Maggie reading the *Economist* and Lisa crocheting a baby blanket. Estelle visited her next-door neighbor, Irina.

Jesús and Dan had gone to the store-front offices and the building site for the new Painted Lady. They felt it necessary to check the properties, especially at night, though they had scant hope they could prevent another fire.

"It's time for me to move home and come back to work," Lisa announced, as if she expected Maggie to thwart her intentions.

"I'm glad you're feeling that well. What are you, two, three months along?" Maggie asked. "You're barely showing."

"That's about right. I sometimes forget I'm pregnant. In my heart, I'm sad, but physically I feel great. I guess having a baby agrees with my body."

"We need you," Maggie said. "Business has been off the charts. Even when you come back, we may have to hire more help. I don't want to pressure you."

"I appreciate everything you've done." Lisa rubbed her baby bump. "I'm due in June. Sophie and Estelle have offered to babysit. ... One more thing."

Maggie's stomach clutched. She feared this "one more thing."

"I've wanted to speak with you about this. Jesús wants to come back to my condo with me. He wants to marry as soon as possible and help raise Robbie's baby. I don't want to leave Juniper Hills and I don't expect him to stay here. In some ways I don't want to think about this. It's not fair to Jesús or myself. He says he's willing to wait until I'm ready."

"If you're asking my personal opinion, It's way too soon for any decision. Robbie's been gone only two and a half months. How does Jesús feel about that?"

"He's sure Robbie would approve. Says he can find a studio in Juniper Hills. Paint anywhere. But I'm afraid he'll miss the inspiration he gets from his culture. He's not finished with the restaurant murals in Hermosillo. He's also an equal owner or more like a silent partner of the restaurant. Joseph and Pablo do the daily management."

"He'll know if he can live here and still paint." Maggie hoped she was right.

"He says we can go back twice a year for inspiration. He loves Mexico and hopes that someday we can have homes in both countries."

"I'm not sure about that. Those laws are changing daily. It's harder now than ever."

"I told him that."

"Do you love him, Lisa?"

"I think I do. He reminds me so much of Robbie I'm not sure I'm being fair to Jesús. But he says he loves me and that's all that matters."

"Sounds very romantic, but it could be a difficult life. You know the troubles Rosa's been having."

"I know. But they're both immigrants. I'm an American citizen. Though I have to admit my feelings are scrambled about the situation at the border. I'd like not to deal with it right now."

Maggie took a deep breath. "If you want my legal opinion, tell Jesús to stay here with us and set up a studio someplace. You two should date for a while and see how it comes together. Mom will be happy to have Jesús live here. He's a big help to her. He can visit you whenever and even help with the baby. If you feel the same at the end of a year, go for it."

"That makes sense. I guess it's too soon to make a serious decision."

"Good. That's settled. We'll all be here to help."

"I know." Lisa stood and smoothed her sweater over the slight swell in her stomach.

"There's something else I wanted to talk to you and Gus about," Maggie said. "I'd like to take on more cases involving Arizona's immigration laws. I won't make as much money, but I'll keep up my responsibilities. There's such sadness out there for families trying to stay together, such a need. A line from a T.S, Eliot poem keeps churning in my head. 'Do I dare disturb the universe?'"

"I think I understand," Lisa said. "But it may be dangerous. These crazies send pipe bombs and start riot in front of your house. What if they injured Estelle? Or Rosa and Sophie?"

"I could move. Dan would be glad to have me live at his house."

"No kidding!" Lisa lifted her eyebrows, short of rolling her eyes. ... But what about our offices? They may be in danger."

"We could hire extra security." Maggie began to see aspects of her decision that she hadn't thought through. She had to talk to Dan and maybe everyone else her decision might affect.

"I want to support you," Lisa said, "but I have to confess. It scares the heart out of me."

"I know," Maggie said, "Estelle and some friends are trying to make Juniper Hills a Sanctuary City. I need to learn more about the Dream Act and how to protect our Latinos under the human rights laws. The government may do away with DACA and withhold funds from the Sanctuary Cities that protect them." She shook her head.

"Oh, Maggie, I heard there's an executive order to turn city officials into federal immigration enforcers."

"That's such a bad idea! Our police hate that. They depend on the law-abiding illegal migrants to help catch the bad guys. The cops say we will be less safe."

"It's hard to tell who really cares about our country these days." Lisa said. "We've gotten so myopic, so selfish."

"How do the authorities come up with these ideas? We'll need more lawyers to challenge the constitutionality of these laws."

"I'm in. Do you think you can bring Gus along?"

"I'll do my best."

A car pulled into the driveway. "The guys are back."

Dan was eager to bring the Leonardo gang to justice. Two more fires in small Latino–owned shops in Juniper Hills and riots in Ridge Wood Valley, the next town over, had left an elderly man badly injured and not expected to live. Dan knew it was a matter of time before they had a hideous catastrophe on their hands.

The next morning, he pumped up his nerve and walked into the Police Chief's office. Gene Strunk slumped in his chair, red-faced above the big belly that hung over his belt buckle. His buzz cut made the top of his head look slightly pointed. He had a mostly clean-shaven face except for stray whiskers jutting from his jawline. Dan missed his former chief and old friend, Charlie Wright.

Dan had spent almost no time with his new superior in the two and a half years he'd been in office. He wondered if Strunk even knew his name. Strunk delegated from afar, through emails and terse handwritten notes.

"We're in crisis and short of personnel," Dan said. "We need to hire another detective to help track down this ugly gang from the south."

Dan had barely gotten the words out when Strunk spoke. "I'll think on it." Strunk picked up a clipboard and red-inked items listed on the attached papers.

"We can't wait," Dan said. "Something horrendous is coming. Our department will get the blame. I've spoken to most of the cops. They agree."

Strunk dismissed Dan with a wave of his hand. "I'll let you know." He hunched his head and shoulders over the clipboard as if alone in the room.

Dan couldn't stand the man. As he closed the office door, he heard the Chief answer his phone. Disturbed by Strunk's response, Dan stood in the hallway listening.

"These damn Hispanics are causing us a lot of grief. Why don't they go back where they belong? The crew is itchy. Nothing's working out like we planned. The shipment is delayed again."

Dan pulled out his phone and pretended to talk while he listened at the door. A stabbing ache shot into his head. Could he believe what he heard? Who was the Chief talking to? Did Dan hear what he'd thought he heard? What had Strunk planned? Was the chief orchestrating something to scare the Latinos out of town? Was that the reason or his solution for the problems they were having? What the hell was going down? The idea that something Strunk expected was delayed nagged at Dan's brain.

He knew Strunk would eventually okay his request for another agent to keep the peace. The chief didn't want a revolt on his hands. Dan went back to his desk and wrote up an ad for a young detective and sent it out through the police network.

In the third floor flat of an opulent brownstone on East 82nd Street, New York City, Chris Watters sat at his computer scrolling through the Police Classifieds.

"What is the master crime fighter doing over there?" his wife teased from the other side of the room at her own desk.

"Please, Cathy, don't make fun of me." Chris chuckled. "You know I'm sensitive."

Cathy rose, picked up her coffee cup, walked over, knelt and put her arms around his waist. "My honey, what is it?"

"I'm the son of a rich doctor who doesn't want to grow up to be a rich scion. ... It's time we moved out on our own. I'm an officer of the law."

"That you are." Cathy smoothed her pajama top over her slightly pregnant belly. It was Saturday morning and they sipped coffee that Lydia, their longtime family maid, had brought up on a tray with home-baked pastries from his parent's kitchen.

"I may have found a new job."

"Really? What is it?"

"An undercover gig. Not sure if it's a one shot or a career position."

"Sounds spooky."

"One problem. It's in Arizona."

"Arizona? Oh my God. It's so hot."

"It's not all desert. The High Country is beautiful. I've been there."

"Well, Mom and Dad are in New Mexico now. They love it. Not too far away."

"They also have mystical vortexes in Sedona, a nearby attraction. Would you be willing to give it a try?"

"What's the name of the town?"

"Juniper Hills."

"Let's do it."

Two weeks later, Detective Chris Watters called Dan from his precinct in New York City. "I saw in our office newsletter you're looking for a Caucasian cop in his twenties to work undercover in Arizona. My wife Cathy and I have been talking about moving West. She's pregnant and her parents recently moved to New Mexico, seems like it's a situation that might work for all of us."

Dan liked Watter's voice and his direct approach. "How soon can you get here?"

"I'll talk to my chief, take a temp leave of absence and be there in two weeks. If we're compatible, Cathy can follow."

"Great," Dan said, "I'll pick you up at Sky Harbor, the Phoenix airport. Let me know your arrival time. We have a serious problem here."

Chris Watters turned out to be an excellent find. A guy of integrity, he was an East Coast native and could do an amazing accent like a nasty thug. He had graduated seven years before from The John Jay College of Criminal Justice with a certificate in Homeland Security.

Dan hired Chris after spending several days with him. Over six feet three, with the body of a football tailback, Chris could rumple his hair, not shave and look formidable. He apologized for being twenty-eight. "I was afraid I'd be too old for this job,"

"You look young enough," Dan replied. He took his new recruit to dinner twice at Estelle's, where Chris made a big hit with everybody. It helped to have Dan's first impressions confirmed by others. As a precaution, Dan never mentioned where he planned to send Chris.

When Dan introduced Chris to Strunk, he decided to hold back his plans for Chris, leaving it at, "Chris Watters is here to help us secure Juniper Hills."

"Fine," was Strunk's reply. "Have a good day."

"Fun guy," Chris said as they left the Chief's office.

"We won't have to deal with him." Dan put his hand on Chris's shoulder. "We're on our own." They drove back to Dan's house.

The next day Dan began to groom Chris to infiltrate the gang in Leonardo. He told him all he knew. Eventually they met with Alan. Dan wanted Alan to fill Chris in on things Dan didn't know or may have forgotten.

"I wish I could do more." Alan still wanted to help wipe out the Leonardo gang.

Dan let Maggie in on their plans because Chris needed a woman to pose as his girlfriend to occasionally act as a go-between for Dan and Chris. He couldn't have Chris calling him at the station. They decided that Chris would use his birth name which was somewhat common and carry a fake ID which he'd claim was his real name if he ran into trouble. They tossed names around for a while. Chris wanted one he wouldn't forget. They both liked Garrison Keillor and his alter ego Guy Noir, private eye. They settled on Guy Black. Dan would have his techs create a criminal background for Guy Black.

"Call me Zoe," Maggie said. "I've always liked that name."

"Good. We've got our cast of characters for this production." Dan brushed his hand through his thick copper hair as if a great weight had been lifted from his mind.

By the time Cathy arrived in Juniper Hills, Chris had rented a room in Leonardo in the large home of Miss Alice Edmonson, a tall, sturdy elderly woman with a perfectly coiled silver bun on the back of her head. She was a sharp lady who asked a minimum of questions. She told Chris she'd never married, led a full life with her charity work and was not interested in his business. "I never meddle in others' affairs."

Chris thought if that was true, they'd get along fine. He spent hours in Leonardo getting a feel for the town. It was an old mining area. Poor people still lived on the south side of the tracks that ran directly through the main street. The wealthy lived higher up in the mountains and out on vast ranches that surrounded the town.

He went to the Texaco Station to ask Terry White if he knew of a cheap car he could buy. He found the bar Alan had mentioned called Mattie's, a dark, narrow, moldy hang-out for the locals. Two nights later he had a couple of beers with Zig Tipton and Joe Santorini. Chris told them he was looking for a landscaping job. He and his father used to build swimming pools and garden walls.

He knew Dan would be pleased as he had coordinated his approach in a short time.

Maggie and Estelle had agreed to meet Cathy's plane and put her up for the night. Dan came over to their house around eight o'clock and the three sat in the living room sipping tea and nibbling warm pecan cookies taken directly from the oven on a tray by Estelle's heavily mitted hand.

"He's doing a terrific job, Cathy." Dan sat in the large velvet chair and tried to put the best positive spin on Chris' work. "I'm sorry I can't be too specific about your husband's activities." He didn't want to upset her, although he figured with Chris being a New York City detective she was used to his dangerous assignments. "We're hoping to wrap up this case in a couple of months. Meantime Maggie and Estelle will get you settled."

"I appreciate the help," Cathy said as she searched Dan's face, trying to decide if it was time to worry about her husband. "At first I was sorry to leave my job teaching art at Pratt. But when I heard the delight in my mother's voice from New Mexico when I told her we were coming to Arizona, I was excited to get here."

Maggie understood Cathy's concern for the safety of her husband in this unknown western environment.

Every day she felt the same concerns for Dan. "Tomorrow we'll look at houses or condos. Know what you want, or do you want to look first?"

"Chris and I decided we'd rent a small house. With the baby coming, we thought that would meet our needs." Cathy was a stunning woman with long straight blonde hair and deep brown intense eyes. She wore a stylish navy maternity suit and low heels.

The next day was Saturday. Maggie had asked the realtor, Stephen Duval, to email her a list of small houses in the area for rent. She said a friend was looking to move to Juniper Hills. Duval offered to show them around, but Maggie put him off, saying they wanted to explore by themselves. Dan had said he wanted no one to know Chris and Cathy Watters were connected to him in any way. Chris' undercover status must be protected for his own good and Cathy's safety.

"Is this job for Chris really dangerous?" Cathy asked Maggie.

"Our town is under siege. What I tell you now is only for your ears. A hateful group of vicious bigots and racists want to make life miserable for Latinos, documented or not, so they'll go back to Mexico. There are four leaders. Dan believes if he can capture them together in one place, the raids will stop and the gang will fall apart."

"I'm feeling uneasy for Chris. He knows the City, but this is such a different environment. More like the wild, wild west."

Maggie laughed. "Dan is careful and thorough. Chris couldn't be in better hands. So, let's look at houses."

Maggie took Cathy's hand and led her to the Honda. "I have three houses in my neighborhood for you to see."

"I can't tell you how much I appreciate your help." Cathy fitted herself in the passenger seat and pulled the door closed.

"I want to introduce you to Lisa. She works at my firm and is also pregnant. She's with Jesús, an artist. I think you have a lot in common. Jesús is looking for an artist group or a studio and maybe you can help each other."

"That would be great. I'd love to keep painting while I'm here. Chris isn't sure if this assignment is for weeks or years and even if we want to make this our home."

"You'll like it here. Perfect climate and friendly people. Great place to raise a child. Most of the time."

CHAPTER 30

CHRIS WATTERS, to rescue himself from boredom, found a small bookstore in Leonardo and spent an idle hour looking over mysteries. He preferred history, politics and philosophy, but was afraid walking around with such titles would blow his cover. He had chosen two Dean Koontz thrillers. Both book covers were sexual and garish enough to discourage questions. In an old pair of jeans and a faded-green tee, he looked convincingly scruffy. Browsing through the lower shelves of used paperbacks, he suddenly stood and whacked the chin of the kid he'd met in Phoenix who had an amazing resemblance to a young Denzel Washington.

"Sorry, did I hurt…. Why the fuck are you hanging over me?" Chris said.

"I'm keeping an eye on you." Alan rubbed his chin and smiled.

Chris quickly switched to his thuggish accent. "Man, I'm new to dis town. Name's Chris. I'm looking for a landscaping job." You never know who might be listening, he thought.

Alan Johnson studied Chris from head to boots. "You got it down good, but your hands and nails give you away. Too smooth. Too clean."

"What the fuck! I've been on the road for over a year. I planned to pick up a pair of second-hand work gloves this afternoon."

"Don't matter. Landscape guys have dirt under their nails forever. Calluses too. All Jimmy Laker will want you to do at first is dig his damn ditches."

"Dan doesn't think it's safe for you to be involved in this take down," Chris said. "We shouldn't even be talking."

"Well if you want a local opinion, rough up your hands. Find a ratty pair of brown work gloves. Wear them."

"Damn. Damn. Am I that obvious?"

"Not really. I've been looking for you."

"We should stay away from each other." Chris took a step back.

"I doubt the gang hangs in bookstores."

"You never know. Maybe one of their aunts or cousins likes to read. This is a small town. Let's be careful."

"I'd sure like to help." Alan pleaded with open hands.

"You just did. I'm going back to my pad and rough up my hands. Thanks." Chris moved toward the cashier.

"Wait. I can introduce you to Laker. He's got the landscaping business."

"Let me think about it. Dan says these guys are killers. I don't want you in the crossfire."

"I live down the road from where you're staying."

"Shit, how long have you been following me?"

Alan smiled and slipped out of the store by a side door.

Chris paid for his books and walked to the startling blue lake in the middle of the park. He dropped his books on a small mound of dry grass, sat down near the shoreline and plunged his hands through the water and into the brownish muck at the bottom of the lake. Squishing his fingers, he worked the mud into his fingernails. Yuck, he thought as he dried his hands on his jeans, picked up his books and walked back to his rented room.

He used his cell to call Dan at the station in Juniper Hills. "I hope I'm not losing my touch. I was just waylaid by Alan at a local bookstore. He's been spying on me since I arrived. I never noticed."

"I thought he understood he's gotta stay out of this."

"He wants to introduce me to Laker, the landscaping guy. He's the only one I haven't met."

"Doesn't he come into that bar?" Dan asked.

"Not yet."

"Are you carrying?"

"My service pistol's in my waistband holster. Got a Glock 26 and ankle holster locked in the secret compartment in the bottom of my duffle with my cell. I haven't been using them. A lot of guys and gals around here have hip holsters. I don't want to appear as if I'm looking for trouble or a showdown."

"Be careful, Chris. These are bad guys and they hate Latinos. They're into some ugly stuff."

"What should I do about Alan?"

"Keep him as far away as possible. He should be in Phoenix working."

"Says he's taken a week off."

"I don't want him to get hurt. If Laker eventually comes into the bar, we won't need him."

Chris started hanging out at Mattie's Bar every night. He wasn't much of a drinker so he had to order and dump most of his drinks in a handy flowerpot filled with cacti on the way to the men's room. He hoped he wasn't intoxicating the sad looking flora. Zig and Joe were often there, so it became natural for them to share a table, play a little three-handed poker. Occasionally he'd whine about having trouble getting landscaping work. For emphasis he'd add, "It's them damn Mexicans."

Nobody took the bait until one Friday Zig invited him to a party the next night. "Lots of booze and plenty of hoes," Joe said.

"I ain't got wheels. Terry White is working on it," Chris said.

"Fuck. I can pick you up." Zig asked, "Where do you live?"

Chris didn't want to be dependent on Zig for transportation, but it seemed a good opportunity to see the gang leaders in one place if they all showed up. He gave Zig his address. "What time?"

"Nine."

"Got ya," Chris said and left the bar.

Zig turned to Joe. "What ya think?"

"'bout what?"

"Him, you dumb shit. Is he with us?"

"Fuck, I've only known the dude for a fuckin' week," Joe said, "Whines a lot."

"Laker will rip off our fucking balls if we bring a freak act into the group. What if he's that way?" Zig flopped his hand around.

"Says he from Kansas. Got a cute punk girl there. I saw her pic. So, he ain't no fuckin 'homo."

"On the road looking for work. Seems pretty strong."

"Yeah."

"I guess Jimmy will have to decide," Zig said.

At exactly nine, Zig picked up Chris in a new Wrangler.

"Nice wheels." Chris said.

"All mine. Paid cash." Zig tapped the horn and lifted his head proudly.

They stopped at Mattie's to have a few drinks and see if anyone needed a ride out to the party. Zig downed three and Chris dumped three. They drove out narrow unpaved roads Chris had barely noticed. It was dark and seemed as if they were changing directions and backtracking until they came to a ranch in the high desert. Chris hoped he could find the place again.

From a mile away, music accosted them, loud and hot. Chris knew these Jeeps were expensive and wondered where Zig got his money. He hadn't heard about the gang being into robberies.

"What is this place?" Chris asked as they approached an attractive ranch house. "Looks like a private home. Gigantic." His heartbeat quickened.

"Belongs to James Laker, Jimmy's old man. "He's a fuckin' big rancher around here. They call it Cobra's End or something like that. It's why we call ourselves the FANGS. You know, snakes have fuckin' poisonous fangs."

"Middle of nowhere. Surrounded by desert. Damn good place to bury bodies," Chris threw out for effect.

"Yeah." Zig licked his lips at the idea.

Chris wondered if anyone else knew them as FANGS. He didn't remember Dan mentioning the gang's name. It was the first he'd heard of the FANGS.

There were close to fifty cars parked around the property. Zig found a space near the barn. Chris slipped his hand over the Glock in his ankle holster. He felt uneasy. He'd left his service pistol and cell in the rented room. The crowd was rowdy and liquored up when they walked in. Someone put a bottle of beer in his hand. Couples hung on each other or coiled together on the five or six settees and lounges in the huge room, reminding him of crack houses he'd infiltrated in New York City. He smelled pot and something he couldn't immediately identify. A young girl came over to Zig, looped her arms around his neck and pushed her ample body into his. "Ziggy, how come so fuckin' late?"

"Hey Cin. Get me a real drink of scotch and one for my bro here. This fuckin' beer is swill." He wrapped his arm around Chris' shoulder.

Chris tried not to cringe. This was going to be harder than he thought. He hated the scene. He had no desire to play with the sexually aggressive young girls. He couldn't just walk out. He was hoping to meet Jimmy Laker, but he didn't feel up to joining in this drug and booze sloshed orgy.

"I'm gonna see who's here," Zig said. "You should do the same. Tell Cin when she comes back with the drinks."

Chris waited for Cin to return, speaking to several people. Cin was angry at Zig's disappearance. He decided to circulate and leave her to deal with Zig. He made his way around the room and headed for the kitchen not knowing exactly what he was looking for. He accidentally stepped on the bare toes of a young girl who looked to be about 16, blue-black hair piled in ringlets on top of her head. "Are Mr. and Mrs. Laker here?" he asked.

"Nah. They're in Ecuador. That's when Jimmy has our fuckin 'parties." She adjusted her flimsy tank top, exposing the curves of her pearly luminous young breasts.

"Too bad. I would've liked to tell 'em how much I like their spread. What's your name?"

"Shelly. You're not from around here. Are you?"

"Kansas. How can you tell?"

"You're kinda polite." She winked at Chris and squirmed against his body.

"Don't be so sure." He hated what he was about to do, but he needed to get out of there before he blew his cover. He put down his glass and grabbed Shelly and kissed her. When she pushed him away, he slapped her face lightly while seeming to slug her. He shouted, "Listen, bitch, we're getting' the fuck out of here whether you like it or not."

He looked around to see if anyone was paying attention before he hoisted her over his shoulder. Statutory rape flashed through his mind. He paraded to the front door and down the steps as dramatically as a movie hero. She was light as a rag doll. Chris was a large man. No one in the room moved, afraid, he hoped, to interfere in a lover's spat. Thank God he'd judged the situation correctly. He hadn't been sure of their rules. Would they come to Shelly's rescue or mind their own business?

Once outside he lay Shelly in an empty lounge chair and said. "Don't move. I have to puke." He staggered into the treed area near the barn acting like he was too drunk to walk straight. How was he going to get out of there?

He was wishing he could call Uber, when from the far side of the barn he heard his name whispered, "Over here."

"Alan. Good God. How...?"

"I've been keeping an eye on you."

"Do you have a car?

"My cycle. Follow me. Are you really drunk?"

"Nah. Haven't had anything. Could use a scotch. I wanted to prove I was a cad. I feel sorry for that young girl. She didn't deserve what I did to her."

"She's Jimmy's sister. Probably used to it. That's the way they treat their women."

"Just get me out of here. Tomorrow I'll say I got sick and hitched a ride back to town."

"Let's go."

"Have you ever heard this gang called FANGS?"

"Nah, they make up new names as they go along," Alan drew in a disgusted breath.

"Do you think they bought my little act?

"Are you kiddin'? You just won an Oscar."

CHAPTER 31

MAGGIE AND DAN, too tired to get up and dance, sat in their favorite booth at Rodney's Café listening to a recorded Sinatra sing "September Song." This first day of November was unseasonably cold. Dan kissed her neck and stroked her hair. They cuddled for warmth, arms wrapped around each other, on the same side of the banquette. Maggie laid her head on Dan's shoulder. "You're worried about Chris? Me too."

"Humm. I'm furious with Alan. He wants to help. Chris can't shake him." Dan slid his hand up and down her thigh. "I'm afraid Alan's going to get both of them hurt or worse."

Maggie put her hand on top of his and brought it to the tabletop. Shivers trickled down her spine. "We have some serious decisions to make, darlin'. I can't think with you pawing over me."

"Pawing?

"Well, caressing. It's not that I don't like it, but...."

"You're right. We need to keep to business. Alan's heart is in the right place, but he's had no training. I'm afraid he's going to get Chris in trouble or even killed. I've got a mind to arrest Alan and get him out of Chris' hair."

"Maybe you could lure him up here as a contact for Chris. Say you're too busy right now and you need his help." Maggie tugged her skirt over her knees and sipped her beer.

"Not a bad idea, Nancy Drew. Funny, but we haven't had much gang activity since Chris arrived in Leonardo."

"That's Sherlock to you, mister. He was more of an analytical detective. Do you think they're suspicious of Chris?" Maggie became aware that her hands were cold and trembling and reached for the warmth of Dan's.

He cradled her hands in his large palms and massaged them as he spoke. "He says no, but maybe he's missing something. He swears they've never seen him with Alan."

"They may be testing Chris." Anxiety for Chris and Alan was building in her own mind.

"Chris hasn't met Jimmy Laker yet. Although he did learn Laker is the chief honcho of the gang."

"So, it wasn't Zig Tipton after all. Now you think Laker ordered Zig to set fire to the offices, but you don't have any evidence," Maggie took a deep breath. ... "To change the subject for a moment, against all our advice, Lisa and Jesús have decided to get married on Thanksgiving Day. You are, of course, invited."

"And you'll get to keep your law partner for a while. How long do you think Jesús will last away from his home?"

"It's hard to say. He has a large adoring family in Hermosillo. But Lisa loves her job. Sophie is counting on being the new baby's big sister and babysitter."

Maggie went on to add that she and Cathy found a perfect house to rent with a beautiful wild flower garden. Cathy and Jesús casually stumbled on an art studio to share. "Cathy says you told Chris not to call. Is that necessary?"

"I'm sorry about that. It's for their safety. He has his cell locked in a secret compartment in the bottom of his duffle." Dan continued, "Remember he's using his own name as a fake name but has a false ID for Guy Black which is supposed to be his real name locked in there with his cell. If anyone checks on him, we've created a long, wicked history of felonies and convictions. He's supposed to call me every Friday. When he's late, I feel sick to my stomach."

"It's painful for Cathy to worry like that." Maggie tried to keep her voice light.

"Alan contacted me and said Chris was a big hit at a gang party. I yelled at him. Said never call me again. Told him if he doesn't stay away, I'll have him picked up and temporally jailed. The kid doesn't realize. the danger he could create for Chris and himself."

"Tell him to call me or text Miss Chloe." Maggie sat back and folded her hands on the table. Dan didn't need her to fall apart on him.

"We don't know what kind of surveillance these punks have. Chris' cell is encrypted. To keep it secret he can only use it in his room or the park."

"I wonder what made Chris such a hit at the gang's party." Maggie looked up as a couple danced close to their table.

"He never mentioned it, Sherlock. Guess it wasn't important." Dan pushed his fingers through his Scottish-red curls. Maggie thought he badly needed a haircut.

CHAPTER 32

CHRIS WALKED from his rented room into town to get a sandwich at an Italian deli he'd discovered. The ratty brown garden gloves he'd picked up in a Salvation Army store stuck out of his back pocket. As he moved at a casual pace, he realized he was walking through American history.

Shop windows displayed old faded pictures from the early Westerns that a variety of Hollywood studios filmed in the area. John Wayne was a popular figure and each of the three hotels in the middle of town claimed that he had been a guest there at one time or another.

Eleven miles from the Mexican border, the town of Leonardo in the nineteenth century was an important mining town for gold, silver and turquoise. It was on the stagecoach route and had a stopover station.

Unfortunately, the ore veins lay close to the surface and were quickly depleted by individual miners. Later the large mining companies brought in heavy equipment for pit mining and devastated the landscape. The mountains remained majestic. There were small communities of bungalows that had been remodeled and still in good shape. Many areas were rundown and uncared for. Several wealthy large cattle ranches like Laker's spread surrounded the town.

Most of the vegetation was scrub oaks, cacti and yucca, but higher up the mountains were lush with blue cypress, spruce and white fir. The town had the wide-open frontier feeling of the Old West. Nearly four thousand residents called themselves "rock-hounds" and loved the gem and mineral shows that were held five or six times a year in the surrounding areas. Rocks, millions of rocks.

A black SUV driven by a uniformed chauffeur complete with an appropriate cap stopped next to Chris at the curb. Chris did a double take, thinking some important county official was stopping to ask for directions to the court house or how to get out of town.

"Yo." A large young man in a short-sleeved beige silk shirt, filled the space where he had rolled down the back-seat window. His stylishly trimmed full black beard moved as he called from the open window. "Come're."

Chris could smell his after-shave lotion from the sidewalk. He stopped walking, his heart thundering in his chest. "You talkin' to me?"

"Yeah. You."

Without moving toward the car, Chris looked into the dark, dead eyes of the bearded bald guy in the back seat. "What?"

"You're Chris Watters?"

"Who wants to know?"

"I'm Laker, Jimmy Laker."

He's come to work me over for abusing Shelly, Chris thought. "What?"

"I hear you're looking for a landscaping job." Laker hung his arm over the open window and Chris saw a green snake tattoo running from Laker's wrist to the hem of his short-sleeved shirt. He also saw a Glock19 holstered under his right arm.

"You got work for me?"

"I think we can do business. My sister says youse a cool guy, real polite."

Like Laker would know good manners. Chris searched Jimmy's face for mockery but saw not a trace.

"Zig and Joe say you're okay. I take their word." Jimmy seemed assured to have two confirmations.

"Where should I go? I ain't got no car yet."

"Tomorrow. In front of Mattie's. I'll send a truck at 7:30."

"I'll be there."

"Let's go," Laker said to his driver.

The SUV drove off as the tinted back window closed.

Chris continued walking. Was he being set up or was the job offer real? His stomach fell back out of his throat and he picked up his pace. Maybe Alan was right. Shelly was used to being poorly treated. Being half drunk or stoned, she didn't realize how abusive Chris had been. It made him lose his appetite for the delicious Italian sandwich his mouth had been salivating for.

CHAPTER 33

"HOW MANY for Thanksgiving?" Sophie looked up from the large stainless-steel bowl of toasted bread slices. She continued with gusto to rip them into small pieces.

"The last I heard it was eleven or, if Chris can make, twelve. Let's count," Estelle said.

"Me and you." Sophie pointed at Estelle. "Mama nd Papa. Maggie and Dan. Lisa and Jesús."

"Don't forget Alan and his mother, Natalie. Cathy nd maybe Chris." Estelle pulled a large bag of potatoes om the pantry.

"What about Gus? Sometimes I think he doesn't ke us." Sophie scrunched up her face.

"He's going home to his mother's in California."

He stopped at a small grocery and bought a packet of Graham Crackers. Ripping off the waxed-wraps, he munched one and then another. As a kid he always found grahams comforting. He missed Cathy and he was anxious to bring down this gang of punks as soon as possible. He wandered over to Mattie's to see who might be hanging around, though he knew two o'clock was early for the gang to start their evening rituals.

When he entered, it took a few minutes for his eyes to adjust to the dark shadows. One elderly woman was sitting at a table in the corner. The rest of the place was empty. Mattie stood behind the bar polishing glasses and hanging them in an overhead rack. Chris was trying to decide whether to sit on a bar stool or at a table when the lone women called to him. "Hey, new guy, come over here."

He hesitated until Mattie said, "She's harmless. Just lonely."

Chris nodded to Mattie, made a gesture toward the beer tap and said, "A cold one." He sat at the table with the strange woman who was drinking something golden in a small tall glass. He offered her a graham cracker and helped her remove the waxed paper on the cracker.

She was small and old, maybe ninety, he thought. She wore a wide-brimmed rose velvet hat adorned with dark pink flowers. Her soft cotton dress may have been fifty years old. "I've seen you with that group of snakes," was how she opened the conversation. "They killed my grandson. A bad lot. You'd do yourself a favor by staying away from them."

"What's your name?"

"Rita Goodwin. Named after Rita Hayworth. I used to be beautiful when I was young."

Chris looked carefully at her face. He could believe it. She had a perfect facial structure with high cheek bones. Her skin was barely wrinkled. Her eyes were like rare gems, maybe emeralds. "Tell me about your grandson. What was his name? When did that happen?"

Mattie brought over Chris' beer, set it on the table and rolled his eyes. Chris thought he'd probably heard her story a hundred times.

"Mike Goodwin. Last year. He was out partying with them and came back dead." Rita carefully sipped her cocktail.

"Sorry."

"Don't be. He was on his way to Hell. They helped him along." Rita took the last sip of her drink and stood or rather struggled to stand. Chris rose to help. "Stay where you are, kiddo. I can still get out of a chair by myself. I have to feed my cat. She gets hungry 'bout now. You take care of yourself. Hear me?"

Chris watched her cross the room at a slow graceful pace. She'll probably live into her hundreds, he thought. He moved over to a bar stool and addressed Mattie. "What's her story?"

"She was born here. Out-lived three or four hubbies. No idea how many kids. She comes in most afternoons, has one stinger, brandy and white crème de menthe, and leaves to feed her cat. I had to buy a special set of glasses to serve her drinks. She used to own a hardware store. Knows everyone born in these parts since forever."

"What happened to her grandson?"

"Just what she said. Out partying with th[...] When they brought him home, his head was [...] in. He fell off a cliff, so they said. Died in the h[...]

"You don't sound like you believe?"

"It's hard to know with those guys."

"Ever party with them?"

"Not me. Are you crazy? They're all bulli[...]

Chris was afraid to ask more questi[...] beginning to sound like a cop, he thought. [...] sure how much he could trust Mattie. He fi[...] his beer and found a sheltered trail through [...] where he ran out of sight until he was ready [...] next day.

"This is a lot of stuffing, Mom. Will it all fit in one turkey?"

"We're having two birds this year. Twelve pounders. I think they're more tender than the huge ones."

"You sure are a great cook," Sophie said.

"What do you want, little one?"

"How do you know I want anything?"

"I'm psychic."

"No, you're not. ... Ice cream." Sophie picked up a spoon and licked it. "May I have a bowl?"

"Of course. Can you scoop it yourself?"

Sophie hopped off the high stool she'd been sitting on, opened the freezer and took out the gallon container of coconut ice cream. She placed it on the counter and opened a drawer to search for the scooper. "Have you met Alan's mother before?"

"Yes. Her name is Natalie. She's been here several times. You'll like her. She's a nice lady and makes beautiful jewelry."

"Alan promised to teach me to dance."

"He's very busy with school and work. He's been driving his mother up here to sell her jewelry at our weekend art fairs."

Sophie spooned out her ice cream and spoke slowly. "I heard Maggie say that Alan must stay away from Chris. Alan could get Chris killed. Is that true?" Sophie's eyes widened with fear.

Estelle took a deep breath and prayed that she was about to say the right thing to this inquisitive child. "Sophie, I'm sorry you heard that. What I'm going to tell you is very serious and you may not mention it to anyone. Can you promise me? Not anyone."

"I can." Sophie paused with the scoop above the ice cream container.

Estelle took another deep breath. "Dan and Chris are trying to arrest this bad gang. Chris is pretending to be a gang member. He's undercover. It is a very secret game and no one must know about it. If you ever see Chris, you must pretend you don't know him. Don't say hello or even show that you recognize him. If you hear anything else, come to me. No one else. Okay?"

"Undercover. I understand." Sophie spoke with great seriousness. "Do you want a dish of ice cream?"

"Not now, honey. I'm too busy." Estelle took a cloth napkin from her apron pocket, wiped sweat from her brow and hoped she hadn't made a mistake. She had always been open with her own kids and felt Sophie deserved an explanation. She was a careful, knowing child. Was Sophie old enough to realize the consequences of a slip of the tongue? Was she herself becoming a careless old woman?

Maggie, Lisa and Gus sat around the antique table in their temporary conference room. "By this time next year, we'll be in our new offices." Maggie said. "I was at the construction site yesterday and the foundation is already poured."

"I can't wait." Preoccupied, Lisa sat back from the table, brushed hair from her eyes and sighed. "I can't believe I'm getting married tomorrow."

"I saw your names, Pérez and Pérez Wedding, on the church sign when I drove in this morning," Gus said. "Are you expecting a large crowd?"

"No. I told Father not to advertise it. We want a small ceremony."

"That's hard to do around here. Townies live for weddings and funerals. What time is your hair appointment?" Gus cleared his throat.

"Ten o'clock. Fifteen minutes."

"You'd better go." He blew his nose.

Maggie looked up from the papers she was preparing. "Gus is right. Go. We'll see you in church. We're finished here for today. ... Gus, stay for a minute. I wanna talk with you." Lisa left.

Gus rose, put on a heavy sweater and sat down. The heat had been turned low for the weekend and the cold affected his arthritis.

"We started this firm together," Maggie said, "and we decided to take whatever cases came our way. We've been very lucky considering the destruction of the Painted Lady. We haven't lost a single client. In fact, if things go the way they've been going, we'll soon have more work than we can handle."

Gus looked at her as if expecting to hear some horrendous news, like she had a fatal disease.

"Please don't look at me like that," Maggie said. "Don't worry. It's not bad."

Gus put his elbows on the table and leaned toward her. "What?"

"I want to do more immigration law. I mean really seek out cases. I know there's less money in it, but there's such a need, so many injustices."

"We're all working to capacity now."

"If you and Lisa can't handle the clients, we'll hire more legal assistants."

He looked as if she had stabbed him in the gut. "We're doing so well. Why do you want to change?

We'll just have a lot of poor, sorry souls in here taking up space and time. But you started this firm and invited me in. You can do whatever you want."

"I'm not looking for your blessings, just your understanding."

"It feels as if we'll be overwhelmed, once word gets out. You're a good rainmaker, Maggie. Will you have time to bring in new clients, paying clients? How will this intention change things around here, the bottom line? Maybe I should look for another firm."

"Gus, do me a favor and wait." Maggie hadn't expected him to jump on the idea, but she'd felt he could be persuaded to accept the new direction she wanted to initiate for their firm. "Let's see how this works out. I'll keep up our image as a top-notch law firm and also deal with the immigration problems. Will you give it a chance?"

"Have you talked to Lisa? ... Of course, you have."

Maggie brushed her hair behind her ear. "She said she'd go along with me."

"Let's see how it unfolds. But I'm not happy were changing plans when we're not even settled in our new offices."

Maggie was sure Gus wouldn't immediately like her new ideas, but she hadn't expected this depth of resistance. He was a good soul at heart. Surely, he would come around.

Maggie and Dan lay comfortably entangled on the sofa in the den watching the ten o'clock news. Dan had brought over two pizzas and a homemade salad of baby greens so Estelle wouldn't have to deal with dinner after spending all day preparing their Thanksgiving feast for the next day. The dining room table was set with orange napkins, autumn leaves and two crystal bowls of yellow chrysanthemums. Rosa and Sophie had gone home to get Sophie's flower-girl outfit ready for the wedding. Estelle was reading in her room, if she wasn't already fast asleep.

Halfway through a PBS report on a hate crime in Alabama, Dan's phone rang. He said it was Chris and moved into the hallway. Maggie was tempted to turn the TV audio down and listen in, but decided to mind her own business. Dan would tell her what he wanted her to know.

From his rented room in Leonardo, Chris said, "Have you ever heard this gang called FANGS? All caps for emphasis. Alan told me they change their name now and then, but presently they call themselves FANGS."

"FANGS. Huh? Never heard of them." Dan paused. "I wonder if they change their name according to the trouble they take on. Attacking Juniper Hills seems to be a specific job for them, something they may be getting paid to do."

"James Laker, Jimmy's father, calls his ranch Cobra's End," Chris said. "They're all snakes, according to this lovely granny I met in Mattie's Bar. ... Which brings me to my next request. Check on the death last year of a young man named Mike Goodwin from Leonardo. See if there was anything suspicious about it. I met his grandmother and she says the FANGS killed him."

"What else do these hoodlums do? I'm almost reluctant to find out." Dan leaned against the wall.

"Lastly, they're planning a rumble tomorrow night not in Juniper Hills but in the neighboring town of Ridgewood Valley. They say it's to enflame the fear of the people in Juniper Hills who they're really after."

"Does that make sense to you?" Dan asked.

"No. Many of the things they talk about don't make sense."

Dan was glad to hear Chris confirm his own ideas.

"I don't think this is a good time to catch them. I'm not even sure who'll be there. Half the time they don't do what they talk about. Right now, their main object seems to be to put the fear of God in Latinos in Juniper Hills. It's sick."

Chris asked Dan to tell his wife, Cathy, he missed her. He was on his way out to Mattie's to plan their strategy for the next night's riot with the gang. Terry White said he had a car for Chris that would be ready in a week. Chris was thinking maybe he could get away and meet Cathy in Phoenix once he had the car, but didn't want to botch his cover or put Cathy in any kind of jeopardy. Chris' loneliness poured through the phone connection.

They chatted for a while and hung up. Dan immediately called the Ridgewood Valley Sheriff who thanked Dan and said he thought he and his men could handle the situation, but would send out an alert if they needed assistance.

Maggie was sitting on the sofa when Dan came back into the den. "Chris can't make dinner tomorrow," he told her.

"Cathy will be disappointed. I'm sorry that they have to be separated and can't share these months of her pregnancy."

"I'd hate to be separated from you, love, baby or no baby." Dan smoothed Maggie's hair, took her in his arms and slid his lips over her neck and shoulders. He held her face in his hands and kissed her warmly.

For a moment she felt that cautious stab in her chest. It was that hollow invisibility that she wanted to call forth, but it wouldn't come. She allowed herself to surrender into his arms.

They locked the den doors, and made tender love on the sofa before Dan went home. Maggie returned to preparing for Lisa's wedding and their Thanksgiving celebration. It was ten minutes to midnight.

CHAPTER 34

WHEN ESTELLE ARRIVED the next morning, the church was brightly lit and smelled of fresh-cut-roses. Lisa and Jesús had planned a small family wedding. Despite everyone's concerns, they'd decided to marry. Robbie had died only three months earlier in the fire at the Painted Lady. Lisa had opted for simplicity. Alan's mother, Natalie, Rosa, Carlos and Chris' wife, Cathy, sat in the front row. Small groups of well-wishers scattered throughout the pews. Estelle recognized several of her friends, local merchants and Maggie's clients. Gus sat in a back pew with a new friend she hadn't met. Weddings and funerals were social events in Juniper Hills, even if you didn't know the bride and groom or deceased. Knowing someone who did was reason enough to attend.

Lisa had told her they didn't want to burden Robbie's large family with crossing the border. They would send them an announcement after the service. Estelle suspected they didn't want to hear his family's opinions about their marriage.

Estelle was sure Lisa felt the same about her family; the couple didn't need any more advice. They also weren't ready to explain how they fell in love. Even though Lisa spoke about Robbie every day, she told Estelle she knew in her heart that he would approve her love for his brother. That she would have someone who would care for her and his child as Robbie would have.

Estelle slipped in next to Carlos as the organist played Pachelbel's Canon. Sophie appeared in a chiffon dress of beige with matching tiara and shoes. Clutched in her hand was a basket of yellow rose petals which she scattered along the bride's path. Maggie, in a simple beige silk dress with a bouquet of autumn flowers cradled in her arms, walked next down the aisle. Lisa, on Alan's arm followed in a mid-calf beige shantung dress, a matching lacey mantilla draped over her blond hair. She carried a bouquet of cascading miniature bronze mums. Jesús and Dan met them at the altar with Father Salvatore. Alan presented Lisa to Jesús. Maggie and Dan stepped back with Sophie. Dan took Maggie's hand and Sophie took Dan's other hand. The ceremony was joyful and short. Sophie giggled when the bride and groom kissed, then turned around and screamed, "Something smells. We're on fire!"

The church quickly filled with a nauseating odor. The air thickened and turned yellowish. People covered their mouths, eyes wide. Heads turned wildly toward exits. Pandemonium was imminent. Dan stood on the altar and shouted, "People, remain calm and leave by the side doors. It's not an emergency. It's a prank. Move slowly and cover your faces." Dan ducked out the nearest side exit.

Estelle moved to the back of the church, pushed open the heavy doors and hooked them in place. Turning, she caught sight of two scruffy boys pedaling their bikes as fast as they could down the street. Dan was already at the curb speaking on his cell. In what seemed like seconds, a patrol car followed by an ambulance pulled up in front of him. She watched Dan explain what happened and indicate the direction the boys headed.

A few minutes later, Dan came back inside the church where Estelle and Maggie and Father Salvatore checked between the pews for anyone who might have fallen. The empty church smelled like rotting garbage.

Outside, people wandered around unsure of what to do. A few lay on the grass, gasping and coughing. Others tended to them. Everyone's eyes were teary and blood-red. Many smaller kids were sobbing, clinging to their parents.

"Did this attack have anything to do with their wedding being listed on the event board in front of the church," Estelle, hands on her hips, asked Dan.

"It's mischief," Dan said. "The boys I saw couldn't have been more than twelve."

"Hatred starts younger and younger it seems." Estelle was upset. "Will we ever learn to live in peace with each other?"

Dan walked to the top of the church steps and shouted for attention. "I've gotten a text message. The cops caught the two boys who did this. They were trying to escape but ran their bikes into a huge patch of bramble and fell in head-first. The officers are taking them to the station, calling their parents and the police reporter from the *Gazette*. This is a racist incident and they want to prevent copy-cat activities. Everyone okay?"

Maggie, who had gone to the ambulance to consult with the medics, called back, "A few bumps and bruises. But we all stink to heaven or should I say like hell!" She wiped the toxic mist from her eyes with the back of her hand and shouted to Dan. "Explain what happened."

"It was a stink bomb. I recognized it right away. The kids mixed sulfur containing chemicals together in glass vials and sealed them with wax. They sneaked into the back of the church, threw them against the brick wall and darted off. Once the glass broke the stink was released into the air."

"Thanks for your explanation," Maggie raised her arm, pointed to Dan. People applauded.

After the ceremony, Lisa and Jesús had planned to stand in the back of the church and shake hands with everyone. Now they stood at the bottom of the steps and urged people to go home.

"Put your clothes in a paper bag and leave them overnight in the backyard. Let the odor disperse. Don't try to wash them today," Maggie told the crowd.

Estelle gathered their out-of-town guests and divided them among her house, Rosa's, Lisa's and Dan's houses. "Go, take long showers. Wash your hair. Scrub. Scrub. Scrub. If you need clothes, we can find fresh ones for you. We'll see you in at my house. Six o'clock."

The aroma of roasting turkey welcomed everyone to the large neo-colonial house. Estelle was elated. Almost by mutual consent the gathered family decided not to talk about the stink bomb attack. Everyone looked a bit damp. It was so childish. The incident could be thought of as comic if the Latino situation wasn't so ugly and it hadn't been a wedding.

Dan opened bottles of white wine then placed them back in the freezer to keep cool. He told Cathy that Chris couldn't make it. "I'm hoping we can round up this gang very soon. Then Chris will be home for good. He's done a terrific job of infiltrating this gang." He didn't add anything about the car Terry White was fixing up. No sense in getting up Cathy's hopes. She did look proud when he praised Chris' work.

Natalie, Alan's mom, wore a pair of earrings she'd crafted that hung like tiny chandeliers studded with chips of rubies. She went straight to the kitchen to help Estelle. They were now the best of friends. Natalie was thinking of moving up to Juniper Hills. "I really like it here," she said as she arranged hors d'oeuvre platters of jumbo shrimp and clams-casino. "Alan decided he wants to be a detective and applied to the Police Academy in Phoenix. He was accepted last week. He can still work part-time, so, it really doesn't matter where I live. This is an art-loving town with lots of opportunities for me." Natalie had brought several boxes of glass baubles and colorful stones for Sophie.

"Sophie will be very pleased," Maggie said. "Already thinks she wants to marry Alan, if he'll only wait for her to grow up."

"That touches my heart," Natalie said. She was a stunning woman with caramel-colored skin, jet black hair pulled back in a chignon and dark eyes that reflected the color of her hair. She wore little makeup and soft pink lipstick.

Rosa had gone out into the backyard to scold Carlos for playing Frisbee with Sophie and Alan. "He's such a fool," she said when she came back. "He's not supposed to stretch his back. You know what he says? If he can't play with his daughter he might as well have been deported. What can I do with him?"

Estelle continued to wipe down the counter top, relishing how much she enjoyed the people circulating around her kitchen.

Maggie hugged Rosa. "Don't be too hard on him. He'll be careful after all that terrible suffering he went through."

Dinner was a big success. Everyone helped clean up. Around eight o'clock most all their guests had left. Dan whispered in Maggie's ear. "Come home with me tonight." He saw her struggle with that tug of self-protection she was always fighting.

There was no one around, but she whispered back, "Okay." They left after checking that the dishes, pots and pans were all cleaned and stored in their proper places.

It was nine o'clock when they arrived in front of Dan's house. Maggie noticed a flashy silver sports car parked at the curb, a shadow of a form sitting in the driver's seat. "I think you have company."

Dan pulled in the driveway and cut the engine. With a look on his face that begged forgiveness, he turned to Maggie, stroked her arm, kissed her check, got out of the car and said, "Wait here." He walked toward the sports car. As he approached the shadowy figure, Maggie heard him groan. "Damn! It is Dolores."

CHAPTER 35

DAN WALKED OVER to the darkened car. Dolores had turned off the lights and rolled down the window. "What are you doing in front of my house at ten o'clock at night?" He fought to maintain control of the tone of his voice. The top of his head was about to explode like some crazy cartoon character. He was furious for many reasons, not just the inconvenience of her appearance.

"Nowhere else to go. They kicked me out of my condo and the bank would have re-poed my car if I hadn't hidden it."

"Who's they?"

"The mortgage thugs, of course. I'm bankrupt."

"What a surprise."

"I don't need your sarcasm right now."

"Hold on. Let me talk to my friend." Dan walked back to his car, slumped behind the wheel and turned to Maggie. "It's my ex, Dolores, in that car. She claims she has nowhere to go. Will you come inside and help me make arrangements for her?"

Maggie hesitated. "Maybe you should drive me home."

"No. I don't want to do that. Help me find a place for her to stay tonight. I don't want to be alone with her even for ten minutes."

Dan was in turmoil. He wanted to help his ex, but he didn't want anything to do with her, except maybe poison her.

"Okay," Maggie said and got out of the car.

Dan could see that Maggie was filled with curiosity. As they walked to Dolores's car, he asked, "Please get her a place to stay tonight? I think Frederick's Inn might have a vacancy."

Maggie nodded, yes.

Dan rapped on the flashy car window. "Come inside and we'll get you a place to stay."

Dolores opened her door, stood for a moment and smoothed the skirt of her badly wrinkled black suit. She smelled like she'd been sleeping in her car. Musty. How far had she traveled?

The three walked to his front door. "This is my friend, Maggie Sweeney." Dan put his arm around Maggie's shoulder. "This is Dolores." He hesitated. "I'm not sure I know your last name now."

"Demarest," Dolores said.

He fiddled with the front door key and they went inside. In the bright lights of the living room Dan saw a haggard replica of his once stunning wife. A tall, lithe blonde stared out through near-dead eyes, looking twice her age at thirty-five. Her shoulder length hair was knotted in nests. What makeup was left on her face had smeared. Dark smudges of mascara appeared on her cheeks.

"Sit down," he told Dolores. He handed Maggie a credit card. "Try the Frederick Inn first." Maggie walked into the kitchen to make the call. After writing down the pertinent information on a sticky note, she hesitated at the door, but the room was silent. Dan and Dolores were seated across from each other at the coffee table. Not a word had passed between them.

Maggie handed the note to Dolores. "They'll be expecting you. Breakfast is included."

Dan stood, turned to Dolores and said. "Maggie is a lawyer. We'll talk to you tomorrow at her offices." He moved next to Maggie as if for protection. "Do you have a card?"

"Not with me," Maggie answered.

"What's a good time for you?"

"One o'clock," Maggie said.

He wrote the name of Maggie's firm and address on a scrap paper he pulled out of his jacket pocket, handed it to Dolores and ushered her to the door. "Call tomorrow and make an appointment for one p.m. with Maggie's secretary."

Dolores mumbled something that sounded like thanks and let herself out the front door. In a few minutes they heard her car engine roar and drive away.

Maggie tossed her coat on the sofa.

Dan stood in the middle of the living room as if in a trance. "Forgive me. I didn't mean to put the burden of that woman on you. I took you for granted. I'm sorry. That woman freaks me out."

"I can see that." Maggie moved closer to embrace him and gently stroked his arms. She tilted her head and smiled. Then nodded toward the open door of the bedroom, He obviously appreciated her attempt to soothe him, but he wasn't into "sexy" right then.

"I want to hire you to see what you can do for her. I can't just leave her on the street."

"Why do you owe her anything? She used you and took off."

"That's true, but in a way, I needed her. Young and lonely when I was posted to D.C., I could just about find my way to the Smithsonian."

"Oh, Dan."

"I was a cowpoke from the Arizona high country. She was beautiful and fun company. Introduced me to the Pentagon party groups. Helped relieve the stresses of living in D.C. I never loved her."

"This is all about guilt? Geez, Dan. I thought I had it bad with Hank. I beat up myself for years because I couldn't make that marriage work."

"Sometimes it's hard to forgive ourselves, even when we know we did the best we could at the time."

Exhausted, they entered the celestial bedroom, slipped into separate night shirts of Dan's and lay, bodies touching, with thoughts of Lisa's lovely wedding in their minds, feeling mutual warmth they wrapped their arms around each other before falling into deep sleep.

CHAPTER 36

DEAR MISS CHLOE: I have lived in San Diego for the last twenty-five years, undocumented. Before I had children, I thought if the police picked me up, I would just go back to Mexico, even though I had no idea where I would go. My family is all here. Recently my ten-year-old son was diagnosed with a rare blood cancer and started on chemo. This experimental treatment can't be duplicated in most hospitals here in the U.S. and certainly not in Mexico I am beside myself with anxiety. The doctors say it could take three or four years to treat his condition. Every time I leave the house, I am filled with panic that I am going to be picked up for some minor mistake and deported. I have a good job and can pay for medical insurance. I don't know what to do or where to go. Can you or your readers help me find a way to feel safe? *Anxious Mother*

Maggie sat at her office desk and for the third time reread the letter she had brought from home. How hopeless this mother must feel! She had to find out who to contact before she wrote an answer. There must be organizations that dealt with life and death problems like this. If there weren't, she vowed to create one. This family was no threat to national security.

Her mind was still whirling with ideas when Dan knocked on her door.

"I came early because I wanted to talk before Dolores showed up." He looked uncomfortable and sad. Her heart ached for him, she wanted him to stand up for himself.

"We have to be fair with her. She spent my money freely, never asked me for anything when we divorced. I didn't have much at the time, but now I can help. You have the reputation as an excellent and fair negotiator. I want you to do your best for her, even though she's a pain in the butt."

"As your lawyer, I'd say move cautiously. The little I know about Dolores tells me she'll drain you like one of our dry creeks if given the chance. Go out the rear door and let me talk to her alone. Come back in an hour."

"How can I thank you?"

"You can't. Go." After Dan kissed her on the forehead and left, Maggie sat back in her rented lawyerly chair and meditated. She couldn't think of any reason to be jealous of Dolores, nor did she want to pity her or Dan. She wanted both to man-up and take responsibility for their actions.

Ten minutes later, Dolores was ushered into her office. "I want to talk to Dan." She stood in the doorway with lips puckered in a sulk.

"Please have a seat." Maggie motioned toward a comfortable chair in front of her desk. Somehow this bedraggled, once gorgeous thirty-five-year-old woman made her feel dowdy. Was this jealousy she was feeling? "Dan wants you to talk to me."

"I want to talk to him."

"He's on call."

"It figures. I'll wait. I want to talk to him."

"Dolores, tell me about yourself. I understand you and Dan were only married a short time. Three years? And you've been married again to Mr. Demarest? Is that your second marriage?"

"Third. There's a George Gillian in there."

"Why have you not gone to them for help?"

"Truthfully? They told me to get lost. They gave me all they were going to give." She ran her hands through greasy blond hair and brushed it out of her eyes. In a way, Maggie admired her moxie. Dolores didn't seem to care if she came across as selfish and greedy.

"And you thought Dan would be a soft touch?"

"He was always kind, even while we were divorcing."

"Where do you live now, or rather where are you coming from?"

"San Francisco."

"Do you have a job? Are you returning there?"

"I model for clothing magazines. It's seasonal. Right now, I don't even have enough money to get my hair styled."

"You're looking for a loan or a hand out?" Maggie was relieved to hear Dolores wasn't planning on hanging around.

"Whatever."

"Dan will help you out, but there are conditions."

"Like what?"

"You get yourself cleaned up and find a steady job."

"How much is that worth?"

What a beauty this one is, Maggie thought. It's no wonder Dan didn't want to talk with her.

"Dan will give you a generous check today. After you get a steady job, he will write another check. He must have proof from your employer in a letter or phone call that you are gainfully employed. Then he never wants to hear from you again. This is a chance to get on your feet. This offer will not be repeated."

"I see you're giving me the steely bitch treatment." Dolores sat with her hands in her lap and sighed. "Okay. I guess it's time to stop depending on the Judas kisses of men to get me through life."

Maggie wrote a check on her office account and handed it to Dolores. "We'll hear from you with records of your new address and place of employment, proof of your new life?"

"Yes, you will." Dolores stood and held out her hand. "Thank you."

Maggie felt reluctant, but decided not to be boorish. She gave her a sincere hand shake. "Don't thank me. Write to Dan and thank him."

Dolores left with a slight bounce in her steps. Maggie hoped she fully realized the next check would depend on her complete rehabilitation.

A few minutes later Dan knocked and strode into the room. "I watched her leave."

Maggie stood. "You should stand in the corner for being fearful of that woman."

"She gives me the willies."

"You owe the firm for the check I wrote, plus $1,000 for my fee. Nothing around here comes cheap, I'm starting a fund for low-income immigrants who need legal services."

"Is that all?"

"If Dolores gets her act together, it'll cost you another check. I want to give her incentive to change."

"You are a wonderful negotiator." He moved closer, took Maggie in his arms and kissed her deeply.

CHAPTER 37

CHRIS WATTERS called Dan a few days later to report the gang had driven up to Ridgewood Valley. "Nothing much happened. We had a few beers in two different bars and looked around for Latinos to bully. The bars and streets were empty. I guess everyone was stuffed with turkey from the day before and taking it easy."

"I'm not surprised." Dan sat back and rubbed his hand through his hair. "I can't make sense of their activities. They seem to have plenty of money. Someone's paying them to make stupid trouble."

"They broke six store windows, punctured tires, dumped over garbage cans and shot out street lamps. No fires though. Nobody called the cops either. It was as if the town temporarily moved to another galaxy, most likely a holiday special or a football game on TV. That gang would have attacked anyone, not just Latinos, at that point. They were mighty frustrated."

"Thank God the town folks will never know the misery they escaped," Dan said.

"I got scared when I saw two teenage girls on the sidewalk texting in the dark, but when they saw the gang coming, they ran into their house." Chris' voice vibrated relief.

"Smart girls." Dan agreed.

"Well, I have some good news and bad. Jimmy Laker says our next 'move' as he called it, is for the FANGS to come to Juniper Hills. Says that's where the Latinos we're targeting live. Apparently, you have all sorts of Christmas activities: parades, music festivals, chorales, pancake breakfasts, Christmas tree-lighting ceremonies. I can't remember what else he mentioned. Lots of people on the street to beat up. Rob. Whatever."

"Great news," Dan said. "We're going to get them this time. We'll be ready. ... Do they ever talk about burning down Maggie's office building?"

"I don't think they did it as a gang. I talked to Joe one night and he said Zig often solos on jobs for money, and Zig has a new Wrangler he bought with cash."

"That would make sense, because whoever did it tried to imitate the small fires the gang had been setting. I'm forming a special force of twenty cops and firemen to work with me to get this gang. When you tell us their plans we'll be waiting?"

"Good," Chris said. "Check the town's schedule of events."

"You won't have to worry about Alan hanging around anymore. Natalie has moved her RV to Juniper Hills. He's been accepted at the Police Academy in Phoenix. He wants to be a detective. I think we've both had a big effect on him."

"Glad to hear it. That's a relief. He's a great kid. He wanted so much to help. I was afraid his enthusiasm would get one of us killed. Okay. I'd better go. There're footsteps outside my door."

"Be safe. Take care. Hopefully we can wrap this up in a month."

Dan had never worked so closely with people he knew and loved and felt he had to protect. Up until now business and his personal life had been completely separate. He was, what was that expression women used, "over the moon" about Maggie. Shit, he'd die if anyone heard his thoughts.

Estelle, Rosa and Carlos were like the parents young Dan lost too soon. Then there was Sophie who had stolen his heart, big time, and Alan and his mother, Natalie, and Lisa and Jesús and especially Chris and Cathy and now even two babies soon to be born. A whole town he had once left and come back to love. How had he allowed himself to get so emotionally involved? He needed a vacation from the FANGS.

Maggie struggled over the latest letter she had received from the undocumented woman in San Diego. Many groups in California helped immigrants. Asylum groups and sanctuary groups were all over the state. Sending the distressed woman a list seemed heartless.

She decided to publish the letter and see what responses it brought.

The next week, MISS CHLOE's mailbox overflowed with replies to *Anxious Mother,* as it did the following week and the one after that. Overwhelmed with the kindness of strangers, Maggie sifted through every response and made three piles: One for racist, hateful comments, one for kind words and one for practical ideas.

She was delighted that the third pile was the largest. It was important to keep reminding herself that many people were big-hearted and loving. She shoved the disparaging letters in her trashcan where they belonged, then read the" kind" pile and pulled out several which she would publish for her general readers. The practical letters she stacked on her desk, preparing to list one and all suggestions. She wanted to start a master list of organizations that specialized in helping immigrants. Her immediate search was for medical assistance.

While California had many programs, she discovered no government programs provided medical care for undocumented children and adults in Arizona, although hundreds of programs and individual volunteer groups offered aid. She began to search through information on the internet and realized it would take hours to create a comprehensive list. For now, she closed her computer. She had to give more thought to the safety of *Anxious Mother* and her child.

She needed to work on two briefs before she called it a night. Lisa and Jesús were expected home that evening from their honeymoon in Philadelphia. They'd wanted to visit the Art Museum and the "Cradle of Democracy."

Jesús said Philly was a must for immigrants and artists.

Estelle planned a welcome home dinner. Sophie asked to decorate the dining room with fresh-cut holly and red bows.

Christmas was approaching. In a couple of days, Estelle would round up a team to drive to the tree farm, choose a perfect tree, saw it down, tie it on top of the Honda and bring it home to decorate.

CHAPTER 38

"WE GO TONIGHT," Jimmy Laker said. The vicious glint in his opaque eyes seemed more prominent with his shaved head exposed. He had removed his cap and was sitting at the gang's usual table in Mattie's bar with Zig Tipton, Joe Santorini, and Terry White. Chris Watters sat quietly between Laker and Joe, watching and listening. Heavy smoke filled the room and an eerie glow emanated from the strings of Christmas lights Mattie had hung around the windows. A straggly Charlie Brown-like tree had been set up in the corner where Rita Goodwin enjoyed her usual afternoon stinger.

"We're gonna hit the High Desert Mall first. I got the Juniper Hills events schedule." Laker waved a bright green piece of paper covered with Christmas doodles. "Next week we'll do the town square and the week after the big parade with fuckin' old Santa. There'll be lots of Latino kiddies running around to hassle. It's time we take a hostage."

"What the fuck. Why?" Joe protested.

"Fear, dumb shit." Jimmy got up and punched Joe hard on each side of his head. "That's what will make them all go back home."

Chris cringed.

"What we gonna do with a kid?" Joe growled, rubbing the sides of his head. "I work on the damn planes at Sky Harbor Airport seven days a week."

"You begged for that overtime." Zig teased.

"Shut up." Joe pointed his gun finger at Zig.

"I could keep it at the garage," Terry said. "There's a room in the back with a bed and toilet."

"Bad idea," Chris said. "Someone's gotta take care of the kid or we won't have a live one to bargain with."

"We don't need any fuckin' ransom money. We want to get the spics to leave town," Zig said. "That's the deal."

"We could take it out to the goddamn ranch and have Shelly care for it. No one would look there. Fuck, we won't even tell my ma and pa. Shelly can say she's helpin' out a fuckin' friend." Jimmy lifted his head proudly.

"How you gonna keep the kid quiet?" Distress was building in Chris' stomach.

"Good old chloroform," Laker said. "Every time the kid gets out of hand, we send it into sleepy land. After a few days we'll only have to threaten a treatment to keep it fuckin' quiet."

"You could kill a kid with that." Chris felt his brain about to explode.

"Nah. We'll just use a freakin' drop."

"Shit happens, man." Desperation clutched at Chris' heart. What if the child died or suffered brain damage? He had to get to his cell and alert Dan. He was disgusted by how they kept referring to a child as *it*. "When do you wanna leave?"

"Ten minutes," Laker said. "That'll get us there by six." He walked over to Mattie.

Chris leaned into Zig and whispered, "I need my Glock. Ain't goin' nowhere without my gun." Chris felt like a character in a Western cartoon.

"Shhh. Don't let Jimmy hear," Zig hissed. "I've got one too. You know he says no guns. We're men. We use our fists and swords and knives. We're willing to kill for the white race. We don't want to stir up no anti-gun protesters. The guys paying us made that clear."

Laker came back to the table and told Chris. "Go with Zig. Get four cans of gasoline. Just in case. I can't believe we forgot them last time. You fuckin' idiots would lose your dicks without me. Joe, you come with me. Terry, get your gang together." He punched Terry in the stomach as he got up to leave. Terry rubbed his gut and ignored Laker, who turned back to the table and said, "Terry has two cars loaded with our guys at his garage ready to take off with us. We meet at the northeast end of the mall and walk. The kiddie choir is at six. Wear black."

Chris and Zig got into his Wrangler. "Stop at my place and I'll run up and get my gun and black jacket." Chris asked, "Laker always give such short notice?"

"Yeah. He's afraid of word getting out. Can I use your john? Gotta piss."

"Sure," Chris said, his mind searching wildly as to how he'd get his gun and cell to contact Dan with Zig in his room. They parked and walked up the inside staircase. Chris had always been careful to prepare for an unexpected visitor; nevertheless, he prayed that he'd left his room in thug-man order.

Alice Edmonson greeted them with a smile. Chris wished he had engaged his landlady more, so she could get a coded message to Dan.

In Chris' room, Zig went straight to the bathroom and Chris quickly pulled down his duffle from its resting place on a wall-shelf. He slid out his Glock, ankle holster and a small ammo pouch. He unlocked the secret compartment and pulled out his cell, leaving the fake ID and his service pistol, hoping an opportunity would present itself for contacting Dan.

He picked up his black leather jacket, locked the duffle compartment and left the key on the dresser where anyone nosey enough to snoop would find it. He stuffed the ammo pouch in one pocket, his cell in the other and zipped his pockets shut. When Zig came out of the bathroom, they were off.

CHAPTER 39

ESTELLE, ROSA AND CATHY huddled around the kitchen table, discussing the list of coming events in the local *Gazette* for the Christmas season. Jesús and Sophie emptied the dishwasher with zest and noise. Natalie was working a new job in a jewelry shop and Maggie and Lisa were at their storefront office.

"There're so many. How do we decide?" Chris' wife, Cathy, kept turning newspaper pages and pointing to one event after another. "Jesús, you and I should take a booth at the town square and display our art work."

"Might be fun," Jesús answered. "Our paintings would make good Christmas presents."

Sophie stopped drying soup bowls for a moment and did a little two-step of excitement. "Tonight, we have the 'Chorale at the Mall.' My class will be performing 'Hark the Herald Angels Sing.' Some of us will wear wings."

Estelle stood and went back to mixing a huge bowl of cookie dough. "We wouldn't miss that in the event of an earthquake."

Everyone laughed.

"Great." Sophie didn't get why everyone was laughing.

At four o'clock, Estelle wrapped the cookie dough in a wet cloth and put it in the fridge. "Tomorrow we cut our Christmas cookies."

"I can't wait," Sophie said, dancing across the kitchen floor, swinging a dish towel over her head.

Sophie and Rosa packed up to go home to their new apartment and get ready for the music festival. "See you in two hours," Sophie called as she closed the back door. "Don't be late."

Chris and Zig headed north to Juniper Hills in the new Wrangler.

"What goin' on with Laker?" Chris asked, hoping he didn't sound like a cop.

"Whatta you mean?" Zig kept his eyes on the road.

"Talk about his childhood. He can't be so violent for no reason."

"Who wants to know?"

"What's his old man like?"

"He's a brutal son of a bitch. Is that a surprise?" Zig's voice was tight with anger.

"Just wondering." Chris got the feeling Laker had knocked Zig around a few times.

"Keep your goddamn wondering to yourself. Jimmy don't like us to go there. He had a baby brother, Gabby. The kid was four when he got shot in the head. Killed. A stupid accident. That's why Jimmy says no guns."

"Oh, my God! How'd he get shot?" As soon as the question let his mouth Chris knew he had crossed a line with Zig.

"Pretty nosey today." Zig turned his head for a second and searched Chris' face.

"Sorry, sounds horrible. Thanks for the warning." Chris couldn't help but feel a genuine sorrow for the psychologically damaged leader of the gang who most likely carelessly shot his baby brother.

"His pop slapped those kids around with a horse whip until Jimmy was bigger than him. He still whacks Shelly if she gets out of line."

"What about their mother?"

"Lots of swollen, black and blue eyes." Zig grunted

"That explains a lot," Chris said.

"Keep your distance."

"I intend to." They sat in silence for the rest of the trip north, while Chris noticed the sky darkening to bruise-like colors. He couldn't think of a way to use his cell to alert Dan.

Twenty minutes outside of Juniper Hills, Chris said, "I need a cup of Joe and a leak."

"Can't you wait until we get to the mall?"

"We'll be busy there."

"Okay. Okay. I guess you're right. There's a Denny's up the road."

Chris let out an audible sigh.

"Is it that fuckin' bad? Didn't you go before we left?"

"You were in my bathroom."

"Oh. Yeah." Zig pulled into Denny's parking lot.

Chris hopped out. "Hey, get us coffees and I'll meet you at the front door." When he entered the men's room, a blond-haired guy, about his age, with a goatee was standing at a urinal. Chris wondered if he could be with one of Terry's groups. He'd noticed two large SUVs full of guys in the parking lot. He hesitated to phone Dan. The stranger seemed to be taking forever to wash his hands and comb his hair. Chris decided the best he could do was pee and text fast.

"Urgent. High Desert Mall at 6 o'clock. Big riot to hurt Latinos. Maybe take hostage. Meeting at northeast end."

Clicking off his phone, Chris muttered, "Women. Heaven help me."

The blond-haired guy chuckled.

Chris tucked his cell in his pocket, zipped up, smiled at the loitering man and left the bathroom. He knew he hadn't given Dan much notice, but that was the best he could do. Dan said he was preparing a group of twenty for a new attack. He hoped Dan was on it.

Zig was already in the Jeep with a coffee in hand and Chris' in the cup holder. "I brought some extra sugar. There's one of Terry's two fuckin' gangs." He pointed to a black Silverado filled with six men.

Chris took a gulp of coffee and a deep breath, thankful that he hadn't revealed himself to the stranger in the men's room. His phone was encrypted with a special app that erased a call or text as soon as he sent it, but he'd never had the opportunity to see if it worked.

Rosa shivered and pulled up her collar. Sophie, with twelve members of her singing class, stood in the cold winter air on a grassy knoll at the High Desert Mall, near a decorated Christmas tree. As the sky darkened, the neon lights blurred silver. Sophie wore a bright red ski jacket and white leggings tucked into white sneakers under a white gauzy gown with two wings strapped to her shoulders.

Their music teacher had stepped in front of the group with her arms raised to get the girls attention when chaos erupted at the far northeast end of the mall. Sophie saw a large black-clad man lunge at a smaller dark man and grab his throat. Two other men tried to trip the smaller man and the four fell in a heap in the walkway. She saw other men, also in black, swinging punches at anyone who came near.

The girls in Sophie's singing group ran in different directions. Sophie stood rooted to the ground, transfixed by the chaos in front of her. Estelle and Rosa ran toward Sophie. A thick-set man gripping a long-curved knife in one hand wrapped his other arm around Sophie's torso, crushing her wings. He picked her up like a sack of fertilizer. Sophie was too stunned to scream. Estelle and Rosa ran after him. "Put her down!" Rosa yelled, "Put her down! Now!"

The man continued to run. People scattered in every direction. Someone tripped Estelle. She went down, tearing holes in the knees of her stockings. Rosa fell on top of her. They tangled together for moments. When back on their feet, they looked around but couldn't see the man who'd carried off Sophie.

Maggie and Lisa, who had arrived from work in their business suits and heels, ran over to them. "Where's Sophie?" Maggie asked.

"What happened?" Lisa screamed as she searched the bedlam unfolding before her eyes.

"A big, ugly guy grabbed Sophie and ran off." Rosa was hysterical. Her sobs were so deep she could barely get out words. "He put a cloth over her face!"

Uniformed police with whistles and clubs arrived. Dan called the group to a circle. "There are too many innocent bystanders to make a move on the gang. We don't want to hurt anyone. Use the bullhorn and command everyone to return to their cars immediately. There are four cars parked at the northeast end. I think they belong to the FANGS. Let's head that way."

Maggie ran up to Dan. "They took Sophie."

"What?"

"Rosa said a large man ran off with Sophie. Estelle said his cap fell off. He had a shaved head and a snake tattoo on his left arm. Mom got that much of an ID."

"They've blended in so well with the holiday crowd, I can't tell the gang from the shoppers." Dan cursed himself. He hadn't finished teaching his special forces the principles of crowd control in a disaster. "I ordered my guys to head down to the northeast end of the mall and see if we can stop them before they escape.

I'll watch for Sophie. Go home. It's not safe here." He ran off.

As Dan headed to the northeast end of the mall, he saw bodies on the ground, bloodied and injured. He tugged out his cell as he ran and called for emergency medical help. "More injured over here," he shouted into his phone.

Three parked cars were already tearing out of their parking spaces in the almost empty northeast area. Some officers fired at the tires. The fourth was a Jeep Wrangler. Dan saw Chris duck down in the passenger seat and ordered his men to hold their fire. "Did anyone get the plates?"

"No," Whitey Smith, his chief lieutenant, said, "but those eyes up there did." He pointed to the security cameras on the walls of the buildings.

"What about the little girl?"

His officers looked at him blankly.

"They abducted Sophie Melendez. Didn't anyone see her?"

Officer Tim Haggerty said, "Oh, my God. I saw a man running with a child in his arms. She had on a white angel costume. I thought he was trying to get her to safety. People were running every which way."

Damn. Damn. Damn. We're bumbling baboons, Dan thought, standing in the vacant parking lot.

CHAPTER 40

ROSA SAT on the sofa in Estelle's den sobbing uncontrollable gulps. Lisa, trying to contain her own trembling, held Rosa's right hand. Cathy, sitting on the other side of Rosa stroked her left arm. Jesús paced the room. Maggie was on the phone with Dan who was calling on his iPhone. Estelle, releasing anxiety and frustration, rattled pots in the kitchen. Carlos had driven his friend Armando, injured in a scuffle at the mall, to the hospital, not knowing that Sophie had been taken.

"How will I tell Carlos I allowed Sophie out of my sight?" Rosa groaned in her agony.

"We were all there, honey," Cathy said, hugging Rosa tighter. "It was pandemonium. Don't blame yourself. Sophie was surrounded by a circle of people who love her. I don't know how we could have prevented that Snake or Fang—or whatever the hell he calls himself—from grabbing up Sophie."

"Why did I let her go to the mall? When we find her, I'm going back to that town in Colorado where Carlos grew up. I hate it here."

Maggie, doing a poor job of controlling her own terror, came in from her office, her blue eyes intense. "Rosa! Stop. There is nothing you could have done to protect Sophie today. This is a planned effort to frighten us, to frighten our whole community. We have to keep our heads and figure out what to do next." Maggie's heartbeat was pounding in her ears.

She closed her cell and stood in the middle of the room, attempting to take control. "Listen to me." Her voice trembled. "Dan says the security cameras captured pictures of gang members, plus all four cars and license plates. He and twenty officers with special training are right now on their way to Leonardo with the car owners' addresses before they have a chance to ditch the plates. Sophie is in one of those cars. Dan intends to bring her home." Maggie was hesitant to mention Chris because she wasn't sure who knew what his relation to the gang was or how undercover he was. "Sophie is in safe hands. Please believe me." Maggie wasn't sure she believed herself.

Chris stayed quiet on the ride with Zig back to Leonardo. He knew Sophie was in the backseat of Jimmy Laker's limo, in the fog of dreams. He didn't want her to wake up and be terrified. How long would she be out from the chloroform? He hoped he could somehow get to her before she recovered consciousness. Did Laker have a soft spot in his heart for kids after what happened to his baby brother? Was Laker the one who accidentally shot his little brother, Gabby? Would he be gentle with Sophie?

"We put the fuckin' fear of God in that town tonight." Zig stepped on the gas and smiled.

"What makes you think so?"

"Latinos are superstitious bastards. We're the FANGS. It's goddamn Christmas. They'll mix it all up and feel guilty. God is fuckin' punishing them. They'll rush back to their homes over the border."

Who was influencing this group? Chris shifted in his seat. His left leg had gone numb. It hardly made sense to him. America had always been a land of immigrants. Each new wave enriched the culture. Many Latinos had lived in the U.S. for decades, not knowing any other home. He'd learned that in grammar school and still believed it. All he could think of was getting to Sophie.

The plan was to meet at Terry White's garage. When Chris and Zig pulled up in the Jeep, Jimmy was already washing down his limo. After changing his license plate, Zig whipped out a screwdriver, removed the false plate and affixed his legal plate in seconds. Two other cars had already been hidden in one of Terry's garage bays.

"The guys will give those cars a fast paint-over tomorrow and put the legal plates back on," Zig told Chris. "By late afternoon there'll be no evidence that they were ever in Juniper Hills."

"Where'd they get those plates?" Chris was astounded by the activities of these guys. They acted like an army squadron with strategic plans.

"Take a fucking guess," Zig said and gave him a silly smirk and a flash of his cleverness.

"All stolen? That's a huge project."

"We have kids working on it all year round. As soon as we get back, we slip on legal plates and nobody can prove we ever left Leonardo. We have a metal shop guy who melts down the stolen plates. No evidence." Zig grinned a nasty smile.

"I'm impressed." Chris walked over to Jimmy's limo and attempted to look through the dark window. "Where's the little taco?" he asked Laker.

"She's still in there zonked out." Jimmy wiped grease off his hands on the bottom of his tee.

"What are your plans for her?" Chris asked.

"Not sure."

Chris racked his brain. He had to come up with an idea that would appeal to Laker. And he had to do it fast. "Can I ask you something? You know I've got a gal in Kansas. She wants kids in a bad way but can't have them. Raped and messed up pretty bad by her asshole old man. If you don't want that kid for ransom, can I buy her from you? Zoe has plenty of cash. She'd probably pay up to $50,000."

"You gotta be shittin' me?"

"I ain't. Think about it. You wanna terrify Latinos? You make their kids disappear. They'll head back across the border by the droves." Chris had no idea if his ruse would work, but he had to get Sophie out of there. This was the best he could do at the moment.

"I can't decide if you're a genius or don't know your head from your ass," Laker said. "Disappear the kids? Humm."

CHAPTER 41

CHRIS THANKED his guardian angels that Laker didn't decide to punch him in the head. He could not have restrained himself from delivering a rapid karate chop. His anxiety was building. While he paced around the garage, a plan began to form. He had to find a way to let Dan and Rosa know Sophie was safe. Revealing his cellphone would be dangerous but a risk he'd take.

Then he'd wake Sophie and talk to her in secret. He assumed that everything he did and said was somehow being recorded by the paranoid Laker. He thought if he slipped in his Guy Noir fake name and they checked his police record, they might trust him more.

Dan was on his way to Leonardo. Three undercover cars followed at a distance, trailed by a police van. With the license plate numbers from the security cameras at the mall, he'd managed to get the four owners' names and addresses. Each unit was to go to a different address and arrest all the people in the house at the exact same time. That way Dan hoped to pick up the whole gang at once, counting on Chris to protect Sophie. He blew out a series of short breaths to gain control as he stopped in front of his assigned house.

When all four squads were in place at the proper addresses, Dan gave the signal to attack the houses. He and three officers surrounded their designated house. Dan went to the front door. The house was dark except for a small nightlight in the hallway he saw as he looked in the window. It was past midnight. Most likely all were asleep. He banged on the door. No answer. He banged again. As he was about to kick in the door, an ancient, bent-over man appeared in the doorway. "Is something wrong?"

"Police." Dan displayed his badge. "Who lives here?" He was not feeling polite.

"Just me," the man said as he smoothed his rumpled blue-striped pajamas. The silver whiskers on his chin poked off in a hundred different directions.

"We need to look around your house and at your car."

"It's in the carport."

Dan directed two men to search the house and took Whitey with him around to the carport. A fifteen-year-old Dodge truck sat under a tarp. Dan felt the hood. It was as cold as a frozen pizza.

"When's the last time you drove this buggy?" he called to the figure now on the porch.

The old man wiped sleep from his eyes. "Last week. I went to town for groceries."

Whitey nudged Dan's arm and turned to the old man. "Where's your license plate?"

"Didn't know it was missing."

A queasy feeling invaded Dan's gut. He went back to his car and flipped on the scanner. Speaking to the three other unmarked cop cars, he said, "Anybody find anything?"

"No," came back three times. "One of these cars is up on blocks."

"Nobody home here. House looks like it's been boarded up for months," came the second report.

"Young couple with a new baby. Not happy we woke up their child after they just got her to sleep." The third report was conclusive.

"Stand down, men. We've been bamboozled. The plates are all false. God damn! These guys are smarter than I thought. Go home," he said to the three other cars. "Take the police wagon with you. I'm gonna look around for a while." Before he left, Dan went back and apologized to the old gent who still stood in the doorway.

"Most excitement I've had in years. Good luck in your search." The old man squinted into the pitch-black yard as if seeking answers for his night visitors.

Dan walked to his car and spoke to Whitey and the two cops in the back seat. "Keep your eyes open for anything that looks suspicious." They rode through the mostly deserted town. There was a garage and gas station on the corner where a couple of men were gathered. Dan remembered Chris talking about Terry White working at a station. He thought he saw Chris in the group but wasn't sure. Dan didn't want to arouse suspicions even though he was in an unmarked car.

He had no probable cause to question the group and didn't want to blow Chris' cover. He headed home. The FANGS had thrown dust in his eyes once again. He would be holding his breath until he heard from Chris.

That night back in Leonardo at the gas station, Jimmy called a meeting at Mattie's for the next day at two o'clock in the afternoon.

"I'm exhausted," Joe whined. "I need some shut-eye."

"Go home. Don't be late tomorrow. We need to regroup and make some decisions."

"What about the kid?"

"I can put it in the back room at the station," Terry said.

"I'll stay near her and the car," Chris said. "When she wakes, I'll tell her we'll take her home. We don't want to scare her." He looked to Jimmy for a sign of confirmation. Nothing. Had he dismissed their talk about disappearing the children? Forgotten it? Decided against it? Chris felt chills creeping along his neck and back. This was not good.

"Okay." Laker brushed sweat off his forehead with a red and black bandanna he then stuffed in his back pocket. It had been a tough evening. "That's our plan until tomorrow. Get outta here now."

Terry locked up the garage. The men got in their individual cars and pulled out. The silence was a gift. Chris sat on an old plastic chair in the dark, thinking about his next move. He thought he had come up with a perfect way to rescue Sophie, but now he wasn't sure he had convinced Jimmy.

He knew Laker's car was bugged. So, he couldn't talk to Sophie in there. When she came to, he would have to get her out of the car. He wasn't sure he could talk to Dan in Terry's garage either. Knowing Jimmy's paranoia, he assumed the entire area would be under electronic surveillance.

He would have to reveal his cell, but once he hung up the message would erase itself. He thought perhaps the gang could hear his side of a conversation, but he wasn't sure if they had the hi-tech equipment to listen to the other side. He didn't want to underestimate them again. He tried to calm himself. What the hell was the name he and Maggie and Dan choose for his fake ID, the name the gang would check and find his fake record of felonies and arrests?

Rattled, all he could think of was Garrison Keillor. Maggie was supposed to be his girlfriend, Zoe, who lived in an apartment in Topeka, Kansas. Lucky for them, Chris' sister was in Paris at an art school and she had allowed them to use her home address for the year. Finally, Guy Noir, private eye, came to him like a bolt from Zeus. He became Guy Black, like Superman emerging from a phone booth. With his new identity in place, he moved into action.

It was safer to call Maggie rather than Dan. He knew it was late, or rather very early in the morning, and hoped she'd catch on right away. She was a smart lady. He entered her number. It rang a few times and a sleepy voice finally answered.

"Zoe? Hey, honey it's Guy."

There was a pause and Chris could imagine Maggie clearing the cobwebs from her brain. "Guy. Guy Black. Don't honey me. Where the hell are you? Why are you calling me at four in the morning?"

Chris's heart stopped hammering in his ribcage. He knew Maggie was with him and aware he couldn't talk. "I've got a surprise for you. Maybe. A child. Not a baby, but she's little. I'm not good with ages. Cute as one of those dolls you like."

"A Cabbage Patch?"

"Yeah."

"How much will this cost?"

"Don't matter. It's what you want, right?"

He could tell Maggie was trying to sound like a thug's girlfriend. "Oh, Guy. When? When the fuck will you be here?"

"There's a small prob. I don't exactly have her right now, but I'm hoping for tomorrow. Maybe three days."

"You ain't gonna disappoint me again."

"Honey, I promise. I'll be there. Maybe I can get Zig to drive me. He has a new Jeep."

When they hung up, Maggie took out a yellow legal pad and recreated their conversation. She didn't want to miss any clues. There might be words that Dan would understand that she didn't. Although she wanted to call Dan, she read for a while, showered, dressed and made coffee. She'd wait until six. She knew Dan's trip to Leonardo had been disappointing and exhausting. It was still early.

CHAPTER 42

MAGGIE COULD NOT WAIT another minute. At exactly five-thirty a.m. after consuming three cups of coffee, she rushed over to Dan's. She needed a face to face with him NOW, without ten thousand interruptions. She expected to find him in pajamas but when she rang his bell, he answered decked out in a charcoal fine-wool suit with a mélange dot wine-colored silk tie and highly shined black leather shoes.

"Wow. You look fabulous."

A blush crept over his cheeks. He chuckled. "Come in and sit for a minute."

She settled in the living room on the long plush sofa piled with a variety of pillows, picked up a satin cushion and hugged it to her chest.

Dan sat beside her. "I'm on my way to Phoenix," he said. "I have an appointment with our new state representative and the governor's right-hand man. Something strange, maybe illegal, is going on in our police department that needs immediate joint attention. Whitey thinks the mayor's involved and I'm sure Chief Strunk is into something that doesn't smell right. We've each heard bits of conversation. We believe the group known as the FANGS has been hired to scare our Latinos out of town. The authorities think drugs are involved, but...."

"It's hard to believe." Maggie stroked Dan's arm.

"Believe it! I won't go into it now, but we've been gathering evidence."

"Before you take off, let me tell you I had a very interesting call at four this morning from our Guy Noir, or rather Guy Black."

"Chris?"

Maggie nodded. "I wrote down our conversation. It was obvious he couldn't speak openly. He's with Sophie. They're taking her to Kansas to his girlfriend's apartment. He said if things go well, they'd be there in three days. We'd better set up our rendezvous right away. He may have Zig and Terry with him. He's thinking 'divide and conquer.' If you take down Zig and Terry in Kansas, that leaves Laker and Joe in the south."

"Good idea." Dan rubbed his neck. "I'm concerned about Rosa. She's probably beside herself with grief and anger, falling apart. Have you told her that Sophie is safe with Chris?"

"I'm worried sick about Sophie. Rosa's devastated. I want to reassure her, but I don't know how much I can say without endangering Chris."

"Hold off for another day. We can't have leaks." He stood and looked down at her. "I've got to leave, Hon. Let's talk tonight over dinner." They hugged and kissed and walked out of his house hand in hand, separating at her car.

It had been a balmy desert night. Brilliant silver winter moonlight illuminated the entire area. At four a.m., Chris paced around the garage property, every so often peeking in the window of Laker's limo to check if Sophie was stirring. They'd sedated her with chloroform. They'd told him it was not much. But still? She was so young and vulnerable. He had to be careful he didn't show too much concern for Sophie. That would surely give away his cover. Someone had draped her with a soft blanket. Her red snow jacket peeked over the top of the blanket. Her skinny legs in white leggings stuck out the bottom. No sign of her angel costume or the crushed wings. The guys must have thrown them in a dumpster along the highway on the way back to Leonardo.

Seeing movement, Chris opened the back door and put his cheek next to Sophie's face. She opened her eyes carefully, as if afraid of what she might see. Chris laid his finger on her lips and then on his own. She got the message. Sophie looked into his eyes, yawned, nodded and whispered "Mama."

"She's safe, honey," Chris whispered back, then raised his voice. "So, you have to pee, do you?" He spoke in a loud voice to let her know it was okay to speak as if they didn't know each other. He gently picked her up in his arms with his finger still on her lips. "The garage is closed. We'll have to use the bushes." He carried her as far as he could into the trees and bushes behind the garage.

"Are you scared?" he whispered, setting her on the ground when he thought they were far enough from possible recording devices.

"Yes and no," she answered in an attempt at an adult voice. "I'm madder than anything else. I was in my angel costume. Where are my wings?"

"Sorry, I don't know. How do you feel?"

"I'm worried about Mama. She must be scared for me. Does she know you're with me?"

"Dan will tell her."

"Good. ... I've seen mean things, Chris. They don't scare me. They make me angry. My friend Gigi was sent back to somewhere she never lived. ICE said they were sending her home, but her real home was across the street from my house."

"I'm sorry to hear that." Chris smoothed Sophie's shoulder and arms where her jacket was wrinkled from sleeping. "Okay," he whispered. "I'm going to say things that don't make sense. Can you play along?"

"Oh, yes," Sophie whispered back to him, still groggy and yawning. "I'm not supposed to know you. Mom told me. But first, I do have to pee." She slipped down her white leggings and panties and squatted over the ground. She pulled a tissue from her pocket, wiped herself and buried it in the leaves.

Chris looked away, to give her privacy and scanned the area.

"I may sound harsh, but don't be scared. We're going to take you to Maggie who we are calling Zoe and Maggie will fly you home to your Mama and Papa. These men will listen to everything we say from now on."

Sophie put her hand over her mouth and her eyes lit up as if she was laughing. "Fly!" she whispered.

Chris thought, OMG. She's enjoying this.

At two o'clock that afternoon, Laker met with Joe, Terry and Zig at their usual table in Mattie's. Rita Goodwin occupied her corner table, sipping her afternoon stinger in a tall crystal glass. No one gave a thought to her presence.

"Terry has something you need to hear," Jimmy said.

Terry removed a portable instrument of some kind from his pocket and hit the play button. It was the recording of Chris's conversation with Maggie.

"Our new boy made this call from the garage last night. First let me say that he asked if he could give that kid we snatched last night to his girlfriend."

"Whoa!" said Joe. "Who the fuck does he think he is?"

Terry took a pull from his beer bottle. "We can get ransom for her."

"I told youse no ransom," Jimmy said. "These people got no fuckin' money. We don't need it anyway. We're getting paid plenty! Besides, Chris' squeeze is willing to pay a lot for a kid. Now listen and I'll tell you what he said to me."

They settled down and Terry played Chris and Maggie's conversation. Both voices were as clear as a high-tech recording.

"Who's Guy Black?" Joe asked Laker.

"That's Chris, you dumb shit. I had our friend in the PD check him out. You wouldn't believe his rap sheet.

What a bad ass. He's only been out of the bucket six or seven months."

"Impressive." Zig smiled. "I thought he was our kinda guy from the beginning."

Jimmy tapped his beer bottle with a spoon. "This is what Chris told me: Make Latino babies and kids disappear. That would put the fear of God Almighty in them. We go sneak their kids away without a trace. Dump them down in Mexico or Central America. Latinos believe in crazy stuff, like voodoo. Witches carrying away their children." He finished on a triumphal tone.

"Sounds like trouble to me." Zig got up for another beer.

"No more than what we're doing," Terry said. "Where's our boy now?"

"Sitting in my car with the kid. They're playing games. Name a dumb animal that begins with C kinda stuff."

Jimmy turned his head from side to side attempting to ease a crick in his neck, surprised that a man would play, let alone talk with a kid. "They don't say very much. Chris told her we'd be taking her home. It worked to keep her quiet. He likes kids."

"His girlfriend seemed crazy to have him bring her one," Terry added.

"What if the kid don't like Chris's lady? Who's gonna silence it when she wants her mommy?" Zig took another swig of his beer.

"We'll deal with that when and if we have to," said Laker. "Meanwhile we make a cool $50,000. He might have a great idea. I'm giving him the kid. I want Zig and Terry to go with Chris and check out this Zoe and her fuckin' place in Topeka. Bring Chris back. You hear? I don't want him on the loose. He knows too much about us."

"What's the penalty for trafficking kids?" Terry asked.

Jimmy slammed him in the head with his beer bottle. "Shut the fuck up!"

CHAPTER 43

"I DON'T FEEL much like eating. I can hardly swallow this wine." Maggie raised her glass and took another tentative sip. She and Dan sat in their usual secluded booth at Rodney's Cafe. "I'm so worried about Sophie. Rosa is an emotional mess. I told her that you know Sophie is well cared for and will be back soon, but I don't think she believed me."

"I'm sorry Rosa and Carlos are suffering." Dan reached for her hand and began stroking it. "Be careful what you say. I can't jeopardize Chris' cover. There're ears everywhere. "Do you still want to go to Kansas as Chris' girlfriend?"

"Of course."

"How are you going to explain the trip?"

"How about I say you and I are eloping?" Maggie tilted her head and winked.

"Not funny. Not that I wouldn't be up to marrying you."

"I'm sorry. No more jokes."

"I can't stop obsessing while being responsible for the safety of so many people, Chris, Cathy, their unborn baby and now Sophie. Then there's the whole town of Juniper Hills ... Robbie and Miguel Castro, that young innocent boy dead.... Did I tell you Luis Gonzales and his family moved? They went to Colorado." Dan pause and sighed. "Apparently, they had relatives there who said they'd be safer. I'm sick about what's happening to our town. Used to be one of the safest places in the country!"

Maggie stretched across the table, took both Dan's hands in hers and brought them to her lips, kissing each finger slowly and lovingly. "I know."

"Here's Chris' sister's Kansas address and apartment key." I received them from Madeline by Fed Ex yesterday. He extracted one hand from Maggie's, pulled a small envelope from his shirt pocket and pushed it towards her. "You should fly out tomorrow morning, rent a car, get comfortable and be ready when the guys arrive with Sophie."

Dan sat back and searched Maggie's face. "You are some special gal. I have no idea how to thank you."

"No need. We all want to get our old town back to peace and quiet."

"Whitey and I and four of my special forces will be waiting to grab Chris, Zig and Terry when they arrive in Topeka. We'll bring Zig and Terry back here to Jupiter Hills. Somehow Chris'll slip through our net and turn up in Leonardo with a story." Dan continued, "You'll fly Sophie back home. Take her to Rosa and Carlos and tell them they must hide her for at least another week. Don't say a word about how you got her. Rosa shouldn't send her to school either. We kept Sophie's name out of the local papers, but I'm sure the story is out, at least in rumors."

They barely touched their dinners and skipped dessert. Dan drove Maggie home. They sat and talked and kissed for a while in Dan's car, enjoying the comfort of each other's warmth.

"I'll make my reservation tonight and leave early in the morning. I'll say I have a new client. I won't say where I'm going."

"Good. That way there's no obvious connection between you and Kansas." Dan got out of the car and came around to open Maggie's door.

"Be careful, Dan. I couldn't bear to lose you."

"Don't go emotional on me." He walked her to the door and kissed her like he'd never see her again. Maggie went up to her room and made a reservation from Phoenix to Topeka.

Chris left Sophie in Jimmy's car with the soft blanket and a snack bar to nibble until he returned. He wanted to get his backpack ready for the trip to Topeka. "I won't be long. Keep the doors locked."

As he walked along the street to Alice Edmondson's house, he realized it had been a foolish thing to say. Of course, Jimmy would have keys to his car. He hoped it would make Sophie feel safe to have the car doors locked. On the sidewalk in front of Alice's house, he met Rita Goodwin on her way home from Mattie's to feed her cat. "Hey, good lookin'," she said, "do you know your buddies are recording you?"

Chris stopped even though he was in a hurry to get back to Sophie. "What are you saying, Rita?"

"I heard those goons at Mattie's play a recording of you on the phone talkin' to your honey."

"I guess they're checkin' me out. Pretty nosey, if you ask me." He was elated his plan was working.

"They know you're using a fake name. Be careful. I'd hate for you to come back dead."

"Thanks, Rita, I appreciate your concern." He entered the house and climbed the stairs to his room. His heart thundered in his chest! His room had been searched. Chris had carefully placed several magazines and two of Alice's, what did she call them, tchotchkes, when he left. He could tell the china tiger had been relocated. He also knew the key he left on the table had been moved, his duffle searched, and the secret compartment discovered.

That was how they'd found his Guy Noir ID and hidden pistol. He still wore his ankle holster and Glock which he intended to keep close until this assignment was completed.

He was sure that he and Maggie had conducted their conversation from the parking lot of White's garage quite well the night Sophie was taken. Anyone listening in would be convinced. Perhaps Jimmy had decided to trust him and sent his goons to see what they could discover. This was a good sign. He was worth checking out. Sophie had been perfect. She'd played along like an actress in a Hollywood movie. Not missing a line. He knew she realized the danger that surrounded her while she acted as cool as a seasoned cop. Where does an eight-year old learn how to keep her cool, or was it a natural part of her personality?

Chris tested his phone. It was empty. No information or traces of calls he had made. The encryption was working. He stuffed briefs, socks and two clean shirts into his backpack. In a lower dresser drawer, he discovered a blank pad and a packet of colored pencils probably left by the previous renter. Perfect! He dropped them in his pack to keep Sophie busy on the trip. He stepped out into the hallway and walked down to the first floor. He knocked at Alice Edmonson's door and from doorway told her he'd be away for a few days visiting a friend in Detroit.

"Have a safe trip," Alice said. "I forgot to mention that Rita told me three of your men came here to visit while I was out. She saw them in the front parlor."

That's probably when they picked my room lock and got into my secret compartment, Chris thought. "Thanks, Alice, for keeping an eye out for me. You'd make a good detective."

Alice blushed. "Flattery will get you anything." She said goodbye and went into the kitchen.

CHAPTER 44

WHEN CHRIS RETURNED to the garage, Terry and Zig were sitting in the front seats of Joe's CRV waiting for him. "Get the fuckin' kid and let's go," Zig yelled.

Chris walked to Jimmy's limo and knocked on the window. Sophie opened the door. "Ready? We're going." He lifted her out and whispered, "Trust me, whatever happens."

Sophie voice trembled slightly, but she assured him, "I will."

They settled in the back seat and Chris said, "This is going to be a long ride." He placed his backpack on the floor under her feet. "Do you want to nap or draw? I have a pad and colored pencils in my pack."

"I'll sleep. The time will pass quicker," Sophie answered. Chris saw her steal a look at the two men in the front seats.

She didn't miss much. If she was ever asked to identify mug shots of Zig and Terry, he was sure she would have no doubts. She propped up the blanket next to the window, knowing they weren't taking her home. Chris could tell she decided to trust him. He hoped he lived up to her expectations.

An hour into the ride, Chris took a few deep breaths and allowed himself to relax.

"How does a tough guy like youse know so much about talking to kids?" Terry asked, turning in his seat to look at Chris. Sophie was snuggled against the blanket, her dark curls spread out on the window, already asleep, purring like a baby kitten through her slightly-opened mouth.

"My old lady was a crazy dipso," Chris said. "After my asshole father took off, most days she left me to take care of my two baby brothers. I guess it comes easy."

"Jeez. I'm glad I ain't had no brothers or sisters." Terry turned back and stared out the windshield. "My old man disappeared after I was born. My so-called mother dropped me with anyone she could talk into babysitting. I left home when I was sixteen. I know old mom died, but nobody ever told me when."

They rode silently into the darkening night as neon lights blazed here and there along the highway. They passed vast stands of ponderosa trees then flat, open desert plains. The terrain changed hourly. Just as Chris saw a sign for the New Mexico border, he heard sirens. Oh, no. Not now. Our plans! ... he thought.

"Are the cops after us? Should I try to out run them," Terry said and hit the gas pedal.

"No. No," Zig muttered, "Drive at a steady pace. It may be nothin'. A broken taillight."

Terry took a sharp turn at high speed unto the first off-ramp. Slowed down and took another right into a residential area of modest one-story houses with postage stamp manicured lawns. He made a few turns along winding treelined streets.

Aware the cops were following at a distance, Chris pulled at the Velcro to release his ankle holster and gun. Then pushed them under the front passenger seat as far as they would go. Sophie sat up and looked out the window. Chris reached for her hand, gave her an assuring nod.

Two squad cars continued to track them. As Terry drove into a cul-de-sac they pulled up alongside the CRV and motioned for him to move to the side of the road.

"Shit," Zig hissed. "What did we do?" One cop approached the car.

"Stay calm," Terry said. "Could be a routine stop. We have an Arizona plate."

"Step out of the car one at a time," the tall, dark, curly-haired officer said. "The little one first."

"Is that me?" Sophie asked.

"Yes," Chris answered. "Walk out slowly."

"Should I put up my hands?"

"If you want."

Sophie climbed over Chris and walked to the cop, who said, "You can put your hands down now. What's your name?"

"Sophie ... Sophie Melendez." She flung her arms around his legs.

"It's okay, little one. You're safe now. ... Yesterday's Amber Alert," he yelled back to the other officers. "We found her." Three cops appeared at his side.

"You guys come out one at a time. Put your hands on the car and spread 'em."

Terry pleaded with Zig. "What should we do?"

"Get out, you loser. What else can we do now? Dumb shit,"

The three men exited the car. The husky black cop patted down Terry and then Zig.

"Not him!" Sophie squealed as the cop put his hands-on Chris' shoulders. "He's my uncle. It's those two kidnapped me and him."

The cop stepped back. "Is that true, sir?"

Chris smiled and nodded, maintaining a calm demeanor. Sophie had given him an escape route.

Zig looked at Terry and mouthed, "What the fuck?"

"The report did say a child had been taken from a mall in Juniper Hills, Arizona by one man," the black cop said. "I think we better sort this out at the station."

"Leave your keys in the ignition," a large blond officer told Zig. "One of my men will drive the car to the station."

The cops handcuffed Zig and Terry and stuffed them in the back of one squad car and helped Sophie and Chris into the back of another.

Unbeknown to anyone, Rosa had become impatient and called in an Amber Alert even though Dan had asked her to wait. The New Mexico cops happened to see Sophie sleeping against the window and stopped the car because they were looking for children.

Once at the station, Zig and Terry were put in cells down the hall. Sophie and Chris were left sitting on a bench outside the sheriff's office. "Why did you say I was your uncle?" Chris asked Sophie.

"I didn't want them to hurt you."

"I'm pretending to be a bad guy. Zig and Terry can't think anything else. I have to slip out that side door over there. I need you to help me. Tell the police and make sure Zig and Terry hear that you lied because I was nice to you. Your Mom and Dad will come get you. Okay?" Chris gave her a fist bump.

"Okay." Sophie returned the bump and looked down the hall where Zig and Terry were locked in cells.

By the time Sophie turned her head, Chris had disappeared. The tall, curly-haired cop came down the hall. "Where's your uncle?"

Sophie started to cry as loud as she could. "HE'S GONE" she screamed. "HE'S NOT MY UNCLE. I ONLY SAID THAT BECAUSE HE WAS NICE TO ME." She let out a shriek that surely would reach the two cells down the hallway. "I DON'T EVEN KNOW HIS NAME."

Chris ran into the pitch-dark parking lot and pulled open the CRV door, glad the police hadn't had a chance to search or lock it. He felt around under the front seat, retrieved his ankle holster, strapped it on, picked up his backpack and hightailed it to the turnpike. He hoped at this hour a tired driver would want some company to keep him awake and stop for a lone hitchhiker.

While sprinting to the highway Chris called Dan and told him about the Amber Alert stop. "Zig and Terry are in custody and Sophie is in Gallup waiting to be picked up by her mom and dad. Call the sheriff of Gallup and tell him under no circumstances is he to release my two consorts in crime even if he has to make up a story. The safety of Juniper Hills is at stake. I'm on my way back to Leonardo."

Dan said, "It might be too dangerous. Laker will be suspicious."

"I don't think so," Chris said. "Sophie is giving me good cover. She's incredible, like a miniature special agent."

"I'm not even going to ask how that will work."

"Did you get a chance to check on Rita Goodwin's son?"

"I did. He was brought into the hospital by three friends after a party. They said he was drinking, horsing around and fell off a cliff into a bed of rocks. Nothing seemed suspicious. They were all sobbing and seemed genuinely distraught. The police reported his death as an accident."

"Contact Rita as soon as you can. She seems to have concrete evidence that her grandson's death wasn't an accident. She's at Mattie's every afternoon. Maggie has my landlady's number and Alice Edmonson is a good friend of Rita's. I believe Rita will testify against Laker for the killing of her grandson. I think Alice is willing to corroborate what Rita has to say."

"How will Laker react when he hears you're the only one who escaped?" Dan asked.

"We'll see."

Next, Chris called Laker, said they had gotten as far as Gallup and related the story about the Amber Alert stop. "The kid's mother called 911."

"How did these people get so fuckin' smart all of a sudden?" Jimmy asked.

"They have Zig and Terry in custody."

"How did you escape?"

"The kid said I was her uncle. Told me I was nice to her. She didn't want me to go to jail. As soon as the cops left us alone, I ran out the side door. I'm heading to the highway to hitch a ride. Do you need me back there or should I go on to Topeka and see Zoe? Is there anything you want me to do here?"

"Come back. I'll send Bert Miller up there and see if he can get Zig and Terry released on bail." Jimmy hung up.

Chris made one more call before he got to the side of the road and held out his thumb. "Cathy? Hi, sweetheart. How're you feeling?

"Me and the little one are thriving, Love. It's so good to hear your voice. We've miss it."

"I miss you two, too. We have this case almost closed. I'm hoping we can finish up in the next few months. I want to be there when our little papoose is born.

"We'll wait for you."

Chris hung up and laughed. Cathy had a special sense of humor. He looked at his watch. It was late. She never said a word about the time. From the side of the highway, he wondered what she was thinking. He had to keep reminding himself how difficult he had made her life with his new career as an undercover agent. He was so tempted to detour to Juniper Hills and spend some time with her that he scared himself. The one thing that kept him going south was the thought that if one of Jimmy's goons was in town and saw him, he would not only put Cathy in danger, but implode the whole scheme he and Dan and Alan had taken months to set up.

It took ten minutes before a car stopped. Chris was on his way back to Leonardo.

CHAPTER 45

DAN CALLED MAGGIE as she dressed for an early flight to Topeka. "Trip is off. Chris and the guys were stopped in Gallup, New Mexico," he said. "Rosa got impatient with me and called in an Amber Alert. The cops have Sophie. Rosa and Carlos are on their way to pick her up."

Dan offered to go with them, but they didn't want to wait. Sophie was safe. That was what mattered. Zig and Terry were in the slammer and Chris on his way back to Leonardo. Chris sounded concerned but confident he could handle Jimmy.

Maggie sat back on her bed. "How will he explain that he was the only one to escape?"

"He told me Sophie gave him good cover. I'm assuming they had a plan."

"Unbelievable."

It had been hours later when Chris finally arrived in Leonardo. The driver who picked him up along the highway had his name, Larry, stitched on the front pocket of his work shirt. Larry turned out to be good company. They both loved football and were rooting for Clemson to finish number one in the playoffs, so Chris never got to sleep. Larry dropped him off at a truck stop south of Tucson.

Chris called a cab and had the driver leave him in front of Alice Edmonson's house. He went straight to his room and collapsed on the bed.

At ten the following morning, he awoke to banging on his door. Chris shook cobwebs from his brain and realized he was still in his clothes from yesterday. His mouth tasted like sand. "Yeah, what's up? I just got to sleep."

"Jimmy wants to see you," Joe yelled through the door.

"Tell Laker I'll see him at noon for lunch at Mattie's."

"He ain't gonna like that."

"Tell him to hang himself."

Joe left, mumbling, "Don't think I'll do that."

Chris sat up in bed, now fully awake and sure he would not be able to go back to sleep. He pulled off his cruddy clothes and ankle holster, slipped on his terry robe and went down the hall to shower in the shared bathroom. There were two other renters on this second floor that he'd never laid eyes on. He'd assumed they worked different shifts.

As he returned from the bathroom, Chris heard the sound of a sewing machine from the room on his left. Although curious as to what that was about, he kept walking. In his room he pulled on a fresh striped polo shirt and clean jeans; he hesitated about the ankle holster. Did he need to protect himself all the time? He was almost convinced that Laker respected him, but did Laker trust him? Chris strapped on the holster.

At quarter to twelve, Chris walked into Mattie's, hoping to set himself up at their usual table before the other guys arrived. Unfortunately, Jimmy Laker and Joe were already there drinking coffee.

Chris sat down, nodded to Laker and Joe and motioned to Mattie. "Turkey on rye and a draft beer. I'm starving. ... Any word from Zig?" He looked first at Joe and then Jimmy.

"Fuckin' nice of you to ask," Jimmy said, and sipped from his coffee cup.

Chris tried to keep annoyance out of his voice. "What?"

"You should know."

"Listen. The kid gave me an out and I took it. "

"So, I heard from Zig."

"Should I have sat there until the cops discovered I wasn't her uncle? Would it be better if three were caught instead of two? My Zoe will probably never speak to me again. She was waitin' for a kid." Sometimes Chris felt like an ass when he played his role.

"Tough luck." Jimmy said. "Burt's up there today trying to get the boys released on bail. The cops told him they both have priors. Might take a while."

"What do you wanna do now?" Chris' sandwich arrived and he began to devour it as if it were his last supper.

Jimmy put his coffee cup down with a clank. "Listen to this. We have a contract, well, sort of an agreement, with these men in Juniper Hills to fuckin' terrify and rough up Latinos," he said. "They want them to stop moving in and not want to live there anymore."

"Somebody's paying you to do this?" Chris tried not to look disgusted. This was the info they needed to close the case!

"I liked your idea about making their beloved kiddies disappear." Jimmy rubbed his hands together and stretched his arms above his head. "I think we should work out a new plan."

"Like what?" Chris hoped he hadn't started something worse than what they had originally set up.

"Like what we're going to do with the goddamn kids after we snatch 'em?" Joe said. "It costs money to keep kids. How about we get somebody to open a fuckin' orphanage in Mexico and sell them or give them to people for free?"

Chris could not believe where the discussion was headed. His heart raced. He feared for the children of Juniper Hills. He had to deflect their plans for more kidnappings. "I've a better idea," he said, "Why don't we get someone to draw up a flyer. Have it say something like 'Your children and loved ones are in danger. GET OUT! A mysterious gang is coming for them. If you don't want to lose 'em, take them back to where you came from.' I think the threats, if we do them right, will work as well as kidnapping them. Save us a lot of trouble. We can have devils and witches and scary drawings on the flyer."

"Sounds fuckin' dumb. Who's gonna believe that shit?" Joe asked.

"You'd be surprised how superstitious people are." Chris had no idea where the idea came from. It sounded farfetched but he wanted Laker and Joe involved in a new scheme so that Dan and his special forces could capture them on the spot. It was like teaching a new project to a class of third-graders. Anything to keep these thugs from hurting people and getting the gang rounded up before they did more damage to Juniper Hills. He had to parse his words carefully in language they would relate to.

"I donno. Let me think on it," Laker said. "You really think the spics will flee for their lives? —My sister, Shelly, is pretty creative, she can draw up something scary."

"I still think we should snatch another fuckin' kid," Joe said.

In an effort to remove himself from the conversation, Chris asked, "What about Zig and Terry?" Chris sensed that Laker was ignoring his question. He finished his sandwich, wiped his mouth, stood and zipped his jacket.

Jimmy brightened. "Not much we can do 'til we hear from Burt. Let's finish the landscaping job south of here before the weather changes. I'll meet you at the site at 7:30 tomorrow morning, Guy Black." Jimmy stood.

Chris half turned and, out of habit, slid his hand along his pants leg toward his Glock. "Whatta ya mean by that?"

"Your jig is up. We know who you really are."

"So? I'd rather be called Chris Watters."

"No more secrets. We checked your record, Guy. You're not wanted by the police right now, but that could be easily arranged."

"Is that a threat?"

"Take it any way you like." Jimmy waved Chris toward the door.

"Don't be stupid, Laker. I probably know more about you than you know about me. If anything happens to me, Zoe will know and alert my friends."

"Maybe I should have two of my guys pay her a visit."

"Forget it. You won't find her. She moved." Chris felt his blood rise to his hairline. His fists tightened.

"Lookie here. The calm man has a hot temper. I like that." Jimmy leered through heavy lids and the scar on his cheek brightened to dark red.

"Don't mess with me, Laker. Remember I'm just passin' through."

"I thought you were staying for the money."

"Well, make it worth my time." Chris opened the door. "See you in the morning."

Still tired from the trip to Gallup, Chris headed back to his room. He wasn't surprised Jimmy had discovered his fake ID. Chris and Dan had planned that knowing Chris was a felon would give him prestige in the eyes of the gang.

He needed to call Dan and tell him about the flyers. Chris was antsy and ready for the charade to be over. Halfway up the staircase of his boarding house, he saw a figure lurking in the hallway and watched her hurry into the room across from his. "Hey," he called as he climbed the rest of the way, two steps at a time. He caught the edge of her door as she was about to slam it shut. "I thought I recognized you. What are you doing here, Shelly? No, don't tell me. Brother Jimmy planted you here to keep an eye on me. Right?"

Shelly sat at the sewing machine and hung her head, letting her long auburn hair cover her face. "Oh, shit.

Please don't tell Jimmy. He'll whack me. You're not supposed to know. I'm undercover. A spy."

"Is this a game?"

Shelly pulled back her hair and gathered the long tresses at the nape of her neck with both hands. Cleared of stringy strands it became obvious she had a very pretty face. "No. I'm to tell him when you come and go, if you have visitors, if I hear you on the phone."

"How's that goin' for you? Have you unearthed any dirt?"

"You're pretty dull, if you ask me." She smiled coyly and looked Chris over with dark eyes speckled with gold flecks. "Once I told him that you went out and Alice, our landlady, wasn't home. He sent Joe and Terry over to search your room. They know your real name is Guy Black. Personally, I like Chris better. That's the highlight of my spy career."

"How old are you, Shelly?"

"Seventeen, almost eighteen. I know I look young. Not young enough though. I'm pregnant. It's Zig's baby. I swear my asshole brother put him up to it to keep me at the ranch." Shelly sat back and drew her hands through her greasy hair. "I was thinking of leaving once I turned eighteen. I heard they can't make you stay home once you reach that age. Ziggy kept playing up to me, and one evening I gave in. I was such a fool."

"Oh, Shelly. There are places that will help you. You don't have to stay on the ranch. There's a Guidance Center over on Bisbee Street. They'll help you get prenatal care, a job and shelter or whatever else you need."

"Oh, the gang will take care of me or I'll scream rape."

"What about your parents?"

"They finally retired to Ecuador and turned the landscape business, ranch and everything else over to brother Jimmy. There's other stuff goin' on out there that I'm not supposed to know about. It's hard to ignore because there's a lot of comin' and goin'. I think my *'rents* are afraid of Jimmy. He makes all the decisions now as far as I know." She stood and wrapped her arms around Chris' neck. "Maybe you can help me."

Chris held her for a second too long, realizing how much he missed the feel of Cathy's body, the curve of their growing baby, more than he wanted to admit. He stepped back. "What are you making on the sewing machine?"

"Baby clothes. A collection called a layette. I have a book that tells me what I'll need. See here." She held up a tiny outfit in yellow. "This is called a onesie. It's yellow cause I don't know if I'm having a boy or a girl."

Chris wondered if Cathy had a layette. They were expecting a boy. He guessed the clothes would be blue. They had already decided to name the baby John Michael Watters after his father.

"Shelly, let's talk later. I don't want to keep you from your sewing."

CHAPTER 46

DAN SAT IN HIS OFFICE in disbelief. When Chris called and told him about the ominous flyers, he'd burst out in a raucous laugh. "You can't tell me anyone is going to take those things seriously."

"They will if more children are kidnapped. The flyer was the first idea that came to me. I thought it was ridiculous, but these goons are hellbent on getting the Latinos out of Juniper Hills, which in itself is an idiotic idea. Someone has offered them a lot of money to 'purify' your town."

"The very thought of those guys makes me feel ill."

"I'm sitting on a bench in the park. I can't talk to you from my room anymore. Laker has his sister stashed in the room across the hall. She says she playing spy."

"Be careful, Chris."

"I've suggested Laker use scare tactics before he goes after more kids. All we need is for his gang to drive up there in three or four cars with those flyers, park in a place known to us and we can arrest them."

Chris knew the flyers need never be distributed. Dan wanted the gang up there together. With Zig and Terry in custody, they would arrest Laker and Joe and charge the four with murder and arson. They may even have a case against them for the death of Rita Goodwin's grandson. The rest of the gang would fall off without their leaders."

"I'm not sure about this, Chris. It sounds crazy to me." Dan sat back in his chair and stared out his office window at his besieged town.

Chris could hear the tension in Dan's voice. "These guys will kill for the white race. Now they just want to clear the Latinos from Juniper Hills. They have some deal with a group up there to scare the Latinos into leaving. I heard Laker mention it. This may be our best way to round them up."

"I'm on to that. I just had a meeting with the authorities in Phoenix. Mayor Buchanan and Chief Strunk are the leaders of a group trying to do exactly that. But they don't have big bucks. We don't yet know who's financing the FANGS."

"You're kidding me."

"Several times I've heard snippets of conversation and at other times so has my deputy, Whitey. That's what triggered our concern. The State Senate Committee and the FBI are going to poke around quietly until they have solid information to move on. Drugs are being distributed. We don't know which came first, drug trafficking or Latino abuse. Meantime we're keeping the investigation close to our vests. I think the whole town council is involved."

"Scary stuff." Chris hung up and thought about the flyer he would ask Shelly to create.

It was Presidents' Week in February. Sophie was home safe and a hero among family and close friends for helping the police capture two gang members and allowing Chris to escape, though everyone was forbidden to talk about it except among themselves. They all knew Chris was still in grave danger.

Many schools were closed. Estelle invited Dan, Maggie, Lisa and Jesús and Chris' Cathy to a dinner party for Alan and his mother, Natalie, to celebrate an award Alan received at the Police Academy. He received the highest score ever achieved in their Criminal Investigation course.

Rosa, Carlos and Sophie insisted on helping prepare and serve the food, although they were supposed to be guests. Because of the Christmas kidnapping of Sophie no one had much of a holiday celebration. This was to be a special dinner. Estelle prepared a Greek leg of lamb, butterflied and seasoned with exotic spices for the grill, roasted root vegetables and a salad with feta cheese. Dessert was a chiffon cake with a lemon glaze that appeared light enough to fly.

It snowed the day before and the woods looked like a Robert Frost poem. Puffy snowflakes clung to tree branches and delicate icicles hung from eaves of houses. Since the Christmas kidnapping, the town had returned to quiet winter serenity. The surroundings felt soft and accepting of all people in Jupiter Hills.

Cathy and Lisa were due to give birth in June, Lisa the first of the month and Cathy near the end. They had been shopping together for baby boy stuff as both expected boys. Even though Cathy's due date was almost a month later than Lisa's, her baby bump was much larger. "Chris is a big man," she explained. "He was nine pounds, eight ounces at birth."

Alan was excited to be the object of much admiration. Sophie followed him around as if he were a rock star. "What's your favorite subject at the Academy?" she asked. "I might like to be a detective. Everyone says I see a lot."

"It's a little early to commit yourself to a career, sweetie," Alan said, tossing her a dish towel. "Maybe you should learn to cook first."

"How can you be so chauvinistic?" Sophie threw the towel back at him. "Women don't only belong in the kitchen anymore. They can do anything they want."

"Where did you learn that big word?"

"I heard Gloria Steinem say the word in an interview on *The News Hour*. It's her birthday. She's in her eighties now."

"I guess you're right."

"I know I'm right. When are you going to teach me to dance? You promised, you know." Sophie swirled in a circle holding out the dish towel.

"I did, didn't I? How about next Fourth of July at the pavilion in Hassayampa Park? They always have a great dance band."

"I'll be taller then."

"Okay. It's a date."

Dan slid a piece of the chiffon concoction into his mouth. When his cell rang, he put down his fork on the cake plate. He saw Maggie look his way and ask with her curious blue eyes if he had to take the call. He nodded and took his cell into the den.

Chris called from his newly found safe park bench in Leonardo. "Sorry to disturb your dinner, but Shelly has created a flyer that will put the fear of God in sensitive souls."

"No! Don't tell me they're going ahead with that cockamamie scheme."

"I'm afraid so," Chris answered. "But first I have to ask. Does the sheriff in Gallup understand he can't let Buchanan and Strunk know anything we discovered about the Leonardo gang?"

Dan's anxiety spiked. He wiped sweat from his forehead with the linen dinner napkin he still held in his hand. "I had a long conversation with him and explained it in several different ways."

Dan and Chris were deeply concerned that the death of Miguel Castro, the Painted Lady fire and the death of Robbie Perez be kept secret until the FANGS were under wraps.

"We don't want the gang to realize we know about the extent of their activities until the entire gang is disbanded," Dan said. "I'm afraid the leaders will take off."

Chris agreed. "That sheriff can't release Zig and Terry until we have Jimmy and Joe. We need to book the four into jail in Phoenix together. It's the only way to decommission this gang for good."

"I'll go over things with the New Mexico sheriff again. So, it looks as if the bogeymen are coming up here?"

"Yep. I'll give you as much notice as I can. ... Is Cathy there?"

"Hold a sec." Dan walked into the dining room and leaned over Cathy's shoulder. "Someone wants to talk to you."

Cathy placed her napkin on the table and stood, her face beaming with delight.

"How's it goin'? Chris asked when she picked up the phone.

"Swimmingly," Cathy answered. "I'm drowning in blue baby clothes. Lisa and I went shopping and bought enough for a small orphanage. The clothes won't go to waste, but our little Jack will outgrow them before he can wear them all."

"I miss you, honey."

"I miss you more. Stay safe. Finish up with those creepy goons as fast as you can!"

CHAPTER 47

GET OUT NOW!
YOUR CHILDREN ARE IN DANGER.
THE FANGS WILL TAKE THEM AWAY!

CHRIS STOOD BEHIND SHELLY as she fiddled with
the design for the flyer the gang planned to distribute.
Scripted in English and Spanish, the black four-sided
border was an inch wide. Out from the darkness peeked
heads of fierce looking beasts. The lettering came
from the wand held by a scar-faced witch with claw-
like fingers. Shelly had used some of the words Chris
gave Jimmy. The drawings were disturbing to look at,
primitive and threatening.

"Shelly." Chris said. "You have real artistic talents. Do something with it instead of making hideous flyers for your brother."

"Jimmy won't leave me be. I have to make the goriest pictures anyone's ever seen."

Scary cats dragged dead mice in their clamped jaws and snakes wrapped themselves around the legs of ugly beasts. Small deformed people stirred boiling pots of desperate children trying to climb over the sides.

Chris shuddered. Those images evoked disturbing emotions, even for him.

When the template was finished, Shelly planned to take it to a friend and have a thousand prints made.

"Do you think they'll be ready soon?" Chris asked. "I wonder if you'll run into problems getting something like this printed."

"Nah. Jimmy has a special guy who does favors for the gang. He'll get them done." She looked up over her shoulder at Chris. "Don't worry. Two or three days max. Unless his guy is behind with other orders."

"Okay. Gotta go." He went back to his room, picked up his leather jacket and checked the gun holstered at his ankle.

Chris had a lot on his mind. He left the boarding house and strolled leisurely to the park. He was in a hurry but didn't want to draw attention to himself. Alone on a path, he called Dan and exhaled with relief when Dan picked up. "I was afraid I might not get you." He spoke in a whisper. "The gang plans to deliver the flyers in a couple of days. I might not be able to tell you the exact time. Stand ready for the next three days.

He looked up and saw Shelly heading his way. "Shelly takes her job as a spy seriously. She's coming toward me now. I'll alert you when I know what's going down." He hung up without saying good-bye and sat down on a nearby bench.

"Hi, Chris." Shelly sidled onto the bench next to him. "Talkin' to your sweetie?"

"Who else? I'm missing her. You followed me?"

"Zoe, right?"

Chris nodded. "Did Zig or Jimmy put you up to pokin' into my personal life?"

"No. I'm just curious. I thought maybe you and I could get a little something goin'." She fluttered her eyelashes at him.

Chris struggled not to laugh out loud. "Shelly, Zoe and I have been together a long time. You're a special person but I ain't interested in messin' around. I'd like to help you, but that's as far as I'm willin' to go."

"I knew you'd say that. Can't blame me for trying. You're a classy guy."

"Let's keep it business."

"Okay," she said, sounding disappointed. She stood, walked a few steps past him, blew a kiss and continued on, headed to the printer with her gruesome flyer.

Chris called after her. "Maybe you should think of acting as a career." He shook his head and smiled to himself. She was indeed an original.

Shelly turned, flashed him a thumb's up and kept walking.

Now I have to watch my back every minute, Chris thought as he hurried to his boarding house. How could he be sure he would be able to notify Dan the minute the gang left for Juniper Hills? He decided he'd have to trust his landlady, Alice. He would give her Maggie's number this afternoon, tell her when he had to leave, to call, ask for Zoe and say, "Our date for tonight is off." That was the best he could do. He would call Dan again and tell him his plan. The FANGS were coming!

CHAPTER 48

THINGS HAPPENED FAST. Two days later, as Chris relaxed in his room at one in the afternoon, he heard bulky boot steps in the hall, followed by a pounding on his door. He knew the time had come. Glad he had earlier written the message for Alice asking that she call Zoe/Maggie if and when he told her he wouldn't be available that night.

"Come in," he yelled, knowing it was Joe. He hoped that Dan had received the message he'd left earlier that morning telling Dan to expect a call from Maggie. After all the planning, he still feared things might go wrong.

Chris, reading a sociology book he'd picked up at a library sale, tossed it into his open duffle when Joe burst into the room.

"Up to your old tricks?" Joe asked. He looked as if he'd slept in his jeans and wrinkled white tee. His greasy black hair fell over his pocked face.

"What?" Chris felt his body tense.

"I know you read all the time."

"What's it to you? I get bored."

"Why so defensive? It's why Laker thinks you're so smart—keeps you around."

"Great. Makes me feel secure. Ha! Why does Laker keep you around, Joe?"

"We've known each other since third grade."

"Ever thought of breaking away and doing somethin' on your own? You're a smart guy yourself." Joe gave him an uncertain look. "I mean a plane mechanic ain't exactly nothin'. What about Carmen? She's a looker. What's her take on the gang?"

"We never talk about it. Laker's orders."

"That's bad, sad and probably the worst start for a relationship."

"Don't know where I'd be without the fuckin' gang. It's family." Joe looked at his watch. "We have to hurry. Laker wants to leave now. Says you and I should wear suit and ties."

"No kidding? We goin' formal tonight?"

Chris moved slowly, wanting to give Dan more time to get his forces in place for the take-down. "Need a few minutes to get ready. Is this an overnight or are we coming back?"

"We'll need gloves. It's cold up there."

Chris gathered his best jacket and a tie, noting that Joe didn't answer his question. "You wanna wait for me downstairs?"

"Jimmy said not to let you out of my sight."

"Still doesn't trust me, huh?"

Joe shrugged. "Likes your idea of those spooky flyers."

Chris already had his Glock strapped in his ankle holster, sure Joe didn't know about it. Laker's policy, because of the accidental death of his baby brother, had always been no guns, but he himself and most of his guys packed concealed weapons at one time or another. As Joe watched he made a show of stuffing his service pistol in the back waistband of his jeans and turned away to slip his cell into the pocket of his jacket. "I can't go without my gun."

"I feel the same." Joe opened the door. "Ready?"

"Let's go. I have to tell Alice I won't be here for dinner."

They walked down the stairs and stopped in the kitchen. Alice was at the range stirring a large pot of lentil soup that smelled of root vegetables and health. Tall, lithe with high-colored cheeks and silver-streaked dark hair, Alice's resemblance to his grandmother always brought good memories to Chris.

"I'll be out this evening, Ms. Alice. Sorry to pass on that delicious soup. Please give Zoe a call and tell her I won't be here tonight. It's Thursday and she's expecting to hear from me."

"I'll be glad to talk to Zoe. You're a lucky guy to have such a sweetheart. She's always happy to talk, even when it means you're not here."

"Thanks, Alice." Chris wondered what Alice thought of him and their telephone arrangement. She never asked.

Joe and Chris walked down the street to Mattie's. "The ladies like you. Even the old bags. What's your secret?" Joe asked.

"Bay Rum aftershave."

"No way."

"Really. It makes them faint at my feet."

"Now I know you're fuckin' with me."

Chris patted him on the back and almost wished Joe wasn't going tonight. He wasn't a bad guy, although misdirected. Every once in a while, a sweetness shone through his eyes.

They walked over to Mattie's where Jimmy Laker sat at the bar talking to Mattie, finishing off who knew how many beers. Three tables of fifteen or so gang members were divvying up the ugly flyers into packets and shoving them into plastic folders. Chris had never laid eyes on half the men in the bar. He figured these were the guys Alan said came in and out according to Laker's plan of the week. A couple of men looked to be in their thirties. Most were kids in their late teens and early twenties.

"Hey," Laker yelled at them. "Don't wrinkle those. Don't wanna pass out shit. Want them to look respectable. People gotta take them serious."

Chris felt faintly nauseous. This disgusting guy was without a soul. He hoped for the umpteenth time that Dan had gotten word from Maggie. He wanted Juniper Hills to be prepared for the onslaught of those dreadful messages.

Jimmy Laker turned, slipped off the bar stool and clapped his hands above his head. "Okay. Let's go." Everyone seemed to move at the same time. "You have your maps and locations, right?"

"Yeah. Yeah." Mumbles rose from the men grabbing packets and moving out the door to their cars.

"You two come with me," Laker motioned to Chris and Joe. "We'll go in the limo."

Chris's heart thundered in his chest. He realized he didn't know exactly what was going down. Laker hadn't discussed the details of the operation with him. Was it because he didn't trust him? Was he under suspicion? When had the maps and locations been decided? Why wasn't he included?

He climbed in the back seat of the Caddy, expecting Joe to follow, but instead Joe heaved himself into the front passenger seat. "Jimmy's going to drive," he said. "This car is fuckin' armored."

Chris felt for his cell and carefully checked his Glock. They watched as Laker gave last minute instructions to some of his men. "Ya know what's goin' on?" Chris leaned forward and asked Joe.

"Nah. Jimmy usually keeps his stuff to himself until the last minute. He's not even using his driver. The fewer witnesses the better, he says."

"What are we supposed to do?"

"No idea. Keep him company, I guess." Joe shifted in his seat.

Chris felt uneasy. Apparently, Laker had decided to place his men at different spots in town, so they wouldn't be meeting at one parking lot as they had at the Desert Mall at Christmastime. He needed to get a message to Dan. He slipped out his cell intending to text Dan just as Jimmy yanked open the car door and settled in behind the wheel. Chris set his cell to silent, not wanting it to vibrate in Laker's car. He dropped it into his pants pocket to wait for a safer opportunity. No one in the gang owned a cell or seemed the least bit interested in communicating with mobiles. Chris didn't think they even knew he had one, although he had used it in Terry White's garage when they recorded him. Even so he was reluctant to take a chance in the back seat of the limo. He would wait until he knew more of the arrangements.

"Do you have a job for me and Joe?" he asked Laker.

"Of course. I want you both to supervise where the flyers go. I want them everywhere, library, post office, groceries, department stores, small dress shops, laundromats ... tacked up on trees and fences, wherever there are people, particularly in the spic neighborhoods. They must look official. You two are the most respectable guys in our group so I'm sending you into the banks and hotels. Don't talk to anyone. Put a pile of flyers on an obvious counter and get out fast."

"Do we go together or alone?" Joe asked.

"Alone. I'll drive up in front of a bank or public building. You get out and go one way and Chris the other the way. Then stroll back to the limo as if you have delivered a very important message. Pretty soon the town'll be raining flyers and we'll have total chaos."

Chris felt as if he was dreaming. He needed to talk to Dan. Was he really in this ridiculous situation with these cruel, uncaring men? He was losing touch with reality. Laker's secretive behavior now terrified him.

CHAPTER 49

"FBI!" The announcement boomed into Dan's office as two brawny men in well-tailored dark suits and narrow silk ties appeared. "We're looking for Detective Daniel Clarke," said the larger agent.

Dan rose from his desk chair. "That would be me. May I see some ID? How can I help you, gentlemen?"

The two men fished in their breast coat pockets and flashed their badges. "We have word that your life is in imminent danger."

"Is this some weird joke?"

"No, Detective. Since your visit to our Phoenix office we've had taps on the homes and offices of Chief Gene Strunk and Mayor Giles Buchanan. This morning we heard Strunk tell the Mayor he hired a man, in his own words, 'to off you.' They believe you and your new recruit are onto their drug running."

"My new recruit? You mean Chris Watters?"

"I'm not familiar with that name, Sir," the taller agent said. "We're taking you into protective custody. You're our prime witness."

"Drug running? I don't know much about their drug dealings. I can't leave now. We're about to bring down the gang from Leonardo that've been threatening our Latino community."

"Detective, we can't guarantee your safety here in Juniper Hills. You must come with us to Phoenix. It's the Governor's orders. Leave your cell. Your position can be traced."

Dan laid his phone on the desk. "I've got to contact Chris Watters. Do the Chief and Mayor know we have an undercover man in Leonardo?"

The FBI agents looked at each other and shrugged. The shorter one said, "Not to our knowledge."

Dan let out a sigh. What a mess, he thought. Nobody knows what anyone else is doing. If Buchanan and Strunk are suspicious of me, they must know about Chris.

"Before we leave, I have to speak with my deputy." Dan walked into Whitey Smith's office. "Call Maggie. Ask for Zoe. She's developed a friendship with Alice, Chris' landlady." As Dan spoke, he grabbed a pad on Whitey's desk and wrote down the numbers for Alice and Chris. "Tell Maggie to warn Chris that Laker is on to him. Then try to get Chris. Leave a voice mail. It's hard for him to answer."

After Dan zipped up his jacket and reluctantly left with the FBI, Whitey dialed Maggie's number. A little girl answered and he hung up. Then he called Chris' cell which went directly to voice mail. "Get out. They're on to you," he yelled into the phone, feeling like an inter-galactic meteor was about to drop on the station.

Jimmy Laker's limo arrived in Juniper Hills during rush hour—lots of cars on the roads and groups of people milling about on the sidewalks. Chris saw nothing that looked suspicious. Stores and restaurants were busy with Presidents' Day sales. No police hovering on corners or cruisers hiding behind bushes and trees with radar guns. On his lap Chris held a heavy packet of flyers in a plastic folder as did Joe in the front seat. Chris didn't notice any men with packets or flurries of activity on the streets. Where were Jimmy Laker's foot soldiers?

Jimmy pulled up in front of The Western Imperial, the classiest golf resort in the tri-city area and told Chris and Joe to get out and place the flyers wherever they would be discovered. As the two gathered their packets, Laker's car phone rang. He hesitated, then answered, "Yeah." Silence filled the limo as Laker listened. Chris and Joe shuffled their flyers around, waiting for last minute instructions.

Finally, without saying a word, Laker broke the phone connection. As Chris and Joe climbed out of the limo, Laker tugged on Joe's sleeve, leaned over and mumbled something to Joe that Chris didn't catch. "Don't forget the restrooms," Laker called after the two as they emerged from the car.

"I'll do the two cafés, snack bar and then the golf shop," Joe told Chris, reading from the directory in the lobby. "You do the reception area, restaurant, health club and restrooms. I'll meet you in the golf shop in fifteen minutes. Jimmy used to play golf here. There's a stairwell on the east side of the reception room. Don't use the elevators. Nobody ever uses the stairwell. We don't want to be noticed."

Joe's face was so serious Chris wondered what he was thinking.

Chris followed directions to the spa and restrooms, thinking he would find the most privacy there. Once in the stairwell, he whipped out his cell, saw he had voice mail messages which he would check later, punched the number for Dan and held his breath. The call rang and rang and went to voice mail. "Damn." Chris tried to think what to say first. "The gang's in town distributing the crazy flyers. Joe and I are in a black armored Caddy SUV, license PTY872. Laker is driving. I haven't seen any other gang members. I'm wondering if this is a test Laker has cooked up for me. Ever since Zig and Terry were picked up in Gallup, he looks at me like he wants to see inside my head."

Chris strolled into the health club and spa and stacked a pile of flyers on the end of a counter in the far corner of the room. He walked outside and stuffed the rest in a green dumpster at the side of the building. No one was around except a young kid helping two golfers load their bags into a cart. They paid him no attention. With his hands empty, he found a quiet spot and called Dan's number again. Still no answer. He tried Maggie's cell. A soft voice answered. Chris was about to say Sophie when he remembered Maggie's fear that their landline might be bugged. "Hi, this is Guy Black. Is Zoe there?"

"Oh, hello, Mr. Black," Sophie said in her best formal voice. "Zoe had to take Mom to the hospital. They think she's had a stroke. Not a bad one though. They didn't have to call an ambulance. Can I take a message?"

Chris marveled at Sophie's composure. "Tell her to call Dan and tell him I'm at the Western Imperial Resort in the back-parking lot. I hope Estelle is okay."

"She's good. I'm sure she'll be fine."

Chris knew he had dropped his cover. At this point in time, it didn't seem to matter. He went back into the spa and started up the stairwell, wondering if Sophie could possibly get his message to Dan through Maggie.

"Stop right there." Joe stood at the top of the stairs. "Take your pistol out of your waist band, drop it behind you and put up your hands. Nice and easy. Back away. I'm comin' down."

"What's this, Joe?"

"Laker decided you won't do. His lawyer, Burt, just called. He talked to Zig. The cops are holding him and Terry indefinitely. Burt thinks you had something to do with the arrest. He don't know what you're up to, but he don't like it. Burt checked on your girlfriend, Zoe, and found out she was staying in a condo owned by Madeline Watters, who happens to have a brother who's a New York detective, named Chris Watters."

"That's some weird coincidence. It's not even my real name. I got it off a book cover."

"Laker don't think so."

"What's he stuck you with, Joe? Bring me home dead? Say I was brained by a golf ball? Fell down the stairs. What?"

"Put these on." Joe neared the bottom of the stairs and tossed a pair of flashy metal handcuffs at him. "Move slowly and don't make me nervous."

"You don't want to do this, Joe. Laker will let you take the fall. You may think of him as family, but he'll be in Ecuador with his parents while you rot in jail waiting for execution. What about Carmen and your own life? Do you really want to give all that up?"

"Laker will take care of everything."

"How can you be sure? Terry and Zig are still in jail. The cops are moving in on Juniper Hills' Mayor and Chief of Police. Help us, Joe. I can make it go easier for you." Chris slowly inched up the staircase. "I'll help you. Think about Carmen. She loves you."

Chris could feel a weakening in Joe's resolve. "We can bring Laker down together."

"I don't know."

"Do you really want to live the rest of your life as his service dog?"

"No, damn it. I don't." Joe's hands were trembling and tears were brimming on his eyelids. "He'll find me. No one can get away from Laker if he's got it in for them."

"We can protect you. I promise." Chris had reached the step below Joe and extended his hand for Joe's gun. Joe released it into Chris' hand, sat down on the top step and let out a sob.

"Where is he now?" Chris asked.

"I'm supposed to handcuff you and bring you out to the limo in the back-parking lot. We'll take you to one of the abandoned copper mines in Bisbee and throw you down a shaft. No one will ever find you."

"Obviously, you've done that before?" Chris let out a deep sigh.

"Yeah." Joe gulped a loud sob back in his throat. "I really like you. This stinks."

Chris handed the pistol back to Joe. "Can I trust you? I've taken the bullets out. We have to get Laker out of the Caddy." Chris called Dan's number and left another message. "We're in the back of the Western Imperial Golf Club. Joe's surrendered and is offering to help us. Laker is riding around in his armored limo. Send help ASAP!" Where were they? Chris was ready for the takedown. Dan and his special forces were nowhere to be found.

CHAPTER 50

"PLEASE DON'T FIGHT ME on this, Mom," Maggie said. "One night in the hospital won't be so bad. Think of it as a vacation. The rest will be good for you."

"When I'm dead I'll have all the rest time I need."

"MOM, you know I hate that talk. The docs have checked you over and say you're fine. They want to keep you overnight so they're sure they didn't miss anything."

"No more tests."

"Okay. I'll tell Dr. Carlton." Maggie smoothed back Estelle's hair, covered her up to her chin and kissed her on the forehead. Estelle looked like a little kid fresh out of a swimming pool. Damp ringlets of hair surrounded her face, cheeks pink with excitement. Eyes dancing. "I'll be back tomorrow morning to take you home. Do you want anything before I leave?"

"You don't happen to have a book in that bucket of a purse you carry?" Estelle pushed down the covers and wiggled up to a sitting position. "I can only stay here if I have a good book."

"I'll run down to the gift shop and see what they have. If not, I'll hop over to the library and bring you a mystery. Louise Penny, okay?"

"Perfect. I've read most of her work, but it doesn't matter. I like to read them again. She's excellent. Look for the newest one."

"Be right back." Maggie took the elevator to the main floor, tried Dan's cell only to get a busy signal and entered the shop. Fortunately, the hospital gift shop had a decent library section. She found a copy of the first book Penny had written in 2005, "Still Life," and figured if Estelle had read it when it was first published, she'd probably have forgotten it by now.

Maggie hurried back to Estelle's room with the book, kissed her good-bye and took the elevator down to the parking lot. She again tried Dan's cell. No answer. She'd stop at the station.

Deputy Detective Whitey Smith ushered Maggie into Dan's office and told her the FBI had Dan in protective custody from Mayor Buchanan and Chief Strunk. "Apparently, the Chief and Mayor were into drug running as well as trying to drive the Latinos out of town. That's all I know." Whitey looked exhausted.

Maggie noticed Dan's cell on his desk. She hesitated, then picked it up.

Whitey rubbed his eyes. "They wouldn't let him take it. His position could be traced if he had it on him."

Maggie slipped Dan's cell into her pocket, pleaded with Whitey to keep her informed. He told her he was on his way to the hospital. His daughter had suffered a seizure at school and been taken to Elizabeth General. She was okay. His wife was driving over, but he didn't want them to be alone.

"I'm so sorry to hear that," Maggie said, stroking his arm.

"It happens every once in a while. She'll be fine." Whitey moved through the door. "I'll keep in touch."

Maggie went out the front door, thinking, so many people have heavy-hearted problems no one knows about. She climbed in her car. Thanked God she had often watched Dan enter his passcode and remembered it. She pushed in Dan's passcode, checked his messages and listened to three from Chris. Holy Hell, she thought, the gang is on to him. Chris was in trouble and trying to contact Dan.

Reluctantly, she called Whitey, hoping he could tell her what to do next. His phone went to voice mail. She called the main police station number and the phone rang and rang. The station was in chaos. Dan's special forces must be out on the streets. The cops in cahoots with the drug-runners had gone into hiding to save themselves from arrest.

She decided to go to the back-parking lot of the Western Imperial Resort and see if she could help. She had asked Whitey if Dan had said anything about taking down the FANGS. Whitey said he thought they had a plan for the next three days to round them up, but he hadn't heard any late news.

Maggie drove over to the Western Imperial Resort.

Chris, not in handcuffs, but faking capture with his arms behind his back, waited with Joe in front of the golf shop. Chris watched Joe's face and couldn't tell if he was scared or sorry things weren't going his way. It didn't take long for Jimmy Laker to pull up in front of the shop. Suddenly, Joe yelled at Chris, "Sorry. No can do." He made a mad dash for the limo door; belly flopped on the back seat and screamed to Laker. "Go. Go."

Chris stood in the doorway laughing. "Snookered," he said aloud. What a performance. He hadn't thought Joe had it in him. He leaned against the wall and considered his situation. They set me up to reveal myself. I misjudged them again.

As Chris watched the limo race out the driveway, he heard the sharp impact of brakes and the squeal of tires on the pavement. A dark gray Honda blocked the exit and behind it was a large white food truck delivering supplies to the Resort.

Laker would be forced to turn around. Chris realized he may yet have a chance to stop him. He grabbed his cell. "Officer needs assistance in the Western Imperial Resort parking lot." He hoped someone not aligned with Chief Strunk might respond. As Laker backed up, Chris aimed his Glock and shot at the tires, but nothing seemed to stop the forward motion of the limo. No one responded to the shots. He remembered from his days in the military that armored cars could move even if the tires were shot out.

As Laker backed up and sped out of the entrance drive, Maggie pulled up in front of Chris. "Hop in," she called. "Wanna chase 'em?"

"Too late. I can't raise any backup.... How did you find me?"

"The FBI took Dan into protective custody. They made him leave his cell on his desk. When I couldn't contact him, I went to the station. Whitey told me they took Dan to Phoenix. Nobody knows who they can trust in the police department. It's almost empty over there.... What do you wanna do now?"

Looking at his cell screen, Chris said, "Dan had Whitey call me. Said the gang was on to me. Told me to get out. We need to come up with a new plan. I think a meeting is called for."

"First stop, new cells. We have to be able to contact each other without leaving traces of our calls." Maggie sat straight in the driver's seat with both hands on the wheel, feeling in command, thinking, what would Dan do?

They stopped at Walmart and bought four throwaways. Maggie, after stomping on her cell and then Dan's with her heel and tearing them apart, threw them in the store's back alley dumpster. Chris kept his.

"Let's go to my house and make some decisions," Maggie said. "We can't go near the station."

"We need a whole new take down plan. Let's see if we can contact Dan." Chris clutched his cell.

They drove to Maggie's house. The sky had darkened. A dangerous wind storm brewed, tossing tree branches and bushes in every direction. Debris lashed their windshield.

To their amazement, Dan was sitting in the rocker on the front porch with a big smile on his face. "I escaped the FBI, promised I'd stay out of sight until they bring down Strunk and the Mayor for their drug dealings. They're mostly interested in the gang's drug activities. The Latinos are our concerns. Can't tell who to trust these days. Let's get Whitey over here and plan our next move to take down the FANGS."

They stood for a few more minutes on the porch. The sky turned dark-purple as they moved to enter the house.

At the end of the street they heard a group of kids roaring with laughter. As Maggie, Dan and Chris looked up, a strong wind gust moved a cluster of the menacing flyers through the air. Groups of kids followed, running, jumping and trying to catch and tuck them under their arms and inside their jackets.

Chris with an impish gleam in his eyes looked up and tracked the twirling flyers. "While trying with those ridiculous flyers to save the kids from being kidnapped—"

"You managed to entertained them," Dan cut in.

Maggie put her hand on Chris' back. "We couldn't have asked for more." Dan took Maggie's other hand and the three still laughing their heads off, entered the house.

CHAPTER 51

Two day later, Maggie, Dan and Whitey slouched around the kitchen table, exhausted with worry. It felt strange not to have Estelle hovering over them. At least her minor stroke hadn't alarmed the doctors. Her vitals, blood pressure, cholesterol, and other tests were near perfect. They prescribed a daily baby aspirin and told her to take things easy for a few days. Carlos would pick her up at the hospital the next morning. Chris had gone to Cathy's house. Rosa brewed coffee and asked if anyone wanted a homemade donut. No one did. She set the platter at the end of the counter.

Maggie turned to Rosa who stood at the sink in Estelle's usual spot. "Rosa, we need to meet right away with Latino groups and make sure people know those flyers are bogus. Who should we contact?"

"What about asking the Mayor or Chief of Police to make an announcement on local TV?" Rosa filled Dan's empty cup.

"NO. NO. That won't work." Dan pleaded with his eyes for Maggie to do something. Rosa should not hear what they had to say. This was police business.

"I can't believe all this." Rosa refilled Maggie's cup. 'I'll tell Carlos. He'll meet with people at our church tonight to spread the word."

"Good." Maggie fiddled with her new phone.

"Carlos should be here soon." Rosa walked around the table to refill Whitey's cup.

Whitey covered it. "No thanks. I'm caffeine saturated."

"Okay, then." Rosa headed for the basement. "Laundry calls." Her mumbling could be heard all the way up from the back staircase.

Dan leaned across the table for the creamer. "We don't know who we can trust. We're now positive Buchanan and Strunk hired the Leonardo gang to attack our community and the neighboring towns. That part I'm sure of, thanks to Chris' undercover work." His eyes met Maggie's. "It was a side activity for those two. Drug running seems to be the gang' everyday business. Chris found evidence that suggests Jimmy's father, James Laker, is the northern contact for a Mexican drug cartel."

"But who's paying for these attacks against our town?" Maggie picked up a pencil and doodled on a legal pad. "Who's paying for the gang's services? Who's the most notorious racist in Juniper Hills?"

"You can't be thinking of that old crotchety headache Horace Grundy?" Whitey stroked his brow with the back of his hand.

"Yeah, him. The man who complains about the noise the garbage trucks make." Maggie wrinkled her nose.

Dan put his hand on Maggie's arm. "More trouble."

"He's filthy rich and at every town meeting griping about the overcrowding, noise and music in the Latino neighborhoods." Maggie tapped her pencil on the table. "His son, Ron, used to be a friend of Hank's, may be still."

"Complaints! He calls the station daily. About thoughtless people not picking up after their dogs around the courthouse square or if the mail isn't delivered on time, but I don't see him poisoning animals or attacking mailmen." Whitey's tone dripped with exasperation.

Dan ignored him. "Grundy belongs to that group of men who meet most mornings at the Crystal Diner. I've seen them sitting around the tables with their open-carry weapons jutting out from under their jackets." Dan added, "Men too old to play cops and robbers. They make the security guys nervous."

"Hank used to meet with those guys," Maggie said. "I have no idea if he still does, but I wouldn't be surprised, if he's in town." She walked to the kitchen counter, picked up the platter of powdered-sugar-dusted donuts and centered it on the table.

"Some are mighty wealthy ranchers," Whitey said as he broke a piece off a donut.

"Others are bankers and real estate agents. They'd have the money to pay gang members for their services." Dan pushed back his chair and stood. "I don't like where this is going. Our welcoming town sounds like a hotbed of bigots and racists."

"It only takes a few to create a real problem." Maggie sipped her coffee. "What are we going to do?"

"The FANGS' Latino activities were a side issue for them. Whitey, Chris and I can corral trustworthy guys from Juniper Hill's special forces, go to Leonardo and arrest the gang members who've been attacking our town. The narcotic agents will take care of Buchanan and Strunk.

"Do we need to call in the National Guard?" Maggie asked.

"We'll be okay with our guys." Dan took a final gulp from his coffee mug. "We're waiting to hear from the Governor's office and the FBI in Ecuador, James Laker and a couple of other thugs are under surveillance for drug running. He's been making crystal meth and has storage sheds for marijuana out at his ranch. The FBI wants to coordinate their drug arrests with our take down of the FANGS. I have to talk to Chris. His contacts in Leonardo can help us. For now, we'll keep all this quiet and meet again tomorrow."

Maggie's stomach twisted. Danger loomed everywhere. She shuddered to think of Dan in the midst of this complicated takedown. One mistake and everything could fall apart.

Chris and Dan sat on a wooden bench beneath a cottonwood tree by Watchung Lake in the center of Juniper Hills. Both men stared across the still waters of the lake in silence. Chris had moved to Dan's house. He feared that if he was seen around town, he would draw attention to Cathy. The FBI had called in experts to comb Dan's house for listening bugs and found it free, but Dan still worried that Strunk knew too much about Chris.

"Two people I know in Leonardo will help us," Chris said. "Alice Edmondson, my former landlady, and Rita Goodwin, the woman who told me the gang killed her grandson. They can spy on the gang without being noticed, especially Rita. She's in Mattie's every afternoon enjoying her favorite drink. She can notify us when they get together. Then we'll raid the place and grab all the gang members at once."

"Why is she so sure the gang killed her grandson?" Dan asked.

"To start with, her grandson never drank," Chris replied. "He was allergic to alcohol and afraid of heights. So why would he be drunk on the edge of a cliff?"

"I see what you mean."

"I'm most concerned about Joe and Laker," Chris went on. "Once we have those two in custody along with Terry and Zig in New Mexico, I'm convinced the gang will fall apart. Laker drinks a lot. Capturing him half smashed would be easier."

"Or maybe he'd be more belligerent." Dan shuddered, thinking of the damage Laker could create. "Damn it's hot." He removed a handkerchief from his pocket and wiped sweat off his forehead.

"Alan called me," Chris said. "He wants to be part of the takedown. Apparently, Rosa mentioned something to Natalie and she mentioned something to Alan."

"So, we'd better move fast before our secret plan is all over town." Dan stood and walked a few feet down to the lake looking for a breeze.

Chris followed. "Alan feels we owe it to him so he can repent for ever being part of that 'hideous' group. That's a direct quote from him."

Dan patted the grass beside him. "It's cooler down here."

Chris joined him on the cool ground with his long legs outstretched. "Okay. Let's bring him in. At least we know he's on our side. These days it's hard to be sure about anyone."

Sunlight sent up a dazzling glare as the water rippled in a sudden breeze. Chris shaded his eyes. "I'll contact Alice; explain a few things I think she already suspects. Ask her to have Rita notify me when Joe and Laker are at Mattie's with the gang. Then we move in. Once we have Laker and Joe under wraps, I'm convinced the FANGS will split and go their separate ways. I wouldn't be surprised if more of them might be having second thoughts."

Dan nodded. "Good. We'll go as soon as we hear from Rita. The FBI can handle Buchanan and Strunk."

"How'll we bring in the Crystal Diner group?" Chris asked.

"I'll have to think about that. Our intel and evidence must be letter perfect. That bunch will lawyer-up before we get them to the station. We can't afford any mistakes."

Two weeks later, Rita Godwin called Chris. "Gang's planning a St. Patrick's Day blast at Mattie's. It's the day after tomorrow. Sounds like a huge affair. Most of the gang will be there. A great excuse to get blind drunk." Rita laughed. "I've often wondered if St. Patrick was a drinker. I know he wasn't an Irishman. Born in England."

"No shit!" Careful, Chris thought. Now that things were coming to an end, he had to watch his language, particularly with sweet old ladies.

Rita giggled.

"Thanks, Rita, and thank Alice. You two stay off the street and out of Mattie's on St. Pat's day. It'll be dangerous."

"At my age, dying would be heavenly. Maybe I'll oil up my derringer and take a shot at that scum, Jimmy Laker. It would be the cherry on top of the best sundae of my life." Her raspy voice raised with her delight.

"See if you can get Alice to keep Shelly home that day."

"We might have to tie her up." Rita let out another throaty giggle.

"Then do it. Take care of yourselves and keep this quiet."

"Consider it done, Boss."

Chris laid the phone down and sat on the edge of his bed with his head in his hands. Were they ready? One false step could result in injury or death to the innocents involved in the case. He raised his head as a nearby car alarm went off. He hoped it wasn't a sign.

CHAPTER 52

CHRIS, DAN AND ALAN stood outside Mattie's Saloon. Chris checked his watch. It was past four and the late-winter sky was beginning to darken over the quiet streets. Twenty carefully vetted plain-clothes officers sauntered around the streets of Leonardo, trying to look like casual tourists. "We walk in, Dan," Chris said. "I'll take Laker's arm and escort him outside like we're still buddies."

"Will he go for that?"

"He's probably shit-faced by now."

"Let's do it." Dan looked anything but confident.

"I'll tell him someone's outside with news about Zig and Terry," Chris said. "I can't imagine he's told anyone what happened with Joe in the back-parking lot of the Western Imperial. Once I have Laker by the arm, I'll motion Joe to the door. They don't know you, Dan, but Alan will look familiar to them. When we get outside, we'll take them to the cruiser. Meanwhile our men will arrest the other guys in the bar and put them in the van."

Chris and Alan went into the tavern, Alan at Chris' side. Dan stayed at the open door. The stink of spilled beer in the room almost choked them. The soles of their shoes stuck to the dried puddles of beer on the floor. They walked up to Laker who squinted up at them with red-rimmed eyes. "Never thought I'd see you again, Black," he said to Chris, laying down a short straw and pushing aside a pile of white dust on the bar.

"I got someone outside with info about Zig. Come on." Chris tugged his arm.

Laker viciously rubbed at his nose with his fisted knuckles and got to his feet. He stood swaying with a dazed expression on his face. Not only was he dead drunk, but by the traces of white powder around his nose, he was jacked up too.

In an unexpected move, Laker dropped behind Chris, pulled a short knife from his pocket and jammed it against Chris' back. "No funny stuff, Guy Black."

Chris walked stony-faced toward the front door, his eyes seeking Dan.

Alan moved closer to Chris.

Laker peered at Alan through rheumy eyes. "Don't I know you, kid? Yeah. Haven't seen you around for a while. Whose side are you on here? Who are you with?"

"Not you, asshole." Alan punched Laker in the chest and twisted Laker's hand until he dropped the knife.

Laker, quick as a striking rattler, pulled an eight-inch blade from his other sleeve and thrust it deep into Alan's chest. Alan's mouth opened wide. He fell against the wall clutching the knife handle, gasping for air as he slid to the floor, eyes closing.

Dan, standing by the entrance door, alerted by the commotion, yanked his Glock from its holster, swung it out and shot. Blood spurted from the side of Laker's head. His body hit the floor with a loud thud.

"Mattie! call an ambulance. Now! Call two!" Chris knelt to feel for Alan's pulse. Blood oozed over the barroom floor. "Come stay with Alan. Bring a towel. Use pressure to stop the blood." He laid a gentle hand on Alan's cheek and brushed back his hair. One look at Laker told him there was no point in checking him for a pulse.

"Where's Joe?" Chris looked up at Dan.

"He must have ducked outside."

"Mattie, stay with Alan," Chris repeated. "Keep pressure on the chest wound. We've got to find Joe."

Dan and Chris ran down the street. Rita and Alice were standing close together on the sidewalk with Joe in front of them on his knees.

Rita aimed a small gold-plated revolver at his groin. "Here's your culprit," she told Chris.

"Get this crazy bitch away from me!" Joe pleaded, hands guarding his crotch.

Dan yanked Joe up. "Let's go, creep. Chris gave you a chance. Now you'll go to Phoenix with the rest of Laker's thugs. Enjoy the company of Zig and Terry."

Two ambulances arrived, sirens blaring, to take Alan to the hospital and Laker to the morgue. Dan rushed to the stretcher that held Alan and reached for his hand. "You'll make a fine cop, my friend."

Alan nodded; eyes half-closed.

"We'll see you soon." Dan squeezed Alan's hand. Devastated by guilt, Dan fought to control his emotions as his heart pounded with fear for the worst outcome.

The Juniper Hills' special forces rounded up the rest of Laker's thugs and ushered them into the waiting vans. Quiet blanketed the streets. Dan and Chris walked back to Alice Edmondson's house where she and Rita sat in old creaky chairs on the porch. "You'll never know how much help you two have been," Chris said. "The District Attorney is going to reopen the investigation of your grandson's death, Rita. I believe they'll convict Jimmy Laker. You may be able to sue his estate for damages."

"Nah, I don't want his filthy money. I just want to clear my grandson's name." A surprising hint of tears choked her words. "I can't thank you enough."

"It's been fun," Alice added. "Ain't had so much goin' on 'round here in years. And to get rid of that gang is a blessing." She reached up to shake Chris' hand. "We're the ones thanking you." She nodded a smile toward Dan.

"We've got to head to the hospital to check on Alan, but we'll keep you informed," Dan said.

They showed their police identification to a no-nonsense nurse who ushered them to a small room off the waiting area.

"Officers, your man didn't make it. The knife wound went directly into his heart. He bled out and died shortly after he got here." She studied their faces before going on. "The strangest thing, I have to tell you. When the orderlies brought him in, he had a peaceful, beatific smile on his face. I've never seen anything like it."

Chris' shoulders slumped. Dan wasn't taking the news any better, but he spoke to Chris. "We have to call Natalie." He felt numb. "I should never have said yes to Alan." He knew he'd carry the burden of that decision for the rest of his life.

Chris looked like he would vomit. "Losing a good man is never easy. Alan had wanted so much to be helpful." Chris, heart heavy with grief, mumbled, "Oh, God, Dan, we have to tell Sophie."

They found Shelly sitting by herself in the ER waiting room. She had come expecting to find her brother. "I don't know what to do, she said. "I called my parents in Ecuador. My father said it was bound to happen. They told me to have Jimmy cremated. They're not coming back here. The police will be all over the ranch. Pop's pretty sure they can't extradite him from Ecuador, but he might go into hiding. He's called his goons to clean out everything and burn down the drug lab." Shelly covered her face with her hands and sobbed.

"I'll have Whitey notify the Leonardo police to get out to the ranch. Maybe they can save some evidence." Dan punched his cell and relayed the information, glad to have something to relieve his grief about Alan for a few hours.

Chris sat next to Shelly. "Alice will give you a hand with your new baby. She could also use help with her boarders. And Rita would be a great baby sitter."

"Thanks." Shelly stood, gave Chris a chaste hug and walked out the door. "I have to go."

Dan turned to Chris. "Arrange for Alan's body to be transported to the Juniper Hills coroner. I'm calling his

Mom." His fingers trembled as he waited for the call to go through.

Natalie was shocked and responded in a faint voice. "I'll have his body cremated," she managed to say. "And, and ..." She took a shuddering breath. "If possible, I'll plan a mass and memorial service on June 20th, his twenty-first birthday." Dan's hand went to his forehead. Twenty-one. He had forgotten Alan was not twenty-one.

CHAPTER 53

SIX DAYS LATER, Dan's ex, Dolores, arrived unannounced from California. Clad in an original Prada suit and coordinated shoes that easily cost thousands of dollars she pranced into the station like a model on a Paris runway.

Newly promoted Detective Whitey Smith, in his recently occupied front office, stood with the phone to his ear. After the Chief was fired along with the Mayor and sent to jail, Dan had been offered the chief's job. "Thanks, but no thanks," he'd told his colleagues. "I'm a detective, not a damn administrator."

The offer went next to Chris, but he and Cathy had decided to go back East after their baby was born. Chris planned to apply to the Columbia University Graduate School of Journalism. He liked investigating, but with the responsibility of a new baby he thought—wrongly, Dan knew—investigative journalism would be less dangerous than police work. So Whitey ended up as Juniper Hill's youngest ever Police Chief.

Dolores pushed around Whitey and banged at the closed door to Dan's private office. "I need to talk to you! I've been locked out of my apartment."

Whitey yelled, "STOP!"

Dolores moved away from Dan's door toward Whitey. With a defiant look she grabbed the gun from his holster, waving it around with nervous jerks. Whitey reached for her arm. The gun went off. Whitey took a bullet in his shoulder and slumped back into the wall, blood streaming down his arm.

Dan bolted from his office with his gun drawn. "What the hell is going on out here?" He growled at Delores. "You shot my friend?" He moved toward her. She stepped back and held out the gun. He pulled it from her hand and pushed her into a chair by the door. "Don't move," he ordered.

Dan went to his friend and gently slid an arm around Whitey's back. "Can you stand? You all right?"

"Yeah. I'm okay. Just a scratch," Whitey said, as blood soaked his uniform sleeve and ran down his hand.

"I've had enough of you!" Dan shouted at Dolores. Turning, Dan yelled into the next room, "Deputy Johnson, call an ambulance for Lieutenant Smith and get this woman out of my sight."

"Wait," Dolores pleaded, almost whimpered. "I need your help. I finally got a good job in Milan, you know that city in Italy, but I'm out of money. I can pay you back."

Enraged, Dan whirled to face her. "Too late, lady. You had your chance. This is how you ask for help? Shoot my friend?

Dan turned to Deputy Johnson, who hesitated by the door. "Get this woman out of my office. Charge her with assaulting an officer and take her to county jail. We'll take care of the paperwork later."

Dan pulled Dolores close to him and snarled in her face. "Do not show up in Juniper Hills again or I'll have you imprisoned for life on an attempted murder charge. Understand?"

Deputy Johnson pulled handcuffs from the back of his belt, jerked Dolores' wrists together, cuffed the still struggling woman and led her from the room.

A shrieking ambulance arrived. An EMT insisted on taking Whitey to the emergency room. Whitey refused to get on the stretcher, saying he'd walk.

"Sir," said the young paramedic, "you're bleeding heavily. Get on the gurney NOW. We need to apply pressure."

Whitey laid himself down, more embarrassed than hurt.

Dan went back into his private office. He blamed himself for Whitey's injury, but having dealt with Dolores empowered him. The guilt and self-loathing he'd carried for years had gone. His first thought was to talk with Maggie. Then he decided. No. This was his success, his alone. He would keep it to himself and walk taller. In his mind he thanked Maggie for making him take a hard look at his relationship with Dolores and at his life. But he would not discuss it. He knew she would notice his new self-esteem. He felt different.

Within the month, pending trial for a multitude of felonies, Joe was incarcerated with Zig and Terry in Phoenix. Mayor Gilles Buchanan and Chief Gene Strunk were jailed without bond for their activities with the FANGS and their drug trafficking with James Laker and his now dead son.

Dolores had been released from jail and ordered by the Judge, a friend of Dan's, never to appear in Juniper Hills again. She'd gotten off easy. Assault on an officer with a deadly weapon was a serious crime. But neither Dan nor Whitey wanted to press charges. They wanted her out of town forever.

Horace Grundy died a natural death at ninety-two, which many thought was brought on by stress from the newspaper articles about his nefarious activities.

The eight members of the old Crystal Diner group were picked up, bailed out on supervised probation and forbidden to leave town. Among the group were Ron Grundy and Hank Leonard. No one seemed surprised. No trial date had been set.

John Alan Watters arrived prematurely. Cathy and Chris named him John Alan instead of John Michael, forever thankful that Alan had saved Chris' life. They planned to stay with Cathy's parents in New Mexico until August and then return to New York City.

Lisa's baby had yet to arrive. She and Jesús were beside themselves with worry. The doctor assured them it wasn't unusual for a first baby to be late. "Both mother and child are in excellent health," he told Jesús. All the Pérezes in Mexico were waiting, not patiently, to gather for baby Robbie's christening.

Maggie, Lisa and Gus returned to their storefront offices. Gus was swamped with work and already complaining about what he would have to do once Lisa took maternity leave. Maggie busied herself hiring two new legal associates. At least once a week. the three strolled over at lunch time to watch their new Painted Lady taking shape.

Josh had grudgingly accepted the fact that he would have to find a new MISS CHLOE. Maggie promised to tutor the new recruit for a few weeks, but Josh's choice of a young Asian woman turned out to be a firecracker who needed few instructions.

The night before Alan's memorial service, Maggie and Dan sat on her porch swing "smoochin,'" as Estelle would tell her neighbor, Irina.

"I'm sorry to lose Chris." Dan wrapped his arm around Maggie.

"He'll make a terrific journalist," she said.

"He was a terrific undercover agent."

"He's only twenty-eight; maybe he'll change his mind."

"Wishful thinking, my love." Dan leaned over and kissed her gently on the lips.

"Chris asked to give the eulogy. He'd developed a strong affection for Alan."

"As I did." Dan looked down at his hands. A wash of guilt came, but he found it easier to let go with Maggie by his side.

"Sophie also asked to say a few words. How could we refuse?"

"We couldn't." He took her hand and swung the porch swing back with a gentle push of his foot. So much had happened. So much to look forward to. The cool evening breezes ruffled Maggie's hair. He leaned over and hugged her. A whole, beautiful life lay before them.

As Maggie and Dan drove into the Sacred Heart Church parking lot to attend Alan's memorial service, Maggie noticed an abundance of new green leaves pushing out from the brown winter tree limbs. Always a joyous sign, but today muted by grief. They walked along the path to the front door of the church, Dan carrying a small step-stool.

They slipped into the second-row pew. In front of them, Natalie, with a totally recovered Estelle's arm around her shoulder, held herself together. Clutching a tissue in her fist, Natalie occasionally dabbed at her eyes. She had decided to remain in Juniper Hills. Natalie had fallen in love with the beauty and warmth of Juniper Hills and the people who lived there. Estelle would serve a special dinner for one hundred in the backyard after the service. It was impossible to slow her down.

Chris and Cathy passed baby John Alan between them, at one point offering him to Natalie to hold, but she smiled and declined. It was too soon. Jesús supported Lisa who looked like she'd pop any minute.

Rosa and Carlos sat like proud pigeons watching their offspring's first flight. Sun rays shining through the lovely stained-glass windows seemed to sparkle the organ music.

When Chris finished his tribute, there were quiet tears and muffled nose blowing. Dan handed off the step-stool to Chris who placed it behind the lectern and helped Sophie as she climbed onto it. Maggie whispered to Dan as he returned to his seat and caressed her hand.

"It's the end of year essay she's been revising monthly since her first day of school and wouldn't let anyone see."

Sophie, in her citrus-colored party dress from the Mexican Fiesta, walked in shiny new black patent leather shoes with slow dignity and stood small at the lectern in Sacred Heart Church. She adjusted a silver clip in her hair and spoke in a firm voice.

"It's a time of hurting once again. I want to tell you the thoughts I've had this year.

HATE is a small word. It only has four letters. It's also a powerful word. It destroys lives, towns and countries. It makes us selfish and ugly. It killed Robbie and my friend Alan who promised to teach me to dance.

There is another small word to help us smile, care for each other, and enjoy life and dance again. That word is LOVE."

Yes, Maggie thought. Love is such a simple, powerful word, often so carelessly tossed around. Without it we become monsters. She watched Dan help Sophie down the sanctuary steps. He looked confident. What was it? He looked somehow different. He'd gone through so much in the past year. Through it all, she could see a change in him. He walked taller, seemed almost lighthearted at times. She liked what she saw.

Maggie was glad she had decided to practice immigration law. She would protect the people around her and at the same time dare to disturb the universe.